The Time of Her Life

OTHER FICTION BY DAVID HELWIG

The Streets of Summer
The Day before Tomorrow
The Glass Knight
Jennifer
The King's Evil
It Is Always Summer
A Sound Like Laughter
The Only Son
The Bishop
A Postcard from Rome
Old Wars
Of Desire
Last Stories of Anton Chekhov (translation)
Blueberry Cliffs
Just Say the Words
Close to the Fire

The Time of her Life

A NOVEL

DAVID HELWIG

GOOSE LANE

Edited by Laurel Boone.
Cover photograph courtesy of Charles Foster.
Cover and book design by Julie Scriver.
Printed in Canada by AGMV Marquis.

10 9 8 7 6 5 4 3 2 1

Canadian Cataloguing in Publication Data

Helwig, David, 1938-
The time of her life

ISBN 0-86492-286-8

I. Title.

PS8515.E4T54 2000   C813'.54C   00-900148-4
PR9199.3.H445T54 2000

Published with the financial support of the Canada Council for the Arts, the Government of Canada through the Book Publishing Industry Development Program, and the New Brunswick Department of Economic Development, Tourism and Culture.

Goose Lane Editions
469 King Street
Fredericton, New Brunswick
CANADA E3B 1E5

for Henry Shapiro

One

IT WAS A SMALL FRAME CHURCH, painted white inside and out, with windows of clear glass, rows of wooden chairs, a piano, and at the front a small raised platform with a lectern for the Bible. Jean sat in front of the piano, and as she pressed down the keys, the sound entered the space and floated in the silence. It was a lonely sound, the playing of a piano in an empty church, but she liked it and liked being here alone. Baxter Dunphy, who was the preacher, also ran the grocery store. The two buildings were on the diagonal at the crossroads, and when she wanted to play the piano, she would pick up the key to the church building at the store. Baxter wasn't an ordained minister, but he'd felt the call and had been accepted as a temporary expedient until the little church could hook up with a larger one and get the real thing. He was a tall skinny man with red hair, a face that looked as if one layer of skin had been peeled off, and big hands, and when she asked for the key, he'd smile in an embarrassed way and give her something from the penny candy counter. It made her feel childish, and when she knew she was going to the store, she'd wear a blouse that was tight over her breasts and wear her hair out so that he'd maybe treat her as more grown up. He didn't seem to notice. Then there was a day when Estelle Dunphy, who was a hard fussy woman, square and muscular and plain, was there, and when Jean walked in, Estelle gave her such a look that it made her start to blush, and when Baxter reached for the candies, Estelle said, "What are you doing?" When she said that, he looked at her, confused, and then he looked at Jean, and it was as if he'd just woken up, and his expression changed, and he told her to remember to bring back the key when she was finished, even though she'd never once forgotten.

Outside the window, she could see the leaves of a black ash. There was a little shimmer on the white walls. She finished a hymn and took out the other music that Mrs. Field, her aunt and uncle's neighbour in town, had lent her, the *Peer Gynt* suite. She liked the strange titles: "Morgenstimmung," "In der Halle des Bergkönigs." She had no idea what a Bergkönig might be, but she saw dark feathered creatures close around her on heavy impassioned feet, reaching out and mocking and tempting her to unimaginable things. Both hands in the bass clef, and then her right hand played two octaves up, the notes glittering and thin, and there was something almost shameful about this dancing in the empty church, and she was frightened that Estelle Dunphy might suddenly appear. Jean lifted her hands from the keys, and there was a moment when the notes were still in the air, and then the silence itself was loud, and she turned to see if she was being watched. She went to the window and looked across the road where the trees of the apple orchard stood in their mute obedient rows.

She sat on the flat rocks by the edge of the water and looked over the lake and tried to make out what colour it was. The surface was choppy, with small whitecaps showing here and there. The water itself was neither green nor blue nor merely both together. Green and blue, and underneath that, black. Then when the sun came out again, a sheen of silver.

Later on they were getting a ride into town with one of the neighbours. It would be crowded, all of them in the front of Buzz Easley's truck, Eg sitting on the floor and Iris on her mother's knee, though she was too big for it now, but they didn't get into town much, and everybody wanted to go. Buzz was a silent kind of man; he was always trying to be helpful, and sometimes Jean thought that he was sweet on her mother, but he had a wife, a tiny woman with frizzy grey hair and a wide mouth. While they were in town, Jean would go round to see her aunt Olive, in the house behind her uncle Wilfred's barber shop. She stayed with them in the winter so she could go to high school in town, and there were a couple of books she'd left behind that she wanted to bring home. One was a book called *Stover at Yale*. It was supposed to be a boy's book, but someone gave it to her, the way people were always giving them things since her father died — she hated that. She had picked the book up and started, and it was interesting enough. It was about Yale University and football.

She knew that when they got to town, her mother would ask, the way she always did, whether Jean was going to visit Margery Perkins. Her mother worried that Jean didn't have enough friends, and since she'd told her mother that she and Margery were friends, her mother was always wanting her to drop in, but Jean was never comfortable in Margery's house, Mrs. Perkins speaking in her careful voice, the father at his office downtown. At first Jean was afraid she'd break something, and then she wanted to break something. She'd look at the fancy plates along the plate rail in the dining room and find herself imagining them shattered on the floor. It was the particular way that Margery's mother was nice to her. It made her want to smash things and talk like a farmer, though at home it made her mad when Eg picked up that kind of talk.

It was better just to be friends with Margery at school. They were the smartest in the class, and so it was natural to be friends, even though they were competing for the best marks. It always surprised Jean a little to know that she was smart. Margery's father was a lawyer and her mother had gone to Bowmanville College for Young Ladies, so you'd expect her to be quite intelligent, but Jean didn't know any particular reason why she should have brains. Maybe her father was smart in some kind of a way, though he didn't have much luck. Getting killed by accident like that. He used to laugh a lot and make her laugh. That's what she remembered best, or thought she remembered; it was a long time now.

South along the shore, she saw Elmer Tisdale's boat moving out into the water, a long shape against the glittering light. He might be going out to fish or to poach ducks. Everyone knew that he shot ducks and geese out of season and sold them to one of the hotels, but nobody bothered about it. He and his wife were Catholics, and she was always having the priest over to talk to Elmer and try to stop him drinking and cursing, but Elmer would just get into a fit and move into the little boathouse for a few weeks. He had a stove in there, and on a cold day you'd see the smoke coming from the pipe that stuck out of the shingle roof. Her uncle Ronald said Elmer was going to burn it down someday.

Ronald was her father's brother, but he didn't look much like him. His nose was bigger and there was something a bit crooked about his face. Her father was a handsome man in the pictures they had of him, with a nice smile. She was only seven when he went away. To fight for the King against the Kaiser.

That was how she thought of it when she was little, and she had pictures in her mind; the King's kindly bearded face looked the way she'd seen it on a stamp, and the Kaiser had a helmet with a point on it and sharp teeth like a cat's.

The sun went behind a cloud again, and the colour of the water changed. The air was full of the sound of bird calls, a small bird's high whistle, a little chirruping song, the throaty unreeling call of the red-winged blackbird, the cooing of a mourning dove along the road. The water splashed softly on the rocks, but over it she could hear the distant clicking of a mowing machine and now and then the sound of a human voice as the farmer, who was taking off a field of hay, shouted to one of the farmhands he'd brought in for the harvest.

Her bedroom had no window, and it was very dark, especially in the mornings. Her mother's room on one side of her, and Eg and Iris's room on the other. As soon as the others woke, they expected her to get up. She never thought it was anyone else's business whether she got up or not.

It was just as well the room was dark, it was such a mess. It was the room where everything got stored when there was no place else for it. There was a trunk belonging to her aunt Elma who was in Toronto. It was locked, and she had no idea what was inside it. She called the trunk Uncle Cec and told her brother that Elma used to have a husband, but she got tired of him because he had dirty habits, so she put him in the trunk and dumped him here. There was a pile of boots of her grandfather's that got saved in case somebody grew into them. Two oars to a boat they didn't have any more, and some rolled-up survey maps of the lakes and islands. A pile of her grandmother's magazines, and a box of the rags she used for making quilts. Two broken chairs. An apple box of old jars. Another box full of screws and nails and bolts. A buggy whip. A six-quart basket of spiles for sugaring, even though there wasn't a maple tree within half a mile. Three old coats hung from nails in the wall. Rolls of wallpaper.

When she got tired of sharing a room with Eg and Iris, the two of them crawling into bed with her or jumping on her to wake her up, she'd made a space in the junk and dragged in her bed and put it in a corner with the head under the sloping ceiling, which made her feel enclosed and comfortable. She drove a couple more nails in the wall and put a string between them and hung some of her clothes there, and she pulled her drawer out of the chest in the other room and brought it in here and set it on top of the apple box. It took a couple of good hard slaps to make Eg understand that she wouldn't have him messing with her underwear and things in the drawer. The second time she smacked him so hard he fell over one of the boxes and hit his head on the wall of pine boards and got a lump on it. He went screaming to her mother, but her mother took her side, and Eg left it alone after that.

Dark as it was, and messy, it was her room now, even if the stairs did come up into it so she heard her mother pass through on her way to bed every night. She could lie there and listen to the branches scratching at the tin roof overhead, and sometimes she could hear the nest of bees in the wall. She could lie there and think about the scrapbook of pictures she'd cut out of old magazines that a neighbour gave her mother, how she'd put them together into stories, and she would imagine new events for them and remember the details of how the people looked in the pictures, how they were dressed.

The first time Bruce Docherty came up to her room, he said he was looking for something, a box of old net floats. She heard his voice at the bottom of the stairs.

"I'd bet it's up there with all that other junk," he was saying.

"Well, I suppose it could be," her mother said.

Earlier, she'd been sitting on his knee. It was her uncle Ronald that started it all. For a while now he'd been after her mother, and she could never make out whether her mother liked it or hated it. That night he'd got hold of her mother as she walked past him and pulled her down to sit on his knee. At first her mother struggled a little, but then she just sat there, and Ronald put his arm around her, and something changed in her face, as if she'd just given up, and she let herself lean against him, and while she was doing that, Jean found Bruce looking at her and saying that she better come and sit on his knee to make everybody comfortable, and she did, and there was something about the size and strength of him that did make it comfortable, and then her mother stood up and gave her a look and told her to get up to bed. It wasn't more than a few minutes later when Bruce said that about the floats, and the next thing she knew he was coming up the stairs to her room, one of the small oil lamps in his hand, then he was sitting on the edge of her bed, and his hand was under the covers, stroking her breasts. He wasn't rough, though she could feel how strong his hands were, and she couldn't have pushed him away if she'd wanted to. She didn't want to. Neither of them could think of anything to say, so he sat there quietly stroking one breast, then the other, then he touched her face with the back of his hand and he was gone, and she lay there with her legs tight together, slippery and as wet as if she'd wet her pants.

She was surprised, but then she figured it out. She'd never understood how you could contain it without getting hurt, but now she knew. It all made sense, and it pleased her to have that worked out.

That was a Saturday night, and the next morning in church, as she listened to Baxter Dunphy talk about sin, she supposed that she'd likely been sinful to let Bruce have her breasts like that and to enjoy it. It was hard to know about sin. Was it a sin for her mother to sit on her uncle Ronald's knee? She remembered the look of strain on her mother's face and then the sad easiness that came over it as she let herself lie against him. He wasn't much of a catch, Ronald. He was out of work a lot, and his luck was bad. If somebody was going to fall off a haywagon, Ronald would be the one. Maybe it ran in the family; her father had got himself killed on the way back from the war in some kind of accident on a truck loaded with cases of ammunition.

All through church, she was thinking about Bruce's hands on her, and she found it hard to concentrate on the hymns. She had a good voice, and she liked to sing out and people to tell her how good it sounded, but somehow, right in the middle of "Come Let Us Sing of a Wonderful Love," she remembered when she was younger seeing a neighbour dog on top of their dog Patsy, and how stupid it looked, and even stupider afterwards, the two of them standing there together with their tongues hanging out. She'd sworn that she'd never do it, just never, it was so stupid, and now here she was in church wondering if she'd let Bruce go any further. Maybe not. She wasn't going to find herself up the stump and laughed at by everybody.

He was a lot older than she was. That's what her mother said to her that Sunday morning, but without looking at her, almost as if she might be talking to herself. "Bruce is a lot older than you," she said, and then she went into the back shed and filled the bowl with sugar from the bag out there. As a matter of fact Jean didn't know how old he was. She thought he must be almost thirty. He'd been in the war, but she remembered something about how he lied about his age.

Ronald was fishing with Bruce pretty regularly now and helping him haul the catch to the broker's wharf, and so the two of them were together in the evenings and would come by so Ronald could flirt with her mother, and she wondered if Bruce was after her just for something to do.

He had come up to her room a couple more times. One night he lay down beside her but on top of the covers, his arm around her. He wasn't tall, but he was broad across the chest, and the bed was too small for the both of them. That night he kissed her before he left, and she liked the feeling of his mouth on hers. They never said anything, either one of them.

"I'll be away a few days," he said to her a couple of times, and she wasn't supposed to know, but she did, that he was taking a load of liquor over to the States and that he could end up in jail or hijacked or shot by the coastguard. It was maybe a month now since the night she sat on his knee and he came up here and started to touch her, and she wanted to know what was going to happen. Was she just supposed to move to town and start back to school in the fall? He was careful about her, in a way, but she couldn't believe he was serious. They'd take a walk together, and he'd hug and kiss her, and she'd feel his hands all up and down her back as he lifted her against him, and she was aware of how strong he was, but he never tried to force her. He could easily enough.

Eg was fishing from the end of the little dock, and Jean was sitting nearby, her arms around her knees, watching him. It was a calm day, and over the edge of the grey boards, through the clear water, she could see the rocks and weeds and sometimes a perch or a sunfish. Eg glanced back toward her.

"Why are you lookin' at me?" he said.

"Because you're so handsome, Edgar. That's why."

"I'm not," he said. He looked at her with his embarrassed smile, and the smile reminded her of the smile on her father's face in some of the pictures she'd got out last night. She wasn't sure what had caused her to ask for the box of photographs, which was kept in her mother's room. It had been a long empty day. She'd pulled a few weeds out of the garden, then helped do down some raspberry jam, Eg and Iris licking up the warm sweet saucers of foam skimmed off the top. Then the quiet, the emptiness, boredom, a kind of loneliness, and a feeling as if she might be on the edge of understanding every-thing but couldn't see quite far enough to do it, as if there were something beyond the horizon of the shining lake but out of sight.

As she looked to the northeast, the islands appeared to hover in the air above the surface of the lake. No one had ever been able to explain to her why that happened. Sometimes she would swim out toward the islands as if she could swim far enough to rise above the water as they did. Far out, she would start to think that she could swim forever. The other way, south, was the United States, but it was invisible beyond the water. Still, you always knew that it was there and that the whisky navy was crossing during the dark nights.

The slack curve of her brother's fishing line hung in the air out to the red and green bobber that floated over its reflection in the water. The bobber jiggled and was pulled partly under. Eg gave a sudden yank on the rod and began to pull in the line, but the fish was gone.

"Damn," he said.

"Not supposed to say that."

"Double damn."

"How about triple? Would you go that far?"

"Nope."

He was examining the worm on his hook, adjusting it to cover the metal.

"You want another worm?" she said.

"Not yet."

As Jean leaned forward, her breasts were pressed against her knees. She pressed them harder and moved slowly from side to side, enjoying the softness and warmth. She thought of how Bruce's wide strong hands would rub them up, and the thought made her face get hot.

"I seen you lookin' at them pictures last night."

"Eg, don't talk like a farmer."

"Not a god damn thing wrong with farmers."

"I was looking at pictures of our father."

"Do you remember him?"

"A little."

"I don't."

"I guess not."

"Elmer says he done somethin' real stupid to get killed after the war was over."

"Elmer Tisdale should keep his darn mouth shut. Any man who sleeps in a boathouse."

Eg didn't say anything. He just stared down at the red and

green bobber, waiting for it to twitch, for one of the fish that moved through the green underwater world to seize his hook and be hauled, flopping and gasping, into the bright air. Jean heard a voice behind her, calling her name. She turned and looked over her shoulder, and there was Iris at the door of the house, waving to her to come. Iris was starting to grow fast, and the skirt she was wearing was getting too short. Her legs were spindly, and the bones of her knees stuck out. Soon she'd maybe be tall enough to wear some of Jean's clothes. Jean knew that Iris needed them, but she didn't really want to share.

She walked up the path to where Iris was waiting. Iris had the Chinese look on her face. Nobody knew where their mother got that expression, but they all knew what it meant, that blank, concentrated look, the eyes dark and shiny as some old Chinaman's.

"Mother says somebody's got to go to Dunphy's for some coal oil and a box of salt."

"You don't want to go?"

"No."

"Why not?"

"I just don't."

"You got your Chinese look on. You must be keeping a secret. Got a boyfriend hidden in the woods?"

"No. I don't."

"I thought maybe I'd go play the piano at the church anyway."

She went into the house and grabbed the handle of the red can that they used to carry coal oil.

"You got money?" she said to her mother, who was checking the bottles of jam to see if any were leaking.

"Tell them to charge it. I'll be in next week."

That explained the Chinese look. Iris hated having to charge stuff at Dunphy's store. Jean didn't much like it, but she did it when it had to be done. It was easier if Baxter was behind the counter. Estelle was a hard one. Jean remembered what she heard Ronald say when he thought she wasn't listening. It would be like sticking it into a cord of firewood, he said. She wondered if Baxter would give her candies. She felt like teasing him to see if his red face would get any redder.

The screen door slammed behind her, and she started off along the road that led to the store, the flat fields behind rail fences on both sides of her, a bobolink on one of the fence posts flying away as she got close, a marsh hawk circling over a field of cut hay, hunting for mice. She could hear the sound of her own footsteps on the road and a little wind in the grass and weeds by the edge, could see a swaying in the daisies and buttercups and clover that grew by the fence. She swung the oil can back and forth.

"Here I am," she said aloud, "going to the store on a summer day, the fields all empty, one hawk up in the sky."

Now she'd said it aloud, that story would always be there just at that point in the road, where a boulder stuck out and a snake slid away through the grass. She stopped for a second and felt the breeze on her face, and she closed her eyes and she could feel time passing.

"I have to go," Bruce said. He was casting off the ropes and stepping over the side of the boat, pushing it off with a paddle, and then the engine started, and he was moving out of the light that came from the house and into the huge darkness of the water. It was a moonless night. She watched the shape of the boat as it vanished into the blackness. She listened as it motored toward the Reach, and finally it was in the Reach and she could only imagine the sound.

It was when she started to walk back to the house that she remembered that Ronald was probably still there. She didn't want to go back in. She wasn't ready to sleep, so she went down the drive and started along the road. She'd never thought about it before, but her father must have walked along this road when he was courting her mother. Her mother had always lived in that house. It had been her grandparents' place until her grandfather died and her grandmother moved into town. So her father had come this way, through the darkness, the road surrounded by tall elms. There would be no light except on nights when a little moonlight found its way through the leaves, and maybe her mother would be waiting for him down by the water, mad because he was late, refusing to talk to him or let him put his arm around her. Then she'd relent and let him kiss her.

There was just enough starlight for Jean to make out the road from the patches of cedar swamp on each side. Mosquitoes buzzed all around her, but she moved quickly and they didn't land, or if they did she brushed them away. By the side of the road, she saw the tiny flashes of fireflies against the black-ness.Then the road turned to the right and back toward the lake, the water washing in softly. There was the long stretch of flat rock, where she brought her brother and sister to swim.

She heard voices. They were coming over the water, must be from a boat anchored just off the shore. The voices of men. She stopped walking and tried to listen. It was something bad. She knew that right away. Where they were anchored. That they were anchored there in the pitch dark. Step by step she made her way over the flat rocks toward the water. She felt, ahead of her with her foot before putting it down.

A whippoorwill cried loudly in a tree somewhere behind her and made her jump. The men had heard it and stopped talking. There was a little wind and the soft splash of water. Then they spoke again.

Afterward she couldn't remember any words they'd spoken, and it was almost as if she hadn't heard the words, that she had understood from silences, from the tones of voice. She heard, half-heard, made leaps of understanding, and then she knew: the men in the boat were going to hijack Bruce when he came back down the Reach and made his way into open water toward the American border. That they had guns.

When she went back to the house, Ronald was gone. Her mother had gone up to bed, but she'd left a lamp burning. Jean turned down the wick and blew it out, pulling away from the oily smoke, and then she went down to the shore to wait for the dawn, though she didn't know at first what it was she was going to do. She sat there with an old tarpaulin around her, listening, and watching for daylight to come. It was a still night, and she heard an engine, probably his, coming out of the Reach and turning south, and then she heard another one, and she closed her eyes to concentrate on the sounds, far off as they were. There was a little whisper of breeze that made it harder to hear, and she held herself as still as a frightened rabbit pointing its long soft ears. She searched the night, her concentration moving across the invisible horizon of the water, and once she thought she heard distant gunshots. All she could do was wait for first light. She would steal the Murton's rowboat and go for him. The night went on and on, and she tried to pretend that all this was different, that she was waiting for him to come in his boat and take her off to someplace, Niagara

Falls maybe, and they'd go to a big hotel and have dinner in a place with heavy silver and white tablecloths and napkins and fine china plates. The waiter would be a Chinaman who bowed when he brought things to the table, and she'd be wearing an emerald green dress with lace at the collar and sleeves. She managed to think that for a minute or so, but not long. It was cold and lonely under the tarpaulin, and coldest when she finally saw the first brightening of the sky over the black water, an icy green light and then pink, and then the sun hauled itself up into the sky, reflected in the drops of dew on the tall weeds. As she looked out across the water into the blinding sun, she saw nothing. There was no heat to stop the shivering that made her press her elbows into her sides and clasp her hands together tight as she could. It was full light now, and she knew that someone could see her from the windows of the house. If anyone got up and saw her bed empty they might look out the window and find her. Elmer Tisdale would rouse in the boathouse just round the curve of shore and notice her as he came out to do his business off the end of the dock.

The sun got higher, and finally she thought she saw something dark far out there, his boat, as still as if he'd stopped to drop his nets, but she knew that wasn't why it was there, and she threw off the tarpaulin and ran along the rocks of the shore to the Murtons' and untied the rowboat. She made too much noise, banging the oars as she got it underway, but she didn't care. She knew what she should be doing was waking someone, banging on the roof of Elmer Tisdale's low boathouse. His motorboat would be the way to get there, but she couldn't do that, she splashed helplessly at the water and then made herself row carefully, trying to imitate the rhythm of Tilly Murton himself, who could move the boat over the water as if it were light as a waterstrider. But she kept going, struggling to hold the oars, leaning and pulling, stopping now and then to look over her shoulder and correct her course, and gradually the long curving shape of the launch came closer. The blisters began on her palms and fingers, but she rowed with determination and all the strength she had. She would get to the boat and find him, although she was sick with the thought of what she would find. There would be blood. She had to be prepared for blood. She thought of animal blood and chicken guts to try to prepare herself, and still nothing mattered but to lean and pull and balance her two arms so that the catch of the oars was even on the two sides of the boat.

Her hands were raw, and there was still a long way to go to get back to the shore. Her fingers were too small to grip the oars properly, didn't reach all the way round, and sometimes as she pulled the oars toward her she felt as if they might slip from her hand and had to cramp her fingers tightly into a hook. Now there were places that had blistered and broken, that hurt her each time she hauled backward, and then one oar would slip out of the water and the force of her pull would make her fall sideways almost off the seat. There was too much weight at the prow. As she leaned forward and down, lifting the blades of the the oars out of the water and setting them for another stroke, they would rattle in the oarlocks, and sometimes she'd lean too far, and the pin would lift almost out. She shifted on the seat, but it was hard wherever she sat. She was thin, and her bones knocked on the wood. She remembered Bruce telling her she was skinny as a boy. She was sore all over, her arms and shoulders and hands, her behind and her legs, from sitting in one place in the boat, and she needed to pee. She could go over the edge of the boat, but if she did that, she'd have to look at what was lying at the prow, weighing it down, and she couldn't look. She was afraid to look. She'd look when she got close to shore, and then she'd do what she had to do. It was hard to steer a rowboat over long distances, but she'd planned how to do it without having to look over her shoulder all the time, using the location of the islands on her left, and the shape of his boat behind her. She was smart enough to keep the launch directly off the stern and judge her direction by that, and later by the location of the two islands. Before long, she'd have to look ahead and make some plan about where to come ashore. There was the chance that someone might see her. If they did, would they send a man out for her? Earlier she'd seen the dark shape of a fishing boat, far off and low to the water, moving to the south, gradually smaller and then gone.

The wind was getting up a little. The boat was at an angle to the waves, and the low chop tossed it and made her miss the water with one of the oars more often. Every time she did, it hurt her. She almost wished someone would come. The sun was well up in the sky by now, catching the tops of the small waves in repeated flashes. For a second she stopped rowing and stared back across the lake, the endless reach of silvery water that went on and on, and just toward the horizon, she could still see his boat, powerless and ruined, a dark spot in the emptiness of sky and water. A cormorant moved along in a straight line, close over the water. She reached down and put one of her hands into the slop at the bottom of the boat, and the cold water made it feel better. She did the same with the other one, and then wiped them on the skirt of her dress. She almost wanted to turn and look. Something in her said, Do it, but she wouldn't. She wasn't ready. Closer to shore she'd look. She gripped the oars. While she was soaking her hands, the wind had turned the boat, so that the islands were off the stern, and the shoreline was on her left but still a ways off. She could make out a tall tree with a crow on a dead branch, and a horse standing in a field nearby. The horse had its head lifted, as if it were looking across the water. Maybe it could catch the smell of the boat from the onshore wind, the smell of the girl and another smell. Then it put down its head and began to crop the grass, and she felt a disappointment. She wanted to be watched by someone. *God sees the little sparrow fall, it meets his tender view. If God so loves the little things, I know he loves me, too.* She figured that God might have given up on her just recently. Not likely he approved of what she'd been up to with Bruce. He'd be better off keeping his eye on those sparrows, though from what she'd seen of sparrows, they had only a couple of things on their minds, eating and the other. She wasn't altogether sure how bad it was, what they'd been up to, from God's point of view. Those few dark tender moments that had ended up here.

She got the boat turned the right way, but it was hard to hold it like that, and she was very tired. The broken blisters raw and stinging, her bones banging the seat, she heaved at the water in this foolish attempt to bring him back to land. There was a bottle of whisky up there in the prow beside him. When she'd tried to pour it in his mouth, it had all spilled down his clothes, and the smell had sickened her. She could try to drink some to give her strength. They gave it to sick people, but she knew that it would make her puke, and besides, to get it she would have to give up her last stupid hope. To turn and know what she wanted not to know, that he was dead, had been since she found him. She wouldn't admit it as she dragged his body into the little rowboat. He'd be alive, somehow, when she got to shore. But she knew that wouldn't happen. She'd turn and look at the blood and the eyes, and he'd be dead. It was so stupid of him to get himself killed. She tried to think what she was going to do.

To bring the body ashore and tell her foolish story. To explain about Bruce, about what they'd been doing, how he came up to her room, how she had to go for him. They'd say she was crazy, laugh at her, rowing a dead man around the lake in a stolen boat. It was a story everyone would tell, like her father getting himself blown up after the war was all over. A real love story, Jean rowing a boat with a dead man. No. She wouldn't have that. She wouldn't have that said. Her whole body was shuddering with cold and tiredness and fear, she was starting to cry. Somewhere, she had to find the strength to finish it all, to push the body overboard and watch it sink like a dark ugly useless fish.

Two

PARIS IN 1917. The city is marked by war and yet life goes on, as it has for the two thousand years of the city's history. Men and women meet under the trees of the Tuileries and stroll the wide shaded walks and later, perhaps, go to a small hotel for an hour of pleasure. Sometimes at night the distant guns can be heard, like the rumble of iron wheels over stone.

Men and women are gathered in a fashionable café, regular customers who have come here for years, soldiers on leave. Two young women get up from a table and walk toward the door. An automobile waits outside.

"Cut," the director shouted, and everyone relaxed. The actor with the thin moustache who was playing a German spy pulled out a cigarette and a package of matches and lit up. Jean and Rhoda stood at the place they'd reached in their walk through the café and waited for instructions from the director. He was one of the Englishmen who were making the movie, young and handsome, and he kissed Jean on the cheek whenever he got near her. He came up to the two of them now and put one arm around each of them and gave Jean his usual little kiss.

"You look splendid, my dear." What she disliked about all these gestures was that they meant nothing at all. She liked the look of the man and the smell of him — it must be some wonderful soap he used — and she would have liked attention from him if it was meant. She intended to have such things, but the director was like the set for the Parisian café, he was an illusion got up for the occasion. He went and got a stagehand to move a couple of tables, some chairs, talked to some of the people who were to walk in after Jean and Rhoda walked out.

"As they walk by," the director said to the spy, "you lift your head and give them a smile. Two beautiful young women, just the thing."

Jean and Rhoda went back to where they started. Rhoda was from the States, and in different costume and makeup, she would play a French country girl in another part of the movie. Jean was hoping they'd propose the same thing to her. Rhoda said she planned to change her name as soon as she got a big part. She had strange eyes and thick lips, and one of the other actresses from New York had made a crude joke about the only kind of big part that Rhoda would ever get. Jean was shocked at a lot of the things these people said, but she liked it, too. It was only a couple of weeks since one of the Englishmen, who saw her in her uncle Wilfred's barbershop one day when she came in to get some money to go shopping for her aunt Olive, had come around and said she could be in the movie if her aunt and uncle would let her. So far as Jean was concerned, the only interesting thing she'd done all year was play a slave girl in the Sunday School pageant at Easter at the big church in town, so she kept at her aunt until she said yes. She got off school two days early to do it. Just a week ago she'd been a schoolgirl, but she was dead sick of it all. She couldn't take it seriously. When Mrs. Tolley had the girls out in the yard doing physical jerks, she'd find herself clowning and doing double somersaults and cartwheels that showed too much. At the house she could feel her uncle Wilfred watching her, and she knew what he was thinking.

She was at home here with the movie people; ever since what had happened with Bruce Docherty, she'd been ready to run away. The Englishman who brought her here was after her, but he was too old, and his skin was ugly. Also she figured he was a crook. She avoided him. Her favourite person on the film crew was Del, the cameraman. Del didn't say much, but last night they'd been sitting around, waiting to do this scene in the café, but delayed because half the furniture hadn't arrived, and he took her out to a restaurant for dinner, and she found that without saying one word he could make her laugh, the shape of his mouth and the way he looked at things. When he took her back to the boarding house where she was staying, he kissed her, and she liked it a lot and knew that he could feel her liking it, and just as he turned to leave he said, Do you want to run away with me, kid? Jean said, Yes, sure. It was the only thing to say, and now she couldn't stop wondering whether he meant it, whether she'd got herself into something. If so, all the better. Last week, she'd heard that her mother was going to marry Ronald, and she didn't want to go back there once Ronald was in the house. She could stay a while longer with her aunt and uncle, but sooner or later her uncle Wilfred was going to get his hands on her. She could feel heat come off him whenever she passed him in the hall, and he tried not to look at her. Jean had begun to have secret knowledge about men.

"Camera ready, Del?" the director said.

Del nodded. She could see that he had his eye on her. Then he got behind the camera and took hold of the crank, ready to turn it. She and Rhoda took their places. They were back in Paris now, where her father was once, during the war. He'd sent a little model of the Eiffel tower, and her mother had it in her bedroom right beside a picture of him with a big grin on his face.

The spy sits in his place in the Paris café where he will be

seen by the handsome young Canadian officer, who is there
with his rich friend whose makeup is so heavy that he looks
like a woman. Jean and Rhoda walk through the café and out
the door into the street. Nearby is a bakery where they stop for
bread, and they will walk up narrow stairs to a small room with
a view over the steeply angled rooftops.

Jean is sitting naked on a straight chair in a hotel room, and a
man is cutting off her hair. She said it to herself that way, and it
sounded like a strange dream or a story she might have been
told, but she couldn't imagine who would ever tell her such a
story; she didn't know people to whom such things happened.
Except now she did. When Del started to cut her hair, she said
it would ruin her clothes, and he said, Well, take them off, and
she looked at him, the way he was laughing at her, and,
defiant, she did it. Now the hair he'd cut was tickling her
shoulders and her back, and it made her wriggle.

"Hold still," Del said. "I don't want to cut your ear off."

"It tickles."

He went on cutting. She could hear the sound of the
scissors as the sharp edges went through the hair. It reminded
her of her uncle's barbershop, and that made her want to
giggle, except that at the same time it made her almost sick.
There was hair all over the floor of the room, the way there
always was in Wilfred's barbershop. There was something
ugly about it, the piles of hair, as if a slaughter had taken
place. Del stepped back for a second, and Jean looked down
at herself. There were tiny hairs fallen all over the white skin

of her breasts. Del was looking at her, and that made her shiver a little.

"That'll do," he said, "we'll just keep your hat on."

They were disguising Jean as a man to get her over the border safely. Del said he could be arrested for driving a girl across the border in his car. He told her that last night, about the Mann Act. He explained that it was so the police could stop gangsters. You couldn't take a young girl across a state line for an immoral purpose.

"What's an immoral purpose?" she said.

"I'll show you," he said. It was very late by the time he took her back to the boarding house.

This morning she'd heard him talking to George, one of the camera assistants who was going to take over after Del left. George was a tiny, fiery Englishman who knew they were running away, and Del told him about the need to get men's clothes for her.

"It's the Mann Act," Del said.

"The man act?" George said, laughing, incredulous. "You mean you've been doing her like Oscar Wilde did the stable boys?"

"It's an Act of Congress, George."

"That's a fancy name for buggery," George said and walked off snorting.

When she asked Del what George was talking about and he explained it to her, she just stared at him.

"Don't worry," he said, "it's not my style. Doesn't seem worth the extra trouble."

As she sat on the chair, the cane seat pinching at her bottom and the little sticks of the back hard against her skin, Del opening and closing the scissors in his hand, she felt a moment of panic, as if she were on the edge of a high cliff and it was too late to turn back, but below there might be anything, she might die of fear on the way down.

Now it was done. They'd sneaked in the back door of the hotel this afternoon, the way they did the night before, past the kitchen with its smell of boiling fat and rotting garbage and up the stairs, stopping at each floor so Del could look down the hall. If anyone spotted her, there would be hell to pay. They got safely into the room, and the hair was cut and lay all around, and now Del was telling her to try on the clothes he'd got for her from George, who was just about her size.

"I got to get all these hairs off me," she said, and went into the bathroom, and there she saw herself in the mirror, naked and helpless, all her beautiful hair gone. She tried to think if she looked like a boy, but she could see too much of herself to believe that. She ran water in the bathtub and climbed in. Del wandered into the room.

"Go away," she said.

"What's the matter?"

"Bring the clothes in here, and I'll come out when I'm finished."

She hated him right then for changing her, and she didn't look or speak when he brought in the clothes. He closed the door when he went out. She splashed water all over herself and scrubbed her hair and rinsed it. The mirror was fogged from the hot water, and she was glad not to see her ruined head. When she was dry, she began to dress, her own underwear and then the white shirt, the trousers and jacket that were stiff and thick and smelled of cigarettes, then the socks and shoes, so heavy they felt like metal weights on her feet. The mirror had started to clear. Through the thin fog that remained she saw the shape of a stranger, and she knew that Jean, the person she'd been and known, was gone now. Jean had fallen over a high cliff and died and been replaced by this other, who would say her words, but they wouldn't be the same words. She knew that she would never go home again. Well, only desperation got you anywhere, she'd always known that.

The last piece of clothing was a fedora. As a joke she'd tried it on in Del's car, but now it was serious. The mirror still wasn't clear, but she set the hat on her head at the right angle, the way her uncle Wilfred set his when he went out to the meeting of his lodge, and she opened the door and walked into the room where Del was waiting for her. His face was empty for a moment, almost frightened, and then he smiled.

"Holy Toledo," he said, "look at you." Jean caught a glimpse of herself in the mirror on the front of the wardrobe where he kept his clothes, and she saw how easy it was to be someone new. She realized that she could be anybody. She walked over to Del and put her arms around him to kiss him, and he almost pulled away, and that made her laugh.

"Are you scared of me, Mr. Delbert Hunnicut? Is that what?" Then she kissed him as a man might kiss.

It was pitch dark when she woke up, and the car was stopped at the side of the road. She was stiff from sleeping in the seat, and she knew there was something wrong. It was so dark that she couldn't tell earth from sky, and at first she didn't know where she was, thought she was alone, then she remembered she was in the United States, running away. She could just make out a shape in the other seat.

"Delbert."

"You're awake."

He sounded far off, as if he couldn't remember who she was. "What's wrong?"

"Nothing. We got a flat, but I can't see to fix it. We'll have to wait till it's light."

They'd got across the border all right, late in the afternoon. She hadn't worn the clothes they'd borrowed from George after all. Del had bought her some boy's clothes and a cap, and he said that she was his nephew John Hunnicut, that they'd been on a fishing trip in Canada but John got sick with something and Del had to get him home to New York City to his family. They got right through, and Jean made Del stop by a patch of woods a few miles away, and she changed back into her own clothes. When she looked in the rear view mirror, her hair was strange, but if she fluffed it up with her fingers, it looked like a bob, well, more or less.

They sat in silence for a while. Jean could hear a soft wind in the leaves and the scuffling of some animal. The buzz of a mosquito. She remembered the night she had sat in the dark waiting for enough light to go out for Bruce when he'd been hijacked. She had bad dreams about that, dreams where Bruce was still alive when she pushed his body into the water. She'd never told anyone about it. She remembered how Bruce's body sank slowly and heavily into the water of the lake, and how she brought the boat to shore and met Tilly Murton and told him she'd heard guns and gone out in the dark to look for Bruce, but she couldn't find him and she got lost. Tilly didn't say much, but he walked her home. Her mother was mad. She thought she'd gone off to meet Bruce somewhere, but she told her the same story she told Tilly. It wasn't until two months later they found Bruce's body and had a funeral. Once or twice she thought of telling the story to Del, but she never did. There was a little light that showed the shapes of the treetops against the sky. She wondered if it could be morning, but then she could tell by the clarity and coldness of the light that it was the moon rising. It would be a long wait until dawn. Del lit a cigarette, and by the light of the match, his face was shadowed and harsh. He looked toward her.

"We could get in the back."

"What for?"

"Can't you guess?"

"If you want."

"It'd pass the time."

So they did. It was crowded, and she had her feet hanging over into the front with Del crouched between her legs. Jean was far away. She looked at the moonlight falling on the trees. The light on the tree branches was thin and bleak, and she closed her eyes. She put her hands on Del's back and he moved in her hands and she listened to his breathing and the empty space inside her was like a huge tickling, getting bigger, too big, as if something might burst, her breathing came hard, and she held onto Del tighter, wrapped her legs around him, and his sounds were in her ears. It was electric and unbearable, and she could hear her voice crying out and she couldn't stop.

When they were trying to get back into the front seat, she had to ask.

"Is that supposed to happen?"

"Yeah, sure," he said. "Didn't you know?"

"No."

"That's why people do it."

"I guess so." She noticed she was crying.

They tried to sleep for a while, and Jean dozed off. Finally it began to be morning, and they took turns going off into the cold woods to relieve themselves. Del found the wrench and the spare and the jack, and Jean went to find a big rock to put behind the back wheel. She stood by the side of the road, chilled in spite of the sunlight, and watched him jack up the car and change the tire. She didn't know where they were, all she could see was woods, and she breathed in the morning air as if she could taste the sunlight and thought about all the things she wanted, starting with something to eat. This was the United States, but it didn't look too much different, though later, when they stopped in the first small town they came to, there was an American flag in front of the store. Del gave her an American dollar to go to the store and get something to eat while he took the tire down the road to the garage. Del said he figured he was lucky to have got paid before he left, the Englishmen were all crooks.

The woman in the store had a round, pleasant face and pink cheeks. "You from out of town? " she said.

"Stopped to fix a flat tire," Jean said.

"You with your family?"

"My uncle."

"Where you from?"

"New York City."

Jean knew that the woman was suspicious, so she bought some cherry tarts and a pint of milk and left. She could see the garage down the road, and she walked along past a couple of small white frame houses, eating one of the tarts, catching the juice with her tongue as the pastry broke. She thought about what it had been like in the car last night with Del, and she wanted it again, right now. When she got to the garage, a short, thick man with no hair at all was working on the tire. He'd taken out the tube and was putting a patch on it.

"You getting it fixed, Uncle Del?" she said.

"Be done soon."

"Wouldn't want to have another night like that one," she said, and winked at him.

He put his finger to his lips when the man was looking the other way.

"You want a cherry tart, Uncle Del? They're pretty good."

"Get them at the store?" the man said.

"Yes," Jean said. "You want one?" She took the lid off the bottle of milk and drank a little from the mouth, trying not to drip on her clothes.

"That's my wife in there," the man said. "She makes them."

"Nice lady."

She could see that Del was mad at her, but she didn't care. She handed him a cherry tart, and he took it without saying a word and started to eat it. In a few minutes the tire was on the rack over the back bumper, and Del was paying the man.

Back on the highway, Del turned to her. "You got to use your head, you know. We could get in a lot of trouble."

"You could."

"You could end up in some kind of home for wayward girls."

"I'd just tell them you made me do it."

Del said nothing for the next few miles. She was scared, but it made her defiant. She didn't say a word. Finally she could see his hands, which had been gripping the steering wheel as if he was trying to kill it, relax a little.

"You're a terror," he said.

"Take me to New York City, Uncle Del, " she said.

She was getting tired of holding the pose. She was stretched out on a piece of cloth on top of a long couch with no back, just a curve at one end. It was better than standing poses, especially those with your arms up. But even lying down like this you soon found that you wanted to move your hip, or your neck itched, or you were cold and coming out in goose bumps. But she got paid, and if she did enough sessions she could get herself the kind of clothes that she saw in the store windows on Fifth Avenue. Funny when you thought of it like that, taking off your clothes to get money for clothes.

She hardly noticed it anymore, that she was naked with all these people looking at her. From the day she'd arrived, New York had been one shock after another, the skyscrapers so high above the streets that she always felt something was going to fall on her from above, the noise, the machines, the shouting voices, the crowds, the lights that were never turned off; there was no real night, no end to anything. Hucksters and thieves and bums and all the coloured people. She'd never seen even one of them before. The first time she went in an elevator, she was so frightened she thought she'd be sick. When Del took her to Times Square at night, she couldn't stop talking about the brightness of it all, the colours of all the neon lights. She still expected things to drop from the buildings onto the endangered streets. She couldn't believe the darkness and racket under the Third Avenue El. After all that, what surprise that she took off every stitch of her clothes and let strangers stare at her.

It started with Del and his camera. While he was waiting for another movie job, and while they were talking about whether to go to California — she didn't think she'd ever become a movie actress by hanging around New York — he drove her out to a beach on Long Island one day, very early in the morning when there was nobody around, and he told her to take off her clothes, and he took pictures of her there, on the wide beach of white sand, the rising sun blindingly bright on the ocean, and other pictures up in the dunes among the tussocks of grass. It was exciting, the way he looked at her, his concentration, and they laughed all the way back to the city. He had the pictures hanging in the big room full of junk he called his studio, and he took more pictures of her in there, and one night a couple of friends of his who were photographers brought some gin around, and they were all drinking the gin and looking at the pictures, and one of the others said would she pose for him. Jean wasn't sure what she was supposed to say, but then he said what he'd pay her and she said yes. She was tired of never having any money.

The photographer's name was Paul, and he was very tall and thin, with very short hair and very bright blue eyes. Jean thought he would probably make a pass at her once she had her clothes off, but he never did, and later on Del told her that he liked boys instead. She thought maybe that was why he made such good pictures of her; he wasn't always thinking about something else. She worked for him once a week now, and he said he was going to have an exhibition of the pictures he'd made of her, and she and Del would get an invitation. If that happened, she wanted to have something beautiful to wear, maybe a pale blue silk dress she'd seen in the window at Bonwit Teller, so people could see that she looked good even with her clothes on.

After every session with Paul, she'd put her clothes back on and look at her face in the mirror to see if she'd changed. She always felt a little as if she might have suddenly grown horns or a beard, and she'd look hard at her eyes to see if the expression was different. Paul said cameras were very dangerous, but most people didn't know it. That was why they couldn't take good pictures. When she told Del, he said it was nonsense, Paul was full of nonsense, but Jean just thought maybe Paul was too serious. He never made jokes like Del and the others. Even when they went out at night to a club where some black men played their music and everybody got drunk, Paul never got drunk and never said much of anything.

One day someone phoned from an art school. They said they were looking for a model and they heard she was available. So now she took off her clothes three times a week in this dusty, drafty room with high windows, and a bunch of people sat around at little easels and painted her. None of them was any good, that's what Del said, and they just came to get a chance to look at a naked girl. She thought that might be true, partly, though they mostly acted very serious about their work and were always asking the teacher if they'd got things right. Anyway, now she had a little money of her own, she could buy what she wanted to eat, and she was saving to get that dress. It was going to take a while, except there was another photographer who wanted to do some pictures. He wanted to put out a deck of cards with pictures of her on the back. Paul, who knew him, said she shouldn't trust him, that she should ask for a lot of money and make sure she had it in her pocketbook before she took off even one shoe.

The teacher said it was time to stop, and Jean got up and went into the little room where she left her clothes. She got dressed and combed her hair. It was growing back in, and Del took her to a hairdresser who trimmed it so it looked more like a real bob and less like a bad accident. It still wasn't right, but it was better. She remembered a tall girl they met in the club where the black men played who kept telling her she liked her hair, just being a cruel bitch. When she asked Jean what kind of a job she had, Jean said, "I get paid to take

off my clothes." That shut her up for a minute but not for
long.

Jean pulled on the dark red cloche hat she'd bought last
week, pulled it down so you could just see a bit of hair at the
side, then she went out into the big room. Nearly everyone was
gone now. The teacher gave her two dollars, and she put the
money in her purse and put on her gloves and went down the
stairs to the street. When she reached the corner, she bought an
apple from an Italian peddler with a cart. The art school was
near Washington Square, so she walked a couple of blocks to
get there and sat on a bench looking at the sunlight in the green
leaves of the trees, the bits of blue sky above. She looked past
the big stone arch at the Fifth Avenue end of the square to the
row of houses with white columns beside the doors. They
looked rich. On the other side of the square a drayman drove
his two big horses and the loaded dray into a narrow alley.
There were two or three cars parked near her, and a man got
out of one of them and came toward her. She recognized him
as one of the men who was in the art class, a short man with
grey hair and a grey moustache and a grey suit and fedora,
even a grey tie, but all that grey emphasised the redness of his
lips and the blackness of his dark eyes. He was carrying a
walking stick. He came to the bench where she was sitting.

"May I sit down?" he said.

"I guess you could. There's room on the bench."

"You're Canadian," he said. "Aren't you?"

"How'd you know?"

"I have business dealings there. I recognize your accent."

"Didn't know I had one."

"Oh yes. How old are you? "

"Are you from the police or something?"

"No. Only that I wondered."

Jean was still suspicious.

"I'm twenty," she said.

"I don't think so," he said, "but if you want to be twenty, that will be fine."

They sat in silence, the man with his hands folded on the top of his stick, his lips thrust slightly forward in a way that made you think he was concentrating on something difficult and far off.

"Would you like to come round to my apartment for tea?"

Jean had been wondering how she'd spend the afternoon. Del was busy these days working on some movie about New York Harbour that had him out on boats, and he never got back until late.

"All right," she said.

As they drove uptown, Jean looked around her at the men pushing racks of dresses across lower Broadway, at the crowds on the sidewalk, the newsboy on the corner, the file of cars that passed them going the other way, the expensive clothes on display in the stores, and all of a sudden she remembered her bedroom at home, with Iris and Eg in the next room, the sound of the waves outside during a storm. They went past Central Park, and the man stopped the car at a small apartment house on a quiet street on the upper East Side. As they were about to get out of the car, the man looked toward her. The corners of his eyes were red, like his mouth.

" My name is Alvin Coortland," he said. "Will you tell me yours?"

"Jean."

"I'll want to be able to introduce you to Mrs. Hamson, my housekeeper."

When he did introduce her, after they'd ridden in an elevator up to his apartment, he said, "Mrs. Hamson, this is

Jean, from my art class," as if she were one of the students, but Mrs. Hamson looked disapproving anyway. She went off to make tea, and Jean and Alvin Coortland sat in high upholstered chairs in a room with large windows that let in the brightness from outdoors but with dark fabric everywhere, heavy maroon curtains, a rug in an even deeper red, like dried blood, tables of some dark wood, and the chairs and the sofa upholstered in a gold colour with a swirling pattern of purple flowers. Even the lamps had deep maroon shades with heavy black tassels.

Alvin Coortland said nothing while they were waiting for the tea. When it came, there was a plate of little cakes for each of them, and Jean was hungry, but she knew enough to know that she wasn't supposed to eat them all. Or was that just small town manners? One of the things she'd learned was that things in other places weren't always what you expected. You could never be sure what was right. Mrs. Hamson poured tea for her and put the cup and saucer and the plate on a small table beside her chair.

"Why are you in New York?" Alvin Coortland said when he had eaten one small cake.

"There isn't any why," she said. "I'm just here."

He considered that for a few moments, drank some of his tea. He took a large drink, as if very thirsty for it.

"How old did you say you are?"

"Twenty," Jean said.

"That's the age you've chosen to be, is it?"

"Yes."

"Do you know that you're very beautiful?"

"You mean without my clothes?"

"With or without."

"My hair's a mess."

He looked at her hair as if to decide.

"Did you cut it yourself?"

"No."

"It takes nothing away from your beauty."

He lifted the cup and finished his tea. Jean sipped some of hers.

"I was in a movie," she said.

"In Canada? Do they make movies there? "

"There's a studio in Trenton. It was a movie about the war. I was a girl in a café in Paris."

"You want to be in more movies."

"Yes."

"Why?"

"Because it's not real. Is that a good enough reason?"

His eyes with their red corners were looking at her. Black, shining.

"Would you like more tea?" he said.

She shook her head. He poured milk into his cup and added tea from the pot and again drank it thirstily.

"Shall I show you the pictures I've drawn of you?"

She shrugged.

"You're not sure."

"It's okay."

"They're like the movies," he said, "not real."

He lifted himself from his chair and walked to a large wooden chest with a series of wide, narrow drawers. One of these he pulled open, and he took out a sheaf of papers which he brought to her and put in her lap. As she looked at the drawings, she remembered each of the days in front of the art class. She could feel each posture and the cool air on her skin. It made her shiver. The drawings were skilled and gentle. Her flesh looked pale and delicate, and once or twice he had drawn her face, and it was, perhaps, beautiful.

"Do you like them?"

"No."

"Why not?"

"You said they're not real, but they are. They make me sad. I don't like things that make me sad."

"Not even sad movies."

"Movies aren't sad. That's what's good about them."

"Come and look at the other drawers."

He led her to the large wooden chest. The curving brass drawer pulls on the front caught the light from the window and shone against the dark wood. But the wood had its own dim deep shine as well, the grain flecked and whorled, with subtle shadings under the softly burnished surface. A flash of sunlight reflected off the brass. All the light in the room sank into the colours, the curtains, the rug like dried blood.

He pulled out one of the drawers. The bottom of the drawer was green felt, and on the felt lay three drawings in dark brown ink, scratchy lines, but you could see the figures hidden in the scratchings, the pattern of dark and light, groups of men and women in strange clothing. A man in a turban. Someone she thought must be Jesus in a long gown. The drawings were just scribbles in brown ink, but she could always tell what was happening. He closed the drawer and opened another, where there was just one drawing, in white on pale grey paper, of a naked woman with chubby thighs and belly and soft breasts, lying on a bed. Jean could feel the texture of the dimpled flesh and the texture of the rumpled sheets. He closed the drawer and opened another, where there were two landscapes, both with a river and oddly shaped trees, little bits of grass. Then the bodies of two naked men with spears, and a small drawing of a man's face, bearded, the skin around the eyes wrinkled and sagging. Then he closed that drawer as well, slowly but with finality. "Enough for today," he said. "I must have you wanting to come back."

"What are they?"

"They are what are called 'master drawings.'"

Mrs. Hamson appeared at the door of the room. "Will you be here for dinner, sir?"

"No, thank you, Mrs. Hamson. I will be going out. Please take the tea things, and then you may go if you wish."

"Thank you, sir." It sounded disapproving. She put all the plates and cups and saucers on a tray and left the room, and Jean could hear noises from a kitchen somewhere.

"Mrs. Hamson thinks I am contriving to be left alone with you."

"Are you?"

"Of course. Come and sit down."

The took their places again in the two chairs.

"Tell me more about those drawings."

"Another time." He said that and stopped, as if all the words were gone from him now. Mrs. Hamson appeared at the door in her coat and said goodbye. Alvin Coortland walked to the door of the apartment with her. When he came back in the room, he came directly to Jean's chair and held out his hand to her, took her hand in his and led her down a hall to a bedroom, a windowless room with a large bed with high wooden posts.

"Will you take off your clothes for me?" he said.

Jean looked at him, the tidy way he stood, the straight nose and thick grey eyebrows, the red mouth. He was as unlikely as some character in a fairy tale. She could almost believe that under his clothes he had scales, claws on his feet, and yet there was something in the place he'd brought her that was rich and comforting. Nothing made sense any more, but then she remembered lying in the bed in her little room at home among all the clutter, and that made no more sense, not really. She began to take off her clothes. When she was naked, he lifted her onto the bed and arranged her as if he might be planning to make another drawing. Then he took off his own clothes and climbed on the bed. He lay beside her, a small man, lighter than Del, but the way he lay beside her reminded her of Bruce coming to her room and lying beside her, the strength and power of his thick compact body.

The man kissed her in a slow, patient way, and fondled her with his thin warm hands, then lay on top and rubbed himself against her, then there was a little fiddling and he was inside her, surprisingly big, and then with a little snort it was over almost as soon as it began.

He was off the bed and dressing, and Jean put on her own clothes, and he led her back into the big room and poured clear brown liquid from a decanter into a small glass with a stem and gave it to her.

"What is it?" she said. It was the first thing she'd said since he led her to the bedroom, and she was surprised to find that her voice still worked.

"Sherry," he said. "I'm sure you'll like it."

He poured himself a glass and drank it the same greedy way he drank the tea. Jean tasted it. It was bitter, like medicine, and she could sense the bite of the alcohol on her tongue.

"This is illegal," she said.

"And it's a very foolish law."

"Where I come from they take it across in boats."

"They do a great public service."

Drinking the gin that Del sometimes gave her mixed with

ginger ale or juice, Jean had found that alcohol went to her head quickly. After only a few sips of the sherry, the swirls of colour in the upholstery held her eyes, it was a jungle; the black eyes of Alvin Coortland were brighter and even more intent.

"Is this heaven or hell?" she said. She was startled as the words came out. She didn't know she was going to say that.

"I think it's only the world."

Jean found she was staring at a picture on the wall. It was very dark, and a face emerged out of the darkness, almost emerged. The face of a woman. In the shadows below, she could make out another face, the bearded face of a man, when she looked closely she saw it was the severed head of a man, the woman holding it by the hair in her left hand, in her right hand a sword.

"As you will have gathered, Jean, I have a good deal of money. If there's any way that I can help you, you must tell me."

The man had poured himself another glass of sherry and was drinking it down.

"I should go soon," Jean said.

"I'll drive you home."

"Just to Washington Square, where you picked me up."

"Will you come again sometime?"

"Yes," Jean said, and after she said it she didn't know why.

The room was full of smoke, and the lights were dim except for those that shone on the musicians who sat on a platform against the far wall. The four coloured men were sweating from the heat in the low basement room and the work of playing their music, and the lights gleamed on their wet faces. Everything was too close and too far off, intrusive and untouchable. Wherever she looked, Jean saw unknown faces, and they grew strange in her eyes.

A tall boy in a suit and with a thin moustache was standing beside her, saying something to her, but she couldn't hear. There was something unnaturally stiff about the way he was standing.

"I can't hear what he's saying," Jean said.

Paul was sitting on one side of her, Del on the other.

"He asked you to dance with him," Paul said. There was a little dance floor at the front of the room with only two couples dancing.

Jean looked up at the boy and tried to smile.

"I'm sorry," she said. "No. I can't."

The boy didn't move. She looked up at him again, and he was staring at her. She realized that he was not much older than she was. He was staring hard at her, as if the force of his look would make her go with him.

"I don't feel well," she said. "I'm sorry, but I can't dance with you."

He didn't move. Jean wondered if he, too, was deafened by the noise of the music and the voices. Del and Paul were both looking at him as he waited there with a stolid animal patience, as if he knew that after he stood there long enough, Jean would get up and dance with him. People at a couple of other tables were watching them. Jean began to feel that something was wrong, that something terrible was going to happen, that this boy's silent determination was bad and dangerous. Paul stood up. He spoke quietly.

"She can't dance, Frank. Not with anybody. She said all

night how sick she was feeling. You know some of this booze you get these days, it's not the best stuff. I think before we came here she drank something that wasn't good."

As she listened to the words, she saw Del look toward her and look away, and she realized that he was frightened.

"You can't expect a decent girl to get up and just throw up on the dance floor, can you, Frank? That's not very nice for anybody. Everybody'd be embarrassed. You can ask her another time. Sometime she's feeling better. I tell you she's been feeling sick all night, wanting to leave."

Jean had never heard Paul talk like that, maybe never heard him say so much all at once. None of what he said was true, but she was glad he could make it up like that and get them out of trouble. If he did. The guy hadn't moved yet.

"You understand, don't you, Frank? We just don't want all the people here embarrassed."

What would happen if Paul didn't get the boy to go away? Would she have to dance with him? She could see the black man at the piano watching while he played. He started to play something louder and faster, his thick fingers moving over the keys more quickly than she'd ever thought it was possible for fingers to move. Some of the people clapped, and as if the clapping had wakened him from a trance, the boy who was standing by their table turned and walked away. Paul sat down and Jean looked at him. The skin on his face looked too tight.

"Let's get out of here," he said.

"I think it's better to wait a few minutes," Del said. He took a sip from the drink on the table. The trumpeter was playing now, something fast and sparky. He pointed his trumpet down at the floor and bent forward, the notes driven out one at a time, like brass nails into dark wood. She didn't know those people, those black men, and they didn't know her. At the next table a guy lit a match and held it to his cigarette, and by the light of the match, his eye squeezed closed in a slow wink. She looked away and stared at the black men playing.

"Who was that guy, that Frank?" she said but without shifting her eyes.

"His name's Frank Delaney." The boy had disappeared. She couldn't see him anywhere in the huddled smoky half-light.

"But who is he?"

"Tell you later."

"Okay, let's go," Del said. They stood and pushed their way between the tables. Some unknown hand touched her bum as she went by, and she knew it had something to do with the scene at the table, a way of proving to her that she hadn't really got away with anything. Once they were outside she started to feel almost safe, but she heard a noise from the alley that ran beside the building, and when she looked, she could see, in the light from the street, that it was the tall boy who'd come to their table. He had another, shorter man up against the wall of the building, and he was holding him with his left hand while he punched him repeatedly, slowly, almost studiously, with his right. All three of them saw it, and then they were a few feet away and walking fast. Jean kept looking behind, but no one was coming. When they got to the car, Del let her in. Paul said he'd walk home.

"Thanks, buddy," Del said. "That was swell, the way you handled it."

"I'm not going back," Paul said. "Not back there."

On the way to the apartment, Del explained to her that Frank Delaney was a gangster who worked for the guys who owned the club. Sometimes he was okay, but a lot of the time he was crazy as a bedbug, especially if he thought somebody was insulting him.

"So should I have danced with him?"

"I don't know. That might have made trouble. He's kind of crazy with women."

"It sounds like he ought to be in a zoo."

"Sure, but who's going to put him there?"

Sometimes when Del had been drinking he was rough with her, but she didn't want him to be tonight. He seemed to know that and he spent a long time, stroking her all over and kissing her, and then he turned her on her belly, spread her legs and lay behind her whispering sweet words into her hair.

Just as she was about to doze off, he spoke to her.

"How'd you like to go back to Canada for a visit?"

"Why?"

"To find a guy with a boat."

Jean was reading the ads in the paper. She was getting restless; maybe what she needed was to get a decent job somewhere.

Female Help Wanted
Attendant for country sanitarium, mental cases.
Middle aged women preferred: wages $50-$60
monthly. Apply office Belle Meade Sanitarium,
666 Madison Avenue, between 3 & 4 P.M.,
Tuesdays, Thursdays and Saturdays.

She turned to another page and looked at the pictures of the cruise ships. It cost a hundred and fifty-five dollars for a cruise to Europe. Once when Del was working on the movie about the harbour, she went down there with him, and she saw the tall white lines of the ships, with the long curve of the deck against the sky, all the brass work polished and shining and rich people going on board to cross the ocean. She saw a liner sail in, the American flag on the front, the ship's horn honking. Someday she'd be on one of those boats.

The phone rang. She was never sure whether to answer it when Del was away. She was always afraid it might be the police looking for her. She'd sent postcards to her mother every week or so since she got here, but she hadn't given her any address because she was scared they'd send someone after her. She picked up the phone, held the receiver to her ear and said hello.

"Are you alone, Jean?"

She recognized the voice. It was Alvin Coortland. She'd been to his apartment again a couple of times after the class, though she couldn't have said why, and when he asked for her number, she gave it to him. It was crazy but she did it. Maybe she was mad at Del that day. For the last two weeks Alvin Coortland hadn't been in the class.

"Yes," she said.

"Could you come to see me?"

His voice was weak and a little hoarse.

"Are you sick?"

"I'm not feeling very well, no. I'd like to see you."

"Is Mrs. Hamson there?"

" No," he said. "Just walk in. The door's open."

He hung up. Jean didn't want to go. She liked the man, in a way, but she didn't like the way his voice sounded, soft and hollow and distant. It was September now and starting to get cool, so she put on a new topcoat she'd bought and a dark blue cloche hat. Her hair had grown in quite a bit, and Del told her a place to go to get it trimmed, it was someone who owed him a favour and did it for nothing. He did a good job, and it looked nice now. Jean decided that she'd take a cab. There was enough money in her purse, though that was the last until she got paid by the school the next week. Maybe she'd ask him for the cab fare. She'd never taken anything from him. He kept saying to ask if she needed anything, but she never had; she wasn't going to be one of those.

In the cab on the way uptown, she tried to think why she went to the apartment at all. Partly because it was another world, so quiet and full of strangeness. The way he showed her things, a teapot from China, a little ivory box from France. The drawings. Every time she went, she would look at the drawings, and he would tell her a little about the artists. They were so old. Two hundred years ago, some woman with pudgy thighs lay there on a bed while a man drew her, the way Jean had let herself be drawn that afternoon. In Holland there was a river, there were trees, and they were in the drawing. The way he would climb on her, so sudden and awkward and helpless, was a part of the strangeness. It was a little ceremony that the two of them performed, nothing to do with pleasure.

When she got to the apartment, she realized that the cab driver had been talking to her, but she hadn't listened to a word. She paid him and went up in the elevator. The hall outside the apartment was long and empty, a carpet leading past the doors to a small window at the end. She could see the fire escape outside. When she tried the door of the apartment, it was open as he'd said it would be. She stepped inside. There was an odour of rotting food.

The silence of the place was all wrong. The strangeness that had hidden behind the furniture, the dark curtains, inside the glass doors of the highboy, behind the books, had now come out and taken possession. Jean wanted to run, but she wouldn't let herself. She walked into the big room where they always had tea, and he was lying there in pyjamas and dressing gown on the davenport. She was glad that his eyes were closed. She'd been afraid that the dead eyes would be staring up at her. She stood a few feet away and looked at him, the grey colour of his skin. He'd hung up the telephone and come to lie down here to wait for her, and he had died while she was putting on her coat and flagging a cab and riding uptown through the streets of traffic.

On the floor beside him were two or three of the pictures of her that he'd drawn. That's what he'd been looking at when he died. Was that what was called love? She walked down to the bedroom where he'd taken her. The bed was rumpled, as if it hadn't been made for days, and the room had a stale smell. On the other side of the hall was a room she'd never been in. She pushed open the door and looked. The walls were full of bookshelves, and there was a desk and in the corner a leather chair. There were papers on the desk, documents and letters. There was some money lying there as well, bills and loose change. She put it in her pocket. She thought she might sit down in the leather chair and read the letters, but instead she looked into the kitchen where there was a mess of old food and dishes. Again she felt as if she might go in, tidy, put everything in order, but she didn't do that, either. Before she left, she went back and got one of the pictures he'd been looking at, one he'd drawn of her.

She went down the stairs instead of using the elevator, and when she had got outside without meeting anybody, she began to walk south. Yellow leaves had fallen from the trees and lay on the pavement, and she marched over them, quickly, never looking back until she was some distance away, and then she got a bus to Washington Square and walked from there to the apartment. Del wasn't home yet, and she hid the drawing in a chest under her clothes.

As they drove along the country road, Del pointed to a field. "You see that field?"

"Yeah."

"That's a baby farm."

"How can you tell?"

"If you look real close you can see the shapes of the babies in the grass. Where they put them out for the day."

His face had that look. She'd been about to take him seriously. Yesterday she saw something in the paper about a baby farm and showed it to him. She'd never heard of such a thing, but Del said the country was full of them. More babies than pigs.

"Wouldn't they need a little parasol? In the summer, to keep the sun off them when they're out there in the grass."

"They got special little ones that clip on their diapers."

The car rolled on. The trees were almost empty of their leaves now, and there was a space between the earth and the blue sky. Jean looked at the ring on her finger. It wasn't real, but she told Del if they were going to see her family, she'd have to tell them she was married, or at least engaged, and he said engaged sounded all right, it might help them at the border, and they bought this cheap little ring at a junk shop. It was pretty. She'd never worn a ring before. Now and then she wondered about trying to get Del to marry her, but she decided to think about that if they got to California. Del's idea was that he'd make a bunch of money by getting a load of bootleg whiskey to New York, and then maybe they'd get a train out to the coast, and they'd have enough that they wouldn't have to get work right away. There was some movie guy with an office on 43rd Street who was supposed to talk to her next week. He'd seen a picture of her, and he was interested. Sometimes Jean thought that every second girl she met in New York was hoping to get into the movies. There were a couple of girls from the Follies at a party the other night, and it was all they could talk about. They talked like they knew all the producers by their first names and had spread their legs for half of them.

"You got to give 'em what they want," one of them kept saying. "That's what you got to give 'em."

If so, Jean thought, they could keep the movies. She liked it just fine with Del, but she wasn't going to be cheap. Funny thing to be thinking with this fake engagement ring on her finger, but she knew what she meant. There was Alvin Coortland, but that was different. She couldn't explain it.

"You going to teach me to drive, Uncle Del?"

"Sometime, maybe."

"You promised to teach me to drive, Uncle Del. You know you did."

Del didn't answer, and she stared out into a patch of woods where the last leaves caught the afternoon sunlight and reflected it into the spaces between the branches and twigs. Spaces, she was full of spaces, a hall of mirrors reflecting one long darkness into another, and no one would know her for what she was, but famous, that too. In the woods, unseen, there were small animals, fast but waiting to be broken, and the birds were leaving.

When she was little, she'd go down the road by herself at this time of year and stand in a patch of woods and look straight up, the tangle of empty branches rising more and more thinly making her excited and then scared, and she'd run all the way home.

"What's his name again?"

"Elmer Tisdale."

Del wanted to find someone with a boat who could be hired to haul a load of liquor, and she thought Elmer might. Tilly Murton wouldn't, everybody knew that. They'd asked him because he was good on the lake, but he always said no. Bruce was good on the lake, somebody once said he must have it in his veins, and look where he ended up. She'd told Del about Bruce to try and talk him out of this smart idea, but he didn't seem to pay much attention. Some guy with a nightclub offered to finance him and split the profit, and all he could see was money.

"What time we going to get there, Uncle Del?"

"We won't get to your neck of the woods until morning. We'll have to stay somewhere tonight."

"Am I going to be your nephew again?"

"Figured I'd say you were my wife."

"Tell them we're on our honeymoon."

The woods ended, and there was a white-painted farmhouse near the road, barns behind, and a field of cattle, thick and slow. Her brother Eg once had a toy farm with cattle like that. Tomorrow she'd be seeing Eg and Iris and her mother and Ronald, who probably lived there now. Maybe Ronald would want to have kids of his own, maybe her mother would have a big belly. The thought made her sick. She wasn't sure she wanted to go back, but it would always be there, those rooms where she'd lived from the time she was little. Her first memory was standing in the room upstairs that was her parents' bedroom, back before her father went to the war, and listening to voices from downstairs. Knowing she was all by herself, she began to cry, and her mother came looking for her and couldn't figure out what she was crying about, and she couldn't explain.

The sun was going down behind the trees and catching the side of a red barn that looked as if it was painted with blood, and in the noise of the motor and the tires she could hear something else, a trumpet far away and the voice of a black woman singing the blues. She knew that this was how it would always be.

Sometime after dark Del stopped at some cabins by a river, and in the night, cuddled up against him, Jean could hear the river outside, the way she'd hear the water at home, and she remembered how Bruce would sit on the side of her bed and put his big hands on her, and she cried for him again. Del slept through it all, it meant nothing to him, it wasn't his home they were going to. Then she slept and woke again from bad dreams that she couldn't quite remember, wanted to wake Del, but he was crabby when she woke him in the night. He was just a goddam stranger, really, in the dark like this, with a river going past that had been a river forever just about, since before anybody came here, Indians even. His body was hot, and she cuddled herself hard against it. If she could get to sleep, it would be all right in the morning.

It was nearly noon the next day when they drove up to the house. It was a grey windy day, the waves were rolling in against the shore with an implacable energy, and a loose shingle on the old boat shed was lifting and flapping in the wind. As she got out of the car, a bit of light came through the clouds, and she saw it reflected on the kitchen window. The air smelled of the water and the grass. They went up and knocked on the door, and when her mother came, she had her apron on and a look on her of shock and an unnameable other thing, bare and insufficient, and she grabbed hold of Jean and hung onto her.

"I thought I'd never see you again."

"I wrote to you. I said I was okay, that I'd come and see you."

Her mother was shivering.

"Come in where it's warm."

She looked toward Del, who was just standing there.

"This is my fiancé," Jean said. The words came hard. She was close to laughing and crying both, chose laughter. "Mr. Delbert Hunnicut."

"How do you do, Mr. Hunnicut," her mother said, and held out her hand.

"Del," he said and shook her hand.

"Come in. Get out of this wind."

"Why don't I go and make my other call first?" Del said to Jean. On the way down the road, she'd showed him where Elmer Tisdale lived, and they'd seen Elmer down by his dock, working on the motor of his boat.

"Okay," Jean said, "but fetch me my little bag from the car, would you?" She thought that was how an American girl would talk to her fiancé. Del brought her the bag and gave her a look.

"Where's he going?"

"He's got some business down the road."

Her mother looked frightened, but she didn't say anything. They went into the house.

"Ronald's in town," her mother said. "He's got some work again at the fish-brokers."

"Is he on the boats?"

"No. Loading and unloading. He does some of the book-keeping, too."

Jean couldn't imagine that, but she didn't say anything.

The kitchen was warm, and there was a smell of cooking fish. A big iron pot sat on the stove.

"Must stink of fish," her mother said.

"I brought some presents, " Jean said. She'd brought makeup and some fancy silk stockings for her mother. When she put them on the table, she saw that her mother was going to cry, and she picked up the bag.

"I'll leave some stuff for Eg and Iris up on their beds," she said.

"Iris's been using the middle room. Your room. Is that okay?"

"Sure thing."

Jean climbed the narrow stairs into the disorder of the dark little room. She opened the case and put the dress she'd bought for Iris on the bed, then went into the end room and left Eg's building set. Outside the small square windows, she could see the grey water slapping against the stones, lifting and dropping a pile of weed that floated there.

It was pitch black as she sat in the driver's seat of the Ford and waited. The car was carefully parked so that no one could get another car or truck past along the narrow road that led to the old farmhouse where they were unloading the liquor. If anyone came, she was to say that she'd got the car stuck and couldn't get it started again. Del had showed her enough that she could pretend to be trying to start it. It was cold, sitting there, and too dark to see. She listened for the sound of voices or the engine of a boat out on the water. She leaned over into the back seat and found the car rug and wrapped it around her to try to get warm, but it didn't seem to help, and in a few minutes, she got out of the car. There were stars out, the same ones she would have seen at the house on the other side of the lake.

They would be asleep now, her mother with Ronald, Eg and Iris. That house wasn't her home any more, she knew that after being there, but if that wasn't her home, she had no particular home. The apartment was Del's, and maybe they'd be leaving soon for California. If Del didn't get himself killed, get both of them killed, running this booze. She'd heard enough stories about the coast guard shooting people up, and she remembered how Bruce looked when she found him, his body flat and dark in a pool of blood and water in the bottom of his boat, how more red blood spread slowly across his shirt as she dragged him over to the side where she'd tied the rowboat. He was already dead, she knew that, even as she found an unbroken bottle of whisky in a smashed case and tried to pour it down his throat. Once or twice, when she couldn't sleep at night, she wondered if he could have been alive when she pushed his body out of the boat, but when she remembered his face the colour of a skinned fish, the blood, and the way his eyes stared, his open mouth, she knew he was dead. She nearly capsized the rowboat getting him out of it, and she found there was blood on her skirt and had to wash it off and got soaked.

She could almost see by starlight now, could make out the tops of trees against the sky, and from back toward the water, maybe a human voice and then an engine starting. It must be Elmer Tisdale setting off back to Canada. She got out of the car and jumped up and down and waved her arms to try to warm herself, jumped higher and higher, crazy with it, her arms wild in the darkness. When she stopped, she could feel the blood beating in her ears. She went to the car and felt around the seat for the car rug, wrapped it around her, sat on the running board and watched the stars, about which she knew nothing, not one thing.

In a while she heard footsteps on the road from the farmhouse.

"Del?" she whispered.

"Yeah."

She got up and went to meet him. Only when he was very close could she see the shape of him, and he put his arms around her.

"We better get out of here," he said.

He started the car and turned it around to drive back to the empty farmhouse, and when they got there, he pulled up in front of the barn, where two men stood beside a truck loaded with hay. Most of the cases of booze were under the hay, but they put a few in the back of the Ford with the car rug and suitcases and a couple of old coats on top. The two men never spoke a word, silent as if their tongues had been cut out, and maybe they had been. They got in the truck and drove away, and she and Del waited in the car until the sound of their motor was gone, and then they started up the Ford and drove over the bumpy track to the road. They drove all night, Del keeping himself awake somehow, and it started to rain. As the slow dim light of morning came into the sky, they were high in the Adirondacks, and they saw a sign for a place with cabins and fishing. When they got there, it was okay, the cabins well away from the road so no one would get a close look at the car, but Del was nervous about somebody seeing it, so they took turns sleeping and watching out the small window with a torn screen. The room was painted a sickly green, and the bed was narrow, with sagging springs. The rain kept up all day, and once it was dark, they both went to bed, laughing like crazy at how the springs sagged and squeaked, but they were up at first light, and by that night they were back in New York.

The room was up a flight of stairs over a flower store, and on the way up the stairs, Jean could smell flowers and wet earth, tropic and sensual. The room itself was painted white and had a high ceiling. Through the crowd, Jean could see Paul at the far end talking to a man and woman, who were both smoking, and the white haze of cigarette smoke around him and the white wall behind made him look pale and almost transparent. Nearby Jean could see one of the pictures he had taken of her, her shoulder, one breast and the edge of her face against a background of black velvet with lighting that made her skin shine like phosphorescence. Near Paul was the man who ran the gallery. He had dark eyes behind round glasses, a mop of hair, and a large dark moustache. He never stopped talking, and right now he was talking to Del, who stood there in perfect silence the way he could, with that observant look on his face that always made Jean laugh, as if this was all a pretty good game. He saw her watching him, his eyes shifted for a second, something passed between them, and Jean thought that she could never have imagined such a thing, that you could know someone that well and read his face at a glance, like seeing a newspaper and picking out the headlines.

A woman came up to her. Her dress was a pale green, and she was all wrapped in scarves and beads of various blues and greens, and her cigarette was in a jade cigarette holder. Her skin was pale and wrinkled around the eyes. "Paul says you're the model," she said.

Jean nodded.

"Lovely, lovely," the woman said. "Lovely."

Jean could think of nothing to say to her, and the two of them stared at each other.

"Lovely," the woman said again, and walked away.

Jean took a sip from her glass. There was a bowl of fruit punch in the corner, and Del had spiked her glass with gin from the flask in his jacket pocket. She didn't much like the taste of it. Beside her were the pictures that Paul had taken in an old warehouse. Jean remembered how cold it had been. He'd brought a couple of blankets for her to wrap around herself while he was setting up the camera and getting ready. The floor was rough and dirty, and standing on it in her bare feet had made her shudder. In the photographs, her figure was small and bare in the large dark room. In one you could see the view of roofs outside the wide window, and Jean was in a corner, almost in shadow, pale and cold. There was a terrible sadness to the picture, that a girl looked like that, with her white breasts and rounded shape, so soft and easily hurt, and Jean wondered who that girl was and what would become of her. She remembered that day and how, when they were almost finished, she'd told Paul that he should take his clothes off, she'd make a picture of him, and how he'd looked at her for a long time, as if he might be about to agree, and then said what a strange idea that was and told her to get dressed. Del said that Paul liked boys, and there was a young man here tonight who stood beside him as if they were holding hands, but there were one or two times when Jean would have said that Paul was in love with her, except that maybe she didn't know anything about love. Paul said that he would make her prints of the pictures if she wanted. She would ask him for that one.

Wherever she looked in here, there were pictures of her naked body and of her face, lit so that it knew more than she could ever know. It made her want to run away, not because she was embarrassed — it surprised her that all these people could look at her nudity and she didn't mind — but because the pictures told too many stories, and that frightened her, the things he could see.

She looked at Del again and met his eyes. It was reassuring to see him there in his brown suit with the pin stripe and the tight vest over his broad chest, so solid and funny and determined. In a minute Jean would go over and stand beside him, in her fine blue silk dress, and everyone would notice what a handsome couple they made.

The car rolled slowly down the street between the dark shapes of warehouses, each lit by a single bulb over a door-way, now and then a store or a couple of houses. Uptown, Broadway would be full of lights, taxis honking, people still walking and laughing on the streets, sitting at tables in the restaurants, but in this neighbourhood there was not a single soul. Del was driving, his friend Tommy hunched over his camera, trying to whistle "The Sheik of Araby," except he couldn't quite get the tune right. It started right and then got lost somewhere, and so he'd start again. Jean had never seen Valentino in *The Sheik*, but a couple of weeks ago she'd gone to see him in *The Eagle*. He was beautiful all right, no two ways about it. He'd been in New York last month for the movie's premiere, but she didn't go and join the crowd. He was in France now to get a divorce. When she tried to think of France, what she thought of was that movie she'd been in, back in Trenton, that and her father being over there.

"So which way?" Del said.

Tommy stopped whistling.

"I dunno. Turn right and then go back that next street."

Tommy had heard rumours from one of his contacts, he wouldn't even tell them what, something about the gangs, maybe he didn't even know what, and they were driving around the streets hoping to get some pictures. He made his living taking pictures for the newspapers. He worked as a freelance, but if he got good pictures he could make money. He had to keep in with the cops and the bootleggers and the theatrical agents and the political bosses, so he knew what was going on. If you looked closely at him, you could see that he was always thinking about three or four things at once.

Jean glanced across the road. Between two tumbledown buildings she could see the Hudson River, black and shining, and a few lights on the Jersey shore. Last night Tommy had been round to their place, talking about his car problems and how he wished he had a driver for tonight. Del offered to drive, and when Jean said she wanted to come, he'd tried to convince her that she should stay at home, but she was determined. Before Tommy came, they'd been arguing about California and how Del kept getting jobs in New York to stop them going, and she was in a mood to insist on getting her own way. Now she was half frozen. The car turned a corner, and beyond the black shape of Del's hat and shoulder, the headlights showed a drunk lying in the middle of the street.

"Stop the car," Tommy said.

He was out the door, and there was a sudden flash of light,

the body of the drunk sharp and detailed, then Tommy took hold of the him by the shoulders and dragged him to the curb and left him there. He was back in the car, reloading the camera and flash.

"Not worth much, but what the hell, it's a picture."

Del drove on. Turned a corner. Another. Tommy was whistling again. They drove down the long silent streets, each small light all but drowned in the larger darkness.

"How you doing back there?" Del said.

"Everything's jake back here, Mr. Hunnicut," Jean said. She wasn't going to admit that she was tired and bored and frozen. So they drove on, through the night streets. Once they saw a diner, a couple of figures sitting at the counter in the dim yellow light, and Jean wanted to go in and get a coffee, but Tommy wouldn't let them stop. Near morning, a few flakes of snow began to fall. Ahead of them, on a corner under a streetlight, Tommy noticed a man standing alone in a dark coat and fedora smoking a cigarette.

"Pull over and wait for me, " Tommy said. He got out and walked toward the man, talked to him for a few seconds, then came back to the car. He gave Del directions and they drove on. A block ahead, by a high windowless building set back from the street, they saw two figures, black and small, just visible in the light that came from an open door.

"Slow down," Tommy said, "slow down, for chrissake."

One of the figures turned to go back into the building, and as he approached the light, the other man reached out toward him. There was a noise, and the man fell, straight forward onto his face, and Jean realized that the hand that reached out had held a gun, and she knew that the man on the ground was dead. The killer had disappeared into the darkness, probably down an alley beside the building.

"Let's go," Tommy said.

Del stepped on the gas, and the car rolled ahead. Tommy was out before it stopped, and he ran to where the dark shape lay with one arm reaching forward as if toward the open door and the light, his hat upside down beside him like the hat of a street musician asking for a nickel. The flash of Tommy's camera lit the area as he shot from the sides and close up, and the blood that flowed from the man's head was a black stain across the pavement. A few flakes of snow hung in the air. In a minute, the still figure on the ground would get up, nod to Tommy, put on his hat and walk into the building, closing the door carefully behind him. In a minute he would get up laughing and come to the car to make a joke. Tommy crouched close to the pavement to get a shot from a low angle, a shot that showed the expression on the face of death, and when the flash went off the body looked swollen and wet.

Tommy climbed back into the car, and Del was driving away, and the door of the place was still open, the light shining out. Jean wanted to go back and turn off the light and shut the door.

"Shouldn't you call a doctor," Jean said, "or the police or somebody?"

"I'll get somebody to call the cops when I get to the paper. Nothing a doctor can do about that mess."

After they dropped Tommy off, they drove back to the apartment. The snow had stopped now, but Jean was shivering again. They didn't talk much. When they got inside, Del poured them each a shot of whiskey and hot water to try to get them warm, and then they had a fight, no reason, they just wanted to, and in bed she bit him and he bit back, and finally he was rocking back and forth on top of her, and she could see the light starting to appear beyond the window, and when she thought of Valentino and the movies, she grabbed onto Del and held him so hard she thought she could break him.

Then they were done, and she couldn't sleep, so she got up and went into the other room and put on the Victrola and sat there in the dark listening to the jazz records that Del had bought her.

Three

"WHAT'S THAT OUT THERE?"

"Illinois."

"There's an awful lot of it." Jean looked at the man in the seat across from her. Once or twice he'd tried to talk to her. She just said yes or no and went back to her magazine, but now she was bored. She could hear the chuffing of the engine and the sound of the wheels clicking along beneath them, could feel the car shaking a little.

"This is America," the man said. "There's a lot of everything."

He had a big head, cheeks very smoothly shaved, hair straight and already thinning though he was still young, slightly protuberant eyes. The eyes took on a shine when he looked at her, and she thought he'd try to get into her berth with her if he was still on the train tonight.

Beyond the window there were steep hillsides, the leaves just beginning to come out on the trees, so that there was an airy haze of green over everything.

"So that's Illinois."

"Later on we'll cross the Mississippi."

"M-i-ss-i-ss-i-pp-i. Learned to spell it in school."

"You can't be out of school very long."

"Long enough."

"How old are you?"

"Twenty."

"You have a boyfriend?"

"There's Mr. Delbert Hunnicut."

"Who's he?"

"I ran off with him to New York City."

"Did he leave you in the lurch?"

"No."

It was hard to explain what had happened with Del, especially to a stranger. The winter was hard on both of them, Jean nagging to go to California as he got one job after another in New York. He got her a part in the movie that they made in Astoria out on Long Island, a girl behind a counter in a candy store, and the director said she was pretty and smart, and he'd write her a letter to somebody out west if she was going. And a couple of times she saw Mr. Finestone in his office on 43rd Street. He was a quiet man with a thick accent — he called her "dollink" — and Jean could tell that he wanted to make a pass but couldn't quite bring himself to it. He acted like there was someone hiding in the closet ready to jump out if he got fresh. Maybe there was. Maybe his wife was in there with a gun. Jean had already decided she wasn't doing it to try to get a job. She'd heard enough from those girls who danced at the Follies. You started out thinking it was going to help you and the next thing you were just a whore.

She looked at the man across from her. No, she couldn't tell him about Del. Too complicated to say that sure she loved him, but she couldn't just sit around waiting for him to take her to California when he didn't want to go. Waiting like that made her mad, and soon she wouldn't love him at all, or would start to whine all the time. She'd met girls like that in New York. It was better to take the money and get on the train.

She looked at the expression on the man's face. It was funny about men, how if they thought they could get between your legs they got all fussed and shiny. One of the things she'd liked about Alvin Coortland was that he didn't. He didn't start to puff up like a rooster. The way the man across from her was holding his head up was just like that.

Back when she was at home, she'd lie in that little bed in the corner under the roof in the dark or first thing in the morning, and she'd think about the world, all of it out there somewhere, all she didn't know about, could hardly imagine. In school, she once pointed to the globe that sat at the front of the room and said to her friend Margery, "I want to go every-where," and Margery gave her a look, as if she might be a little bit touched. Now she was going places, and she liked it, but she could imagine that you could know too much, that you could see more than you wanted.

She wasn't sure she wanted to see so clearly that this man was fussed as a rooster from the thought of getting her.

"What comes after Illinois?" she said.

"Missouri. We stop at St. Louis."

As she looked out the window at the spring fields, she hummed to herself.

"I'll bet you're a good singer," the man said.

"I sang in the church choir," Jean said. "Back home."

"Where's home?"

"Canada."

"So you're a pretty little Canadian girl."

"Most people say beautiful," Jean said. She was in a mood where she couldn't resist devilment.

"Well, yes," the man said, as if he was thinking it over. "I guess beautiful would be the right word."

"I guess it would."

"So where are you headed?"

"California. To be in the movies."

"I hear a lot of girls go out there to be in the movies, and some of them get in real trouble."

"I've already been in two movies. I didn't get in too much trouble. Except for running away with Mr. Delbert Hunnicut, but that turned out all right mostly."

"Where is he now?"

"Back in New York."

"So he did leave you in the lurch. Put you on the train all by your little lonesome."

"No," she said. "It wasn't like that."

When she told him she was going on her own, Del just shrugged and said if that was what she wanted. He had given her some of the money from the booze they smuggled and said maybe he'd come to California later on and meet her.

"But still, this fellow of yours is back in New York, and you're all by your lonesome, isn't that so?"

Jean was bored with the man, so she picked up her copy of *Photoplay*.

"Do you think it was Mable Normand who killed him, that Taylor fellow?"

He was reading one of the titles on the cover.

"No," she said, "I think it was Peavey."

"I was going to write a book about that case," the man said.

"You write books?"

"I expect I'll write a great many books, but right now I'm working for magazines. Travelling."

Jean looked out the window. They were near the front of the train, and the smoke from the engine blew by the window and dropped little black flecks of cinder on the ledge outside. Through the screen of smoke, she saw a low hill where a man was ploughing up the earth, the plough hitched to the leaning grey body of a mule, and something, maybe the way they were talking about books, made her think that she'd read about this or seen it someplace else. The man was talking to her, but she couldn't quite take in his words. She was seeing herself in a movie, in the farmhouse where this farmer returned after he'd finished his ploughing and unharnessed the mule.

"You are beautiful, yes you are," the man was saying, and his voice was different now. She turned and looked at him, and when their eyes met, she saw a life with this man, keeping house for him while he worked on his books. She wanted him to say something stupid so she could laugh at him.

"Where are you going to?" she said.

"I planned to get off in St. Louis. I have a magazine article to write, about shipping on the Mississippi."

"Will you ride on the boats?"

"Yes, I expect I will. Have you ever read a book called *Huckleberry Finn*?"

"No, I never read that."

"It's about the Mississippi, about a boy and a black man riding on a raft. You should read that book."

"Mr. Delbert Hunnicut dressed me up like a boy to get me across the border."

"I wish I could have seen that."

"My hair was an awful mess."

"Do you read books?"

"I read quite a lot of books."

"Maybe someday you'll read one of mine."

"You better tell me your name, so I'll know if I do."

"No, I like better to think that maybe you'd just know." He took a small silver flask out of his inside pocket. "Would you like a little nip of this?"

"No," she said. "I don't think so."

He took off the cap, put the flask to his mouth, and she watched his Adam's apple bob as he drank two swallows. Then he wiped his mouth with his fingers, put the cap back on and put it in his inside pocket. The liquor made his face pink.

"What I'd like," he said, "is if you'd get off the train with me in St. Louis, and we'd go someplace nice and I'd look after you."

"No," Jean said, "I don't think so."

"Maybe I won't get off the train in St. Louis. I'll buy a ticket to Los Angeles and go out there to look after you. I'll write a book about the movies."

"I don't think you better do that."

"You should have somebody to look after you."

He leaned across and put his hand on her knee, and for some crazy reason Jean wanted to cry. She hadn't cried when she left home, and now some man she didn't know and didn't much like almost made her cry. Dammit, why did she never feel what she was supposed to feel, or never even know what you were supposed to feel? She stopped the tears and looked out the window at a white farmhouse with a horse and wagon tied to a small tree and two children sitting on the flat bed of the wagon.

"Look, mister," she said, "I guess you're okay and you mean what you say about wanting to look after me. But mostly you want to get between my legs. I don't mind. Lots of men want to. But don't let it go to your head. You just get off the train and ride down the M-i-ss-i-ss-i-pp-i and write about it for the magazine, and someday you can put me in one of your books."

Evelyn was lying on her bed, bawling. She and Jean shared a small room in a house in Glendale. The house had a big green lawn, with gardenias and hibiscus and red bougainvillea growing on the fence. The man and woman who owned the house said to call them Mom and Pop, but Jean and Evelyn didn't, and when they tried to talk about why and practise doing it, all that happened was they started to giggle. The man was very thin and nervous and soft spoken, the woman fat and unhappy. Jean couldn't imagine calling them Mom and Pop ever, but Evelyn said they should keep trying.

Evelyn was tall and very slender, and as she lay on the bed crying, her skirt was pulled up, and her long thin legs were pale against the mauve bedspread. The room was all decorated in pink and mauve, and Jean hated it. Evelyn said she didn't half mind, those were colours she liked, though not her favourites. Both of them wanted to get out, but they'd have to make more money. They got regular work as extras now, with the promise of something better. That's part of why Evelyn was lying on the bed crying, her thin shapely legs bare and helpless, her face buried in the pillow.

Suddenly she sat up on the edge of the bed, her legs together and her hands in her lap. She had white skin and very large blue eyes, but her mascara had run from crying so there were black streaks all around them. Jean was standing by the window. There was an orange tree outside. It still amazed her to see oranges growing here. It was something she could never have imagined, living among orange trees and flowers all year long.

"It's bad enough," Evelyn was saying through her tears,

"having to do it. But then he goes and says to come in tomorrow and he's got a real part for me. A whole week's work maybe. But I don't dare wait, and I don't dare say anything."

Jean went and sat on Evelyn's bed beside her and put her arm around her.

"It's just all so awful. I've just got everything in such a mess. I knew when I had that dream about all the broken china that it meant everything was gonna go wrong. I knew it."

Evelyn was pregnant and had arranged for an abortion. The man was an assistant director who offered to help her get a part in a big movie for Paramount but never did. Jean could remember the day he had taken the two of them to the beach, the sunlight on the bright sand, and how he kept picking them up and carrying them into the waves, or giving them piggyback rides, or starting wrestling matches, everybody laughing through it all at his old jokes — "She's so dumb she even asked me how electric light poles grow in a straight line" — and then more touching and giggling until all three were giddy, sunstruck and hungry, and it must have seemed to him that he had his choice, and he began to brag about how he could get any girl a job if she was good to him. It was Evelyn who ended up going to his hotel with him. Jean had kept her promise to herself not to do it for what was offered, though that day and some other times she'd been tempted. Sitting here with her arm around Evelyn, feeling the heat of her body as it shook with tears again, she was reminded of how lonely she was.

"Do you suppose I'd dare wait two weeks?"

"I don't know," Jean said. "I don't know much about it." She heard stories sometimes, gossip among the other extras, but she knew nothing. She knew how it happened, and she knew you missed your time of the month and then you were in trouble, but that was about all.

"It took me so long to find him, that doctor, and they say the longer you wait the worse it is, and you could bleed to death. I better just go and do it. And I'm so scared. I don't want to bleed to death like that."

Jean tightened her grip on the slender body.

"Lots of people do it," she said. She didn't really know if that was true, but probably.

"They're starting to shoot tomorrow. I said I'd be there. What else could I say? That I think maybe I'm gonna be sick tomorrow, that I can feel it starting. I couldn't say that, could I?"

"No," Jean said. "You couldn't say that." She thought the best thing to do was agree with everything Evelyn said.

"I better phone and tell him I can't do it. If I just don't show up, my name will be mud and I'll never get a decent part. But I'm not phoning from here. I'll have to go down to the United Cigar Store, they got a phone there. I don't want those two figuring it all out."

"Don't tell Mom and Pop," Jean said and gave Evelyn a look, and Evelyn started to giggle, she couldn't help it.

"You go wash your face," Jean said, "and we'll go down there. I'll buy you a strawberry soda."

Evelyn was always drinking sodas to try to put on some weight because she thought she was gawky. With her big blue eyes, her thinness sometimes gave her a comical look, and Jean thought she might be good in comedies, but Evelyn said that wasn't what she wanted. While Evelyn went off to wash her face, Jean looked out the window again at the orange tree, and she thought of what was growing in Evelyn as if it was something as round and hard as an orange.

They walked down the street to the United Cigar Store. There were three men wearing grey hats standing by the door, one with a cigar, the others smoking cigarettes, and Jean

breathed the heady smell as they walked past them. Jean went
to the counter and sat down and ordered two strawberry
sodas while Evelyn went to phone the director who'd offered
her the part, but when she came back she still had a long face.

"What did he say?"

"He's gone, he won't be back today, and they don't know
where he is."

"You could leave a message."

"But what if he doesn't get it? My name will be mud, and
I'm going to be all messed up inside, I know it. At least I don't
want my name to be mud."

"What time is your appointment?" Jean said. The soda
jerk was further down the counter serving a man in a dark
blue suit, but she thought he might be trying to listen. Evelyn
was sucking noisily on her soda.

"Eight o'clock. And I'm supposed to be at the studio at
seven. I don't know why I didn't just tell him I couldn't do it.
I kept thinking, I have to tell him, but I couldn't. But what's
going to happen when I just don't show up?"

"Why don't I go instead? " Jean said. She had the thought,
and she said it. "Then at least there'll be someone there. If he
doesn't like it, he can send me home."

"I'll be so jealous if you get to do it."

"Do you want to go?"

"No, I can't."

"If it works and I make the movie, I'll split the pay with
you."

"I wish everything wasn't such a mess. I really do. I really,
really do."

Jean was at the railway station. She was saying goodbye to Evelyn. The engine had its fire up, ready to pull out of the station, and little bits of ash were falling on them. One fell on Evelyn's forehead, and she wiped it away, but it left a tiny dark mark on the perfect white skin.

"I guess I just didn't have the luck," Evelyn said.

"You'll come back when you're better."

"No, I won't come back. I'll go home to Syracuse, and I'll find something to do there."

Jean was about to say, Oh, you'll be getting married, but she stopped herself in time. Evelyn was all messed up inside after her abortion, and the doctors she went to couldn't seem to help her. They said probably she'd never be able to have babies.

"When I'm back in Syracuse I'll see every movie you're in, and I'll tell all my friends that I know you."

"You write me letters," Jean said, "and tell me everything you do."

Jean knew that Evelyn would write her for a while, and Jean would answer, and then the letters would get less frequent, and finally someday they'd stop. It was one of those things she thought she shouldn't know, but she couldn't help it.

"I'll send you the money," Evelyn said.

Jean was in the movies now, and she had been helping Evelyn out, she'd paid for her ticket back to Syracuse.

"No," Jean said. "It's just a present. You don't owe me one thing."

"You could have got me an upper berth. That would have been good enough."

"Don't be silly," Jean said.

Evelyn reached out and grabbed her and hung onto her hard. Jean couldn't help noticing her slightly sour smell, and there was something frightening about the strength of her hug.

As Evelyn let go of her and she drew back, she saw someone watching them from further down the platform. He was wearing a pale cream-coloured suit, fawn loafers and a fawn hat. He held himself very straight. He knew how beautiful he was. She could hear him thinking to himself, I look just perfect, and she knew that after Evelyn got on the train he would speak to her and they would leave the station together.

In front of her, Jean could see the long, powerful and dangerous white-capped waves of the Pacific Ocean. Somewhere on the other side was China. Behind her, there were hills in strange brilliant colours, mountains, deserts. She was someone else now; she had a movie name, Cora Heart. The studio made up stories about her for publicity. They said that her father was a Canadian war hero. Well, maybe he was. A handsome, attentive man stood beside her as they looked over the ocean into the sky. Like her, he had two names, a movie name and another one, and it always seemed to her that he had no name at all. Like her he was trying to learn to be the person with the movie name, beautiful and perfect. She turned to him, and she could see the texture of his skin in the bright light from the ocean, the slight darkening of the whiskers that he shaved so carefully, the long eyelashes, the clear eyes. You couldn't look at him without wanting to touch him, and when she did touch him, his skin had a soft silky quality. She wished he was someone she could love, but he wasn't the man for that. While she was thinking about how beautiful he was, probably the same thought was crossing his mind — how beautiful I am, standing here by the ocean, with the hills of pine and chaparral behind my back.

The night before, Jean had written a letter to her mother. It was the first time since she'd left New York, and she was arranging to send some money along with it. She tried to tell her mother what it was like, that she had a contract to make movies, that people did her hair and gave her pretty clothes to wear and told her what to do when the cameraman started to crank, that at first she was a bathing beauty and in comedies, but then somebody liked how her face looked when she was sad, so now she was making those sad movies with happy endings. When she wrote it all down, it sounded like a lie, and she knew her mother wouldn't believe it. Jean only believed it herself because she was busy all the time, because there was always someone telling her what to do. She worked six days a week, the hours were long, and it was easiest if you just did what you were told. At first she read the scripts and tried to understand, but now she didn't bother. She did what she was told, and they paid her money for it. Yesterday Mr. Bliven came, in his black suit like an undertaker's, a man with a big nose covered with blackheads and sweaty hands that held hers too long. He came to talk to her, and what she said was going to be in a magazine, and Jean hoped that she didn't say anything to embarrass herself. She tried to say what she thought Mr. Bliven wanted, but it was hard to guess. She'd read the magazines, and everyone in them said the same things, so Jean figured she was safest to say those things, too, and she did.

As she listened to the sound of the surf, she glanced at the man posed so perfectly beside her, and then she looked across the white-capped waves toward China.

Gladys Clawson sat across the room, smoking cigarettes. She wore a pale green dress with a little lace collar and matching shoes, and her hat and gloves were on the table beside her, but she had a thick body, and the way she smoked cigarettes made the clothes look as if they belonged on someone else. She was going to be writing Jean's next movie, and she had come to talk to her about it. Jean didn't want to. She wanted them to tell her the story and what to do and what to feel. The musicians on the set played sad songs or cheerful songs and you followed the music. That was the way it was supposed to be. Gladys Clawson kept asking questions about where Jean came from, and Jean had to say something, and so she started telling about the lake and the boats, but she could see that the woman wasn't interested, and then she was sorry she'd mentioned it. At parties people told exciting stories about rumrunners, and she tried not to remember what had happened to Bruce.

The director had sent some pages ripped out of a magazine for her to look at. It was the beginning of what Gladys Clawson was supposed to write. A girl sees a murder, and then she falls in love with a man and doesn't realize at first that he is the killer. Jean was to be the girl. Just as the wedding is about to start, she sees a walking stick and some gloves she remembers and knows that the man she's going to marry is the murderer. When they were talking about it, Jean realized that Gladys Clawson wasn't really listening to anything she said, though the wide yellow eyes kept staring at her while she was talking. She kept lighting cigarettes and asking questions and staring, and then she got up and put on her hat and gloves and went out to the car where a tall coloured man was waiting for her, and they drove away.

"Would you like a cigarette?" Gladys Clawson said, holding out the package, but Jean refused. Sometimes she liked the smell of other people's cigarettes, but she couldn't see the point of smoking them herself. Gladys Clawson lit her own cigarette, put the package away in her purse, then got it out again and left it on the table beside her. Then she opened her purse and took her lighter back out and put it on the table beside the cigarettes, and when she had done that, she put the purse on the floor at her feet. The movie she'd written was over, and Jean didn't know why she'd got her out of bed on a Sunday morning. Gladys Clawson hadn't taken off her hat today, and she looked awkward sitting in the chair with the cigarette in her mouth. She shifted her purse again. While they were shooting the movie, she told Jean she wanted to come and talk to her about something important. Gladys Clawson had written some good scenes for her, so Jean agreed.

"My friend knows Mr. Lasky," Gladys Clawson said. The yellow eyes were watching her again, curious, empty. Jean didn't know why she was telling her this. Everybody knew those names, Mr. Lasky and Mr. Zukor and Mr. Mayer, but she didn't need to know those people. Everyone was frightened of them, and the best thing was to stay far away. She lived in her bungalow on its wide lawn among the bird-of-paradise and the red hibiscus, and when she wasn't filming all day, she was waiting for a new script to arrive with the shooting schedule, and at the end of each month there was a cheque. She tried to find time to write letters to her mother and to Evelyn back in Syracuse. Gladys Clawson said she needed a manager, and she wanted Jean to meet some friend of hers.

"Everybody knows Mr. Lasky," Jean said. "But Mr. Lasky doesn't know them."

Gladys Clawson blew smoke out of her nose and took another drag on her cigarette. "He knows my friend. He knows my friend very well. You're going to need advice about handling money. My friend knows a good stockbroker. He can make your fortune."

"I don't need a fortune."

"You don't like money?"

"Yes, I like money just fine."

"You like nice clothes."

Jean was wearing white trousers and a flowered silk top. She knew that they looked good on her, and they did cost a lot of money. Around the studio, she heard people talk about buying and selling stocks, and she didn't understand a word of it, and she wouldn't get involved in things she didn't know about.

"If you made money, you could buy yourself a house, in the hills or out on the beach."

"I'm all right here. I like it here."

Gladys Clawson waited, sucked on her cigarette, stared, spoke again. She had a flat urgent way of speaking.

"You know, when your contract comes up, they'll cheat you if you don't have good advice."

"Why are you telling me all this? Does he pay you, your friend?"

"I just want to see you well looked after. You're a pretty little girl from the country, and they could take advantage of you. A girl needs someone to look after her. Some of the girls here, they have their mother or a special fella who takes care of them."

The yellow eyes stared. Jean was sure that Gladys Clawson wasn't telling her the truth, but she didn't know exactly what the truth was. The studio publicity said that her father was a war hero, and sometimes she started to believe it.

"You're in the movies now, and the movies are very important. This is just the beginning. Everybody knows that. There's a lot of money in this business and a lot of bad men. You need someone to watch out for you. You'd know that, if you thought about it." She butted her cigarette and picked up the package to take out another one. When she picked up the lighter, her fingers were shaking. Her nervousness was making Jean nervous. Probably the woman was right, that she was just a stupid little girl from the country; when she signed the lease for the house, the man who owned it had to explain everything to her. She didn't even know what stocks were or why you bought them. She did what she was asked and took her cheque to the bank.

"My friend will come right here and talk to you, and he'll explain everything." She reached out and put her thin hungry lips around the cigarette, and Jean saw that she had small teeth with spaces between. "You know that would be the thing to do, don't you?"

"No," Jean said. Stupid maybe, but stubborn too. "I don't want to talk to him. I want to go on just like I am."

The room had six sides, and the table had six sides, and six of them sat around it on straight chairs. The room was called the Temple, and the walls and ceiling were painted a very dark red-brown, with a stencilled pattern in a purple that was almost black. The floor was a dark mahogany, and the table and chairs were all black. There were no windows, and after they had filed in from the other room, where they waited and one or two tried to chat amiably, the door was closed. Against one wall was a low sideboard, and on it rested a sword, a book, and a silver goblet. Above them a representation of a sun and a crescent moon hung on the walls. The ceiling of the room was very high; it was as if the room were at the bottom of a long tube leading up into space.

"Are we ready?" Regina Queen said and looked around the table. The others turned obediently toward her. There were two men and three women. One of the men was tall, with damp eyes and a tonsure of hair around a bald spot. He had a small mouth and the expression of someone lying in wait. The other was Jean's beautiful friend, who had brought her here. He said it was important to know about the future; then you could be ready. Of the women, one was very old, with a widow's hump and thinning hair, one was little more than a child and had a child's perfect complexion, though she had large breasts that hung awkwardly from her thin shoulders, and the third was a handsome woman, with dark eyes and hair, probably Mexican. Regina Queen herself was a fat woman in a flowing black dress that hung loosely over the roundness of her body. But her hands on the table were very white and rather small. She was the only one of the women who wore no ring. Jean had got in the habit of wearing her pretend engagement ring, though she wore it on the wrong hand now. Even though it was cheap and second hand, it was pretty, and she liked it. She had enough money now to buy other rings, but she didn't do it. The other women all had rings. You couldn't help but notice, as they sat with their hands spread out on the black surface of the table. Jean had never looked at hands so carefully before, the lumps around the knuckles of the Mexican woman's fingers, the liver spots on the old woman's and the silvery pallor of the skin. They had not been told each others' names. Regina Queen said communication was better without. She was a quiet-spoken woman, but she had a certain authority. She had been famous since she predicted the death of Valentino a month before it occurred. Many people drove to this quiet street in Santa Monica to consult her.

Jean had driven here with her beautiful friend, and as they drove, the sun, which had been shining, disappeared, replaced first by cloud and then by waves of December fog rolling in from the ocean. The trees and houses vanished, and there was nothing but the chill looming whiteness. They had to drive slowly and stop at every corner. It made Jean remember foggy days in the house by the lake where she had grown up. There was a day when she was very young and had never seen fog before, and her father took her hand and led her out into it toward the vanished lake. This Pacific fog was even thicker, and the smell was different.

Now in the Temple, waiting to begin, she imagined invisible figures walking slowly toward them.

"Are we ready?" Regina Queen said again, and everyone spoke or made some sound to indicate that they were. Jean looked at the face of the woman, sunk in the heavy jowls, and thought of her predicting the death of Valentino. Often she didn't want to see the things she saw, that's what she told the newspapers, but she had no choice. She could only see what was given to her. If there was death, she saw death. Now she instructed them to put their hands on the table so that they just touched the hands of those on each side.

"Be very still," she said, "and don't speak unless you are

sure you must. Now it will grow dark." She didn't move, but the lights went out, and the darkness was full of after-images of sight. Jean's fingers touched those of the young girl on her right and those of the man with staring eyes on her left. There was a soft sound, a kind of humming, the voice of Regina Queen. It went on and on, and the darkness grew heavier, a pressure on her face. Regina Queen's voice was whispering, things that were almost impossible to hear, but slowly words could be made out.

"Blessed Anastasia, Blessed Anastasia, Blessed Vincent, Blessed Vincent, all the Blessed Ones, Blessed Anastasia, Blessed Vincent." The voice disappeared again into the humming. Jean could hear music, a piano, someone was playing "In der Halle des Bergkönigs," and she realized that she was playing it herself, back in that white empty church. The music was getting louder, and she could hear a repeated mistake, the one she always made, missing an accidental. She wondered if anyone else could hear the jagged series of notes.

"Is that you, Mother?" a voice said. It was the young girl, but her voice sounded unconvincing, as if she was pretending because that was what was called for. Jean felt angry at this childish pretence, wanted to slap the girl, but Regina Queen went on quietly evoking her saints. The music played its awkward way on in Jean's head, shapes moved in the consuming darkness of the room, and the dark creatures began to dance heavily in their feathers, bowing and showing their naked parts, and then Bruce was there, as if he were the object of their dancing, and Jean thought that this was not what she had come here for, this bad comedy, and yet all the while tears were running down her face. She felt a tingling in the fingers that touched the man on her left and the girl on her right, as if some sort of electricity had begun to flow between them, and shapes continued to move in front of her eyes, the man beside her breathing heavily, a hint of panic in the sound, and Jean felt her own breath quicken but knew as it did that if she allowed herself to breathe with him she would catch his panic and scream. The girl beside her was mumbling now and groaning, but it was all fake. It made her furious, and she wanted to pull her fingers away, not touch this foolish self-indulgent child with her inappropriate big bosom. Other voices were speaking, and some of them were known voices. This is where the dead speak, she thought. There is a silver goblet on the table, the sun and moon on the wall, the book and the sword. The sword moving through the air. She could see a figure now, appearing out of the umber shadows, a woman in a pale robe, a look of satisfaction on her face, and held in her hand, by the hair, the head of a man, bearded, the eyes closed, blood dripping, and in her other hand, a sword. She recognized the pale face of Alvin Coortland. Animals looked brightly toward her out of their dark forest. There were other voices in the room. She tried to see them in her mind, the others who had been sitting there, the old woman, the Mexican, and to make out who was speaking. There were noises and loud breathing and a sound of weeping. She heard someone speaking her name and telling her that she had lived a thousand lives and must live a thousand more. Here were all the lives she must live, story after story. Among the voices, she could hear her own, though what she was saying made no sense. It was in some other language, and the silver goblet was being offered to her, full of blood, but she wouldn't drink it, and then there was nothing but the growing noise and a terrible headache.

They were standing in daylight, in the moving banks of fog, she and the beautiful man, and he had his arm around her to support her. They were in a grove of orange trees, and she could see a branch close to them, the perfect orange globes just visible through the fog, round and bright and perfect. The skin of her face was wet. She couldn't bring herself to ask what had happened, how they had come to be here outside the house, not even when they were in the car driving away, but by the time the car had reached her bungalow, the fog had cleared, or they had driven out of it, and in the sunshine in front of her house the great flowers bloomed, red canna lilies and yellow roses and purple azaleas, and the trees were thick with green leaves. The beautiful man looked pale and frightened as he drove, so she spoke of ordinary things, the part he was to play next week, a prince in disguise. She invited him into the house with her. When they were inside, she led him into the bedroom, took off her clothes and undressed him in front of the full-length mirror that pivoted on its mahogany stand — it was what he liked, he had taught her what to do — and still in front of the long shining observer, she took his part in her hand and stroked it slowly, and he watched her do it in the mirror as he admired his perfect body. He had been polite and attentive, even though she had frightened him, and she was happy enough to be able to please him.

Her shoulders were bare, and her arms, and the soft material clung to her body when she moved. A string quartet was playing softly in the corner of the studio. The camera was turning, and Jean felt more naked than in the days when she had taken off her clothes to model in that big bare room in Greenwich Village. Above her, banks of lights were blindingly bright, a dozen white suns concentrating their light on her. She remembered what Del had taught her, to imagine herself in the eyes of the cameraman. To act past the camera into his brain, since he was the only one who could see the pictures. The director might shout his orders and think he was in charge, but it was the cameraman who made the movie, Del said, and by thinking about him, she lost her awareness of the machine he was cranking. This cameraman was a good one, very quiet, and she could imagine herself a small figure inside his brain, an unhappy woman waiting for her lover to arrive, terrified that he might not come.

"Walk to the window," the director whispered, "and look for him."

Jean took three steps and waited for a moment. Once she looked, she would know that he wasn't there. She looked. No sign of him.

"Then turn around slowly and look at the camera, and just then you see him, and you are so happy."

Jean began to turn, and as she turned, she told herself that she would see Del behind the camera, that she would look through the lens and into his eyes, and as she stared into the circle of glass, she believed it, that he was there.

"Cut."

People began to move onto the set to get it ready for the next shot, her view of the man standing in the doorway of the room. Then they would come together for a kiss.

The director was talking to the cameraman. Tubby Pringle, the still photographer, came up to her. His fat face was shiny with sweat.

"Can I get a still of that last shot? It will be a great one for the magazines."

"Okay. I'll try."

The cameraman had moved his tripod for the new shot, and Tubby was setting up where the camera had been. Jean wanted to find a mirror and check her hair and makeup before the kiss, which would be shot very close up. Just beyond the lights, she saw the beautiful man who was her lover. This was the first time they'd worked together. There was going to be a story in *Photoplay* that hinted that they were madly in love. They weren't, though Jean was comfortable enough with him. It always surprised her that someone who spent as much time as he did looking in mirrors could have such nice manners, but he did. She thought he was like a woman, and he was as gentle in bed as she imagined a woman might be. It was all pleasant but a little unreal. It was like a movie about a love affair, and Jean found it oddly consoling.

"Hurry up, Tubby," she said, "I've got to get ready for the next scene."

"Keep your pants on, miss," Tubby said. "We need a good one for the magazines."

"There will be no need for the magazines if we don't get this picture made."

"What an efficient little cunt you are," Tubby said. He had a bad mouth if you annoyed him. There was a rumour that he once got fired from United Artists for saying something like that to Mary Pickford.

"Don't lose your temper, sweetheart. I'm just a poor little working girl trying to make her way."

She was looking flirtatiously at him and gave her shoulders a little wiggle. He ignored her, but she thought he was probably mollified. She'd better give him a little kiss on the cheek after the picture was taken. It was hell on a set when people started to get crabby.

"Okay," Tubby said, "give us the look."

Jean tried to remember how she looked when she turned from the window, her excitement and longing. The lens clicked.

"One more," Tubby said.

She tried again. The lens clicked.

"Did I look beautiful, Tubby?" she said.

"You'll make them come in their pants, honey."

Jean went behind the camera and gave Tubby his little kiss, standing close so her breast rubbed against his arm.

"No more calling bad names, Tubby," she said. She was aware that Olga Dmitrievna was watching her. The woman was nearly six feet tall. She had black hair wound around her head, and she was dressed in black. It was said that she lived by the ocean in a beautiful house filled with strange modern paintings. She was designing Jean's next movie, and they were supposed to be getting together to discuss costumes. It displeased Jean that Olga Dmitrievna had seen her playing up to Tubby Pringle. The woman's dark eyes under the thick brows were very clear and very astute. Jean felt suddenly ashamed of herself, rubbing against Tubby like that, but she had to keep him sweet. She'd worked on one angry set recently, and she couldn't stand another. She did what was necessary.

The next shot was set up, her lover coming through the doorway of the room, then she would run into his arms, and they would kiss. She checked a mirror. Her face was white and unreal in the camera makeup, as if she were in the grip of some terrible sickness. Her hair was still all right. She turned back to the set as the cameraman began to crank.

"Okay, you come through the door and you see her."

He came in and stood. He didn't act, and sensible directors knew better than to try to make him act. Jean would do the acting, and his beautiful face seen in a giant close-up would reflect whatever the audience wished to see in it. When they tried to make him act he lost all his magic. Jean would bring all the passion to their kiss, and the women in the audience would understand this, that this was not a man who would grunt and smell of sweat and use coarse words. They would look at his untouchable beauty and long for the perfect things it embodied. When she kissed him, Jean would express their hunger. She would kiss as if she might suck the soul out of him. Let Olga Dmitrievna watch that, if she cared.

The door opened, and the woman stood in front of her, quite naked. She was tall and white, small breasted, her ribs visible under the skin, black hair wound around her head, and the other patch of hair as black and thick. As Jean stood there, she was aware that she could hear the ocean from behind the house, and there was a strange smell in the air, like cooking fruit.

"You must come in. Dmitrievna will send the little ones away now that you have arrived."

She led the way into the house. In the hall just inside the door was the figure of a man crudely carved out of brown wood, with bulging eyes and a thick-lipped open mouth and a male organ that hung along the short legs almost to the knees. On the other side of the hall the figure of a woman with ponderous breasts and immense hips and a small animal appearing out of her mouth. On the wall was a woven carpet with birds in brilliant red and orange. At the end of the hallway, a mirror, and Jean saw herself in jodhpurs and a white shirt, looking slight and tidy between the two carvings, and in front of her the tall white figure of Olga Dmitrievna moving through the door into another room. Jean followed her. On a sofa between two high narrow windows sat two small young women, both blond, both naked, their mouths and nipples pink, their eyes bright.

"Dmitrievna has company, little ones. Go away, and later we will have a picnic on the beach. Dmitrievna will make something very good. Something rich and sweet with butter and honey and *noix de grenoble*. That will be later. Go away now."

As the two of them looked at each other, bright-eyed, like two small mute animals, Jean realized that they were twins.

"Off with you now, or Dmitrievna will be angry."

She clapped her hands loudly. The two got up and ran quickly out of the room, their breasts bobbing.

"They are Dmitrievna's apprentices," the woman said when they were gone. "They are studying ecclesiastical embroidery."

She stood in the middle of the room, tall and imperious. Near her was a large wooden chair, with wide arms and a carved back. Across the room was another like it.

"Yes," the woman said, "you must sit down," and gestured toward the large chair. When Jean sat in it, her feet scarcely reached the floor. The naked woman did not move. The dark hair looked as if it might be something that would grow to cover her whole body.

"You have heard that Dmitrievna is a sapphist," she said, "but you are not, not at this stage of your development. Regina Queen says she has seen a long and intricate history for you, with many and complicated incarnations. For now you will be more comfortable if Dmitrievna wraps herself." She turned away. The bones of her long spine made little knobs all down her back. From behind the door, she took a long black gown that looked as if it might have belonged to a priest, and she put it around herself.

"You are very silent," the woman said.

"There's nothing I need to say," Jean said.

"Do not be too wise too soon. There is always time for wisdom later on." She sat in the big chair.

"Now," the woman said, "Dmitrievna must look at you. You understand that in this film, *Eternal Woman*, you must play woman through all the ages, from Cleopatra to a modern girl. Dmitrievna must make you beautiful in all these times and places." The woman's eyes were on her, acute and cold.

"The face is perfect, as they say. Now you stand up, please."

Jean did as she was told. She was no longer nervous. She looked at a painting on the wall, a portrait of Dmitrievna, but angular, geometric.

Jean turned obediently, stood still while she was measured, walked when she was told, lifted her arms. She was used to it, doing what she was told, being looked at.

"You have a perfect body. Dmitrievna can make you all women, the beauty of all women."

Jean sat back down in the chair like a throne. She studied the portrait on the wall.

"Do you like the picture?"

"Yes."

"A great Russian artist. He is dead now."

"I've heard you have many interesting pictures. I'd like to see them."

"You mean the work of Pablo Picasso."

"I don't know the names."

"The pictures that people laugh at."

"I don't think I'll laugh."

"Dmitrievna will show you, and you will be astonished.

98

Pablo Picasso is in Paris. You must go there. A friend of mine is coming here, a French director of films, an artist. I will introduce you to him. You will go and make movies for him in Paris."

She stood to leave the room and indicated with her hand that Jean should follow her. As they passed a window, Jean saw the emerald green endless Pacific.

Jean stood by the ship's rail and stared over the grey ocean and watched the movement of wind and light in the clouds. They were out of sight of land. It was growing familiar now, the ghostly emptiness when everything familiar was left behind. Somebody asked you, and you said yes, and you moved on. Land fell away behind the boat, and new land would appear in front. That was how her people had got to Canada. Now she was going to the continent they had left. The only person she knew there was Jules Michaux, the director who had hired her. She had met him through Dmitrievna, and he had sent her a telegram, offering to pay her way to France where she would star in a movie about a female Pope. Pope Joan. She had never heard of such a thing, but Dmitrievna had assured her that such a figure did exist, somewhere in history.

Maybe it was a stupid thing to do. Otherwise she would have signed a new studio contract for a lot more money, but California wasn't a place she belonged. She did what they told her, and the movies got made, and she saw her picture in the magazines, and she was learning to be Cora Heart, but it was as if she never stopped being in the movies, and everything they wrote about her in the magazines was a lie. She could tell lies if she had to, but you wanted to stop sometimes. She knew that part of the reason she'd said yes to the movie in France was that the trip gave her an excuse to stop in New York and see Del. So she stopped in New York and found that he'd moved another woman into the apartment. That's who answered the door when she knocked. The girl called to Del, and he came to the door in a new silk dressing gown she'd never seen before. Jean didn't say a word, just waited for him to speak, and he handled it pretty well, invited her in, told the girl, whose name was Dorothy, that this was Cora Heart, and how lucky she was to be meeting a real movie star. At first Jean thought that was a cruel joke, but it wasn't. Del had seen her movies and said they were very popular in New York, that people were talking about her. Jean was aware that her clothes were better than the other girl's clothes, that she could never afford something like Jean's coat with the fox collar, and she was tempted to put on the dog a little about money and famous people.

Del finished dressing, and, leaving Dorothy in a pout, they found a cab and drove to a place on Broadway near Times Square for lunch, and Jean realized that people were looking at her, though she couldn't tell if they recognized her or if it was just how she looked in her best clothes. She saw someone that she thought she recognized, and the woman looked at her and smiled. It was one of the girls who danced in the Follies, one she used to meet at parties. She saw the girl talking to the other one in the booth with her and pointing to Jean, and then they came over and asked for her autograph. As she signed the piece of paper they held out to her, Jean watched Del to see if he was laughing, but she couldn't make out the expression on his face. The girls wanted to talk about the rumours that there would soon be talking movies, but Jean said she didn't know.

After they went back to their own booth, Del asked her about the stories in the newspapers about her and the beautiful man, and she said yes, there was something to them, but he wasn't going to France with her. She could see that Del was jealous, and she figured he had a nerve, when he was living with Dorothy and he was the one who wouldn't come out west with her.

After they finished lunch, Del told her that *Eternal Woman* was playing at the Roxy, and he convinced her to go there with him. She kept her hat pulled down and her collar up — she didn't want to be recognized. She hadn't been in the Roxy before, and the size and splendour of the place was wonderful. As she watched herself on the screen, she couldn't help crying a little because she did look beautiful.

After the movie they went and sat in Central Park, and Del seemed to be offering to start up again if she wanted, to get rid of Dorothy, but Jean chose not to understand, and they talked about something else. By the end of that afternoon Jean knew two things, that she still loved him like crazy and that she couldn't wait to get on the boat and leave New York. When she first got on the boat and the steward, who was very blond and handsome, a German, showed her to her cabin, she went inside and sat down on the bed and tried to understand why she loved Del and why she wanted to run away.

There was a cold wind as she stood by the rail of the boat, and she pulled down her hat and wrapped the fur collar of her coat around her face. It was cold out here, but she didn't want to go inside. She had books, but she couldn't read. Dmitrievna had given her a book in French. Her beautiful lover had given her something by Madame Blavatsky. Del had come to the boat to see her off, and he gave her a book called *In Our Time* that he said was his favourite book, and she could see why, but

she could only read a little bit some days after she'd had a glass
of wine, sitting by herself in the lounge. She would read a few
lines, and she'd think about the people in the stories, and
about Del, and then she'd close the book and finish her wine.

Before she left New York, Jean had written to her mother to
say she was going to France and sent some money. That was the
best she could do. Why are you going to France? her mother
would say to her if she saw her, and look worried, and Jean could
only say, because somebody asked me and I said yes.

A pleasant-looking man with grey hair and a moustache
walked past along the deck. He tipped his hat to her as he always
did when he saw her. Jean thought that he would probably ask
her to have a drink with him, or afternoon tea. He was French,
and under his moustache he had a small perfect smile.

Now they were out of sight of land, Jean thought it was
time to meet people, to go to the dances in the evening, to
meet the gentlemanly Frenchman, to flirt with the handsome
German steward. She was nowhere now, on her way to a
country where people spoke another language and the fields
were planted with the dead of a hundred wars.

There was the grey ocean, and more ocean, and more
beyond that. A sky that was never still. In the middle of all this
sky and water was an ocean liner, and on the ocean liner a
young woman stood by the rail in a coat with a silver fox collar,
and that was what there was.

Four

THE SEA WAS AS CLEAR and brilliant as amethyst or emerald, the colour changing from perfect green to perfect blue. White cliffs rose from the water, marked here and there with the dark shapes of small plants that found enough soil in cracks of the rock to propagate themselves. The sailboat was anchored, but Jean could feel it roll a little as she crossed the deck. On both sides of them the white rock walls of the *calanque* rose steeply, and it was as if the light came from the rock itself. Where the sides of the *calanque* came gradually together, there was a small beach of stones.

Jean dived into the clear water. She saw the rocks beneath her, patterns of filtered sunlight, and then she came to the surface and began to swim toward the shore, riding high in the buoyant salt water, watching the light on the tiny wavelets as she approached the beach and walked awkwardly ashore on the sharp small stones.

She looked back to the boat, where Jules and his wife had come on deck in their bathing suits, their bodies almost in silhouette against the background of pale rock. Pascale was tall and long-waisted, with narrow hips. Jean had never met Pascale before they arrived at the dock at Martigues, where she waited on the dock for them in a smart wine-coloured suit, hampers of groceries at her feet. Jules introduced Pascale, who smiled and was efficient about getting them on board. They had slept on the boat, ready to sail out in the morning, and Jean, lying awake, had heard their sounds during the night, and it made her lonely and unhappy. She remembered the invitation to go and visit *M. le comte*, the man she had met on the boat, who had unexpectedly come to visit her on the set, and she thought maybe she would accept.

The two of them began to swim to shore, Jules briskly, his wife with a slow, inefficient sidestroke. She took a long time to arrive, and when she began to stumble over the stones, her long legs made her look awkward and easily broken.

"Well," Jules said, spreading his arms to indicate the water and rock, "what do you think?"

"I've never seen anything like it," Jean said.

"You grew up by the water."

"It was not like this."

Pascale was lying on her back, and the shape of her hip bones was visible through her bathing suit. Jules looked down at her possessively.

"I grew up in Paris," Pascale said as she lay there with her eyes closed, "and I never imagined anything so beautiful as this. Until Jules brought me here, I never could imagine what it would be like."

"Me, I'm Provençal," Jules said, "and I could never understand the rainy north."

Pascale sat up, reached out and touched his leg.

"You smell like Provence," she said.

"I'm going to swim," Jean said.

She got up and walked carefully into the water, stumbling as the stones pressed into her flesh. She swam out past the boat, to the steep rock side of the *calanque*, where she hung on for a minute to rest, then pushed off again, putting her face in the water and looking down into the aquamarine shimmer of the depths, the planes of light. She swam back to the boat, looked towards the shore, where the two of them sat side by side, both in the same position, their arms around their knees. Jean went down to the little cabin she'd been given, stripped off her bathing suit and rubbed herself briskly, rubbing her hair dry and then brushing it, then rubbing it again and brushing it until it was almost dry and lay properly around her head. Then she opened the small case that held her makeup, and, bending awkwardly over the bed in the small cabin, she arranged her face.

Back on deck, she set the bathing suit and towel to dry in the sun. By now, Jules and Pascale were swimming back to the boat. He arrived first, puffing and shaking like a dog. Pascale came after, all legs and arms as she climbed aboard. The two of them went down to dress and came back on deck with the hampers of food and wine. Jean sat on a wooden chest that contained coils of rope and drank the white wine, and her head began to spin with all the brightness of sun and water and the white rock of the cliffs.

After lunch, they raised the anchors and sailed out of the *calanque* and around the island and docked, and when the boat was tied, they began to walk up an old road that led past a couple of tiny houses and between the chalky hills, with here and there cactus plants lifting their fat branches covered with sharp spines. At the top of the hill was a large complex of ruined buildings overlooking the blue water and, two miles off, the city that curved round the old harbour and spread upward toward the mountains, a black and white church at the summit of a hill, and below, fishing boats and the dark freighters docked to take on cargo.

There was something ominous about these ruins, buildings

grouped around an open square with a little imitation Greek temple in the centre. Everything empty and overgrown. A wine bottle lay on the ground.

"What is it?" Jean said.

"A lazaretto . . . a hospital."

"Why would they build a hospital here, so far from the city?"

"But that was why. Bad fevers. Contagious diseases."

They were brought across the water, wrapped like mummies, taken away from the city where they might spread their fever, and brought somehow up the hill, in little carts perhaps, it was too far for a sick person to walk, and they were shut away here to wait for death or the chance of health. She looked at the little temple and wondered why it was here.

"I don't like this place," Pascale said.

"No," Jean said. "I don't like it either." In spite of the hot sun, she was shivering.

"I wanted to see it again," Jules said. "I thought one might make a film here."

"No," Jean said. "No one would come to see a film made here."

"Don't be so American," Jules said.

Jean moved away from him, across the bare ground of the square. A breeze off the water blew against her face.

"Let's get out of here," Pascale said. "Let's go." They turned away from the ghosts, went back down the hill and found the boat, and after they had drunk some more wine, they sailed back round the island and into a different bay. When they were anchored, Jean looked into the blue water, defiant, being called so American like that, his condescension. *M. le comte* didn't condescend to her. Without speaking, she took up her bathing suit, went to her cabin to change, and then came up and dived into the water and swam beneath it, white and perfect, the strength of her arms pulling her through the bright depths, the amethyst, the emerald.

She stood in the garden and looked at the peach tree that grew by the wall, the way the branches had been pruned and trained horizontally, then vertically on a frame attached to the wall, so that the tree had become flat and geometrical. *Espalier.* That was the word. Guillaume had told her that. *Le comte.* M. de Seviède. She had all these names for him and hadn't quite settled on one. He explained to her that the tree was grown like that against a south-facing wall to catch and reflect the sun's heat and to shelter it from cold winds. Each of the peaches, now nearly ripe, was wrapped in brown paper and neatly tied with string. The gardener did this to keep off the wasps which might otherwise find a taste of sweetness and eat their way into the fruit.

In front of the peach grew three gooseberry bushes and two black currants. Madame Roussel would use them to make desserts and sweet liqueurs from the old recipes that had come to her from her grandmother, who had also been the cook to the family. Everything here went back a thousand years. They were still arguing about what had happened to the king a hundred and fifty years ago. Guillaume and his family were loyal to the king, even though there was no king. The family had once lived in a great chateau, but it had been burnt down, and now, when they were not in Paris, they lived here, on the edge of Les Sourcelles in a stone house behind a wall with a little stone barn and gardens and white doves and the sound of chickens clucking happily on the other side of the garden wall where the peach tree had been trained to grow in its perfect pattern. On the streets of the town, men would tip their hats to Guillaume and call him *M. le comte.*

She turned back and looked across the lawn to where his brother Robert sat in his chair. It was a wooden chair on wheels, and Berthe, who worked around the house and helped Madame Roussel, had brought him out in it to sit in the sunlight. He had been maimed in the war and couldn't walk more than a step or two, and he had only one eye, and the side of his face where the eye was missing had shiny skin with a mauve tint. The war had done something to his voice as well, and it was throaty and harsh. He, most of all, was ferociously loyal to the king who didn't exist. His anger, comprehensible enough in one who had been so ruined, was always ready to burst out. His life had been narrowed to anger and a few loyalties. It was clear that he loved Guillaume and Guillaume's son, Philippe. And the church. Guillaume pushed his chair down the street to mass early every morning, and when they returned, Robert would drink coffee and eat the fresh pastries that Madame Roussel took from the oven. On his face the anger was altered into a kind of triumph, and he and Guillaume would gossip a little about those they'd seen in church and about local politics.

Jean reached out and picked one of the black currants, rubbed it between her fingers and smelled the rich perfume of the fruit. One of the white doves was sitting on top of the wall, a bright eye watching her. She knew that Robert was watching her as well, uneasy and distrustful. Almost certainly he knew what Guillaume had said to her last night. The dove turned its head as if listening, then spread its wings and flew away. Now only Robert observed her as she stood in the garden and tried to put into words what she would say to *M. le comte.*

He wanted her to marry him. Last night he had explained
this to her, slowly and carefully, in case she might not understand
what he was saying. Now and then he would stop or translate
a word into English, but she had come to understand French
very well. Speaking French was like being in a movie. It was
its own world, and you were a different person while you
were there. Apart from what she'd learned in school, she had
learned it while she was making the movies for Jules Michaux,
first *Pope Joan*, and then the other one, the comedy, and it was
part of the pretence. She pretended she was Pope Joan, and she
pretended that she could speak French. So she had understood
his slow, detailed, thoughtful explanation of what would be
involved in marrying him. His son, who was a only a little
older than Jean, would inherit the title, but should Jean have
children, he would certainly undertake to make provision for
them. There was, too, the question of Madame de Coulanges.
She had been very good to him since the death of his wife, and
he wished to treat her with dignity and propriety.

The dove returned, and another with it, and she heard
their soft sounds in the air. Were they a pair? Should she take
that as some indication? She supposed all this was the sort of
thing that you might discuss with someone, but there was no
one nearby to discuss it with. In a week she was going to Paris,
and Olga Dmitrievna would be there to work on a film with
Jules, and there might be a part for her. It was to be a film with
talking, and her French wasn't good enough for that, or so they
believed. Jules had some idea of making her a German
woman, and that would explain her accent. Jean wasn't
convinced that a German would have the same accent as she
did, but Jules didn't appear to be worried about that, though he
was very nervous about making a talking film. He said the
talking would destroy the art.

Guillaume wanted to get married very soon, and she hadn't raised the question of this movie. Or other movies. Whether he would expect her to stay at home. When she first met Guillaume on the boat, and he spoke to her in his difficult formal English, she knew that he was a serious person, and she admired him for it. They sat together at a table in the lounge, and he asked her questions, one at a time, as if he had a plan of the things he wished to know about her. He began to teach her French expressions. Though he had never heard of Jules Michaux, he said that he would learn about him. He had, in fact, never watched a movie — it had not seemed necessary — but he had heard that fine work had been done by a French director named Abel Gance. They would walk around the deck, even when the wind was strong and there was rain and salt spray, and his face would grow bright, the blue eyes and salt-and-pepper moustache against the pink freshness of the skin. She could see that he liked being with her. Still, she was surprised that he arrived when she was working on the film about Pope Joan in the south. They were shooting in the ruins of the Roman theatre at Orange, and she looked up and saw a familiar figure in the seats — the dark suit and hat, the walking stick, against the dim grey stone of the seats high above her. When he introduced himself to Jules, it was clear that he had learned about him and had seen one of his films. When he brought up the name of Abel Gance, Jules stiffened — they competed and were not friends — but Guillaume managed that smoothly enough, and after shooting ended for the day, when he took Jean out for dinner, he invited Jules to come with them, and the evening went along comfortably. He asked her to come to Les Sourcelles, but there was a second film, and he came to the south once again, appeared one day in the distance watching. She was pleased to see him, his careful, serious eyes observing her. He was unlike any other man she had ever met, so quiet and full of certainty. He knew the world and what it was worth.

The two white doves flew away, first the one, then the other following. Jean went past the end of the wall to the small yard where the chickens walked on their stiff yellow feet, bundles of loose brown feathers with reptilian eyes and bright red combs. The rooster was on top of one of the hens, his wings flapping to balance him. He fell back off, shook himself and strutted away, ran a few steps, then stood still surveying his world. His eye, cold and malign, reminded her of Robert's one remaining eye, bright with rage.

One morning, Jean had gone along to mass with them, and as the priest began to offer the host, Guillaume had pushed Robert's chair forward, and with Guillaume and another man holding him, he had stood, taken slow steps to the altar rail through a patch of sunlight cast by one of the windows in the thick grey stone walls, the light emphasizing the unnatural colour and sheen of the skin on his face, each step a huge effort of will, Guillaume struggling to hold him up as the hopeless legs tried to walk, lurching but going forward until he knelt in front of the priest to receive, then was lifted like a broken thing being reassembled, turned, the good part of his face pale and tight with pain, staggering back into the patch of light as if into the random blessing of some fierce god, and finally, reaching his chair, Guillaume and the other man helped him back in and set him upright.

Jean walked past a climbing rose on an arched trellis and toward the row of chestnuts that marked the end of the garden. Just beyond them was the stone wall, and beyond that a long sloping field of grain.

Philippe was arriving this evening from Paris. Guillaume had not yet told him about this possible marriage, and Jean was certain that he would not approve. She had met him once in Paris, and he was cold and supercilious. He had met Dmitrievna and made a remark about artistic Jews.

She walked back up the green lawn, and as she passed Robert's chair, she said something about the scent of the roses, and he growled a response in his rusty voice and turned his head so that his one cold eye looked her over, weighing, measuring, like a farmer about to buy a domestic animal. The way he was looking at her made her sure that he knew about Guillaume's proposal. He would disapprove, of course. She knew that he and Philippe would both dislike the idea.

Guillaume was in his library writing. Jean went up to her room and put on her hat and coat. She would walk up the hill past the rock grotto where a spring of water ran down the rocks to form a stream that found its way to the small river that ran near the town. She liked to sit by the spring and listen to the sound of water coming from the earth. Guillaume told her old stories about a pagan god who was found here. It reminded her how once, when she was very young, when her father was still at home, they had gone to visit a friend of his, and there was a spring near the house, a tin cup hanging beside it, and she was given the spring water to drink as if it were the most precious thing in the world. That was the way Guillaume spoke about the springs here, life arising out of the French earth, the same earth where his family had lived and where, all through these low hills, they had been buried.

Past the spring, she would go up a steep path through a small area of woodland. From the top, she could look over a vineyard and the town, the geometry of the tile roofs meeting at odd angles, the low steeple of the church rising just beyond.

Jean sat in a chair in the hotel room and looked out the open
window at the rain pouring down on the metal roofs and
splashing into the courtyard below where the clerk left his
bicycle. A minute ago she had looked down and seen the
bicycle there, black and narrow in the rain. She was chilled
with the window open, but she wanted to watch the rain, to
hear the sound and smell the heavy damp of the air. As she sat
alone in the bare room, she was waiting to be married.
Guillaume had said that she ought to come to the apartment,
where they would be living after the ceremony tomorrow
morning, but she wanted to spend this last day alone. Perhaps
only to be aware of her loneliness and solitude. Tomorrow she
would have a place to be and someone there with her. But
now she wished to be alone to think, and watch the rain.

She had written to tell her mother that she was to be
married and that after the wedding she would be *la comtesse de
Seviède*, and her mother's answer sounded worried and
disbelieving, telling her that Eg had been sick, they said he'd
never walk right, and things were tough, Ronald was out of
work but doing a little fishing. She said she was hoping for the
best. At the bottom was a note asking whatever happened to
Delbert Hunnicut, Jean was supposed to be marrying him,
wasn't she?

What happened to Delbert Hunnicut? He got left behind
when I caught the train, that's what happened to Delbert
Hunnicut. She wondered about writing to let him know about
her marriage, but she decided against it. That was all a long
time ago now. Like everything before France. Only Dmitrievna

was left. Dmitrievna had come to France to work for Jules, and she said that she was going to stay. The girls in the United States were very pretty, she said, but they had no flair. They were naive and stupid and soon boring. Her friend in Paris was an older woman, short and heavy, with thick hands, who seldom spoke but paid the bill when they were in a restaurant or café.

The rain was heavy, loud on the roofs of the buildings nearby. On the table beside her was a *petit bleu* from Jules about the movie they were starting next week. He had decided that she was not to be a German woman but instead a beautiful and mysterious figure who never spoke, even though the other characters did. He would show them that silence could say more than all those words, he said.

Guillaume had agreed that she would go on making movies, at least until they had a child. It satisfied him that she didn't use her own name. Cora Heart and Jeanne de Seviède would be different people. If they had a child, Jean would stop. It was hard to think of having a child. It wasn't something she could quite believe in, but it was possible. If she did, it would be an orphan, somehow. Philippe was the true son who would become *le comte de Seviède*, while her child would be nothing. Philippe had made clear that he disapproved of this marriage; she had overheard him saying to his father that he might better have married Madame Roussel, who was a peasant but at least a French peasant. All very well to have an actress for a mistress, as he himself did, but to marry one was entirely beyond reason. Since she disliked Philippe, it didn't especially matter what his opinion of her might be. She knew how Guillaume felt about her. Sometimes she would catch him watching her with a look of intensity and pride. As she thought about it, Guillaume's love for her and what it meant, she wanted to go out and stand in the rain, in the pouring, soaking rain until she was wet to the skin and cold and shivering. Because it was dangerous, the idea of marriage and the possible child she might have.

She would wait, and what would happen would happen. After the wedding, she would move into the large apartment on the Boulevard Haussmann, and she would learn to deal with Madame Roussel. It would come to her when it was needed.

She sat at the table of the café and watched the men and women going by with a kind of astonishment at their existence, that they had lives, each one of them, that like her they could watch things and have thoughts. The city was caught in some strange light. She could see the inside of everything while at the same moment knowing she understood nothing. All this, perhaps, because inside her there was an invisible thing, the secret child that had begun to grow. Across the table Dmitrievna sat in a black suit almost like a man's, with trousers and a vest. Her black hair was cut short now. Jean knew that the waiter thought she was Dmitrievna's lover as the two of them sat, each with a glass of white wine, and watched the men and women move through the streets on a bright spring day.

Two workmen went by, pushing a wheeled cart with a ladder on it, a box of tools and several long pieces of wood, and beside the toolbox a baguette and a bottle of wine. Two tables away, a man in a dark suit was reading a newspaper. The papers were full of dire prophecies. Everyone was worried. People were losing their money. She didn't understand quite where Guillaume's money came from. There was land, and he had something to do with a bank, and investments. He gave Jean a sum of money every month, and she still had her own from the films she'd made. There was a pile of notes in the drawer where she kept her gloves. Once or twice she had thought that perhaps she should ask Guillaume what to do with it, but for now she did nothing. Today when she came out to meet Dmitrievna, she took a hundred-franc note and put it in her purse.

The man lifted his eyes from his newspaper and looked toward her. She met his eyes and then looked away.

She was someone men noticed. That was why being looked at had become her *métier*. It was a very strange *métier*, and it required an inward stillness, but now inside her, instead of that stillness, there was a child growing, and now she had become like the eyes that watched her, was one who saw everything.

Across from the café, a narrow street entered the boulevard. Between the tall buildings with the many windows, each with shutters and ornate ironwork forming a little balcony, it was like a deep valley, and she could see the water running along the gutter, and a woman in a dress, without a hat or coat, came out of the butcher shop with a chicken in her basket, the head and feet hanging out on each side, walked two doors along the street and vanished through the entry of a courtyard. Above her, some of the shutters were closed, but others were wide open to let in the fresh spring air, and those high up, where the sun came over the rooftops to shine in the windows, had plants set out to catch the light.

Jean could smell the street and the coffee in the cups of a man and woman near her who sat talking, books on the table in front of them. She could smell, from somewhere, a slight, sickening odour of fish. There must be a *poissonnerie* nearby.

She almost imagined a damp green smell from the leaves of the plane trees that were just beginning to open.

"It will be important for you to work with this man," Dmitrievna said. She was speaking English. Her French and English were equally good, and neither was her native tongue. She had grown up speaking Yiddish and Russian. She learned French and English in school, then came to Paris before the revolution to study art, and when the revolution occurred she decided to stay, then found her way to America to make American dollars. She knew Jean wouldn't be one of her girls but was crazy about her all the same and took a great interest in her career. One day Jean would tell her about the baby and how that would change everything.

"Why is it so important to work with him?"

"Because he is a genius."

Dmitrievna was only interested in knowing a man if she thought he was a genius, or that he might soon become one, or at least be someone whose failure to be a genius was itself important.

Jean sipped her wine. Across the boulevard, a woman in high heels and a maroon hat stood on the corner. Then a large black car appeared, and she got in. The car drove away, and Jean would never see her again. Jean wondered how many people lived in Paris, and how many she saw each day, and if she lived here for the rest of her life how many she would see. She had met only a few. Guillaume's friends visited, but the women were older and uncomfortable with her, envious of her beauty perhaps. Jean had got used to knowing that she was beautiful, it didn't seem any different to her than any other way a person might look. It was part of her *métier*. Being beautiful and being looked at. But that was to change: perhaps when she was no longer looked at, she would no longer be beautiful. She would like to ask Dmitrievna about that, it was the sort of thing she would have thought about, but she wasn't ready yet to tell her about the baby.

Jean reached for her glass. Dmitrievna was looking at her, the dark, almost black eyes very still. Jean knew what it was all about. She could not prevent it, that the woman loved her, could only accept it as it was, something as inevitable and unlikely as the sunlight that shone on a beggar who sat by the wall of the church only a few steps away, a beggar who would stay there until dark and then go down to the Seine and find a place under one of the bridges, cover himself with rags and cardboard and sleep.

When they finished their wine, she was going with Dmitrievna to an art gallery on the rue Bonaparte to see an exhibition of photographs by a man whose work Dmitrievna admired, another genius, and Dmitrievna and her friend were planning to buy one of his photographs. After the gallery on the rue Bonaparte, they were going on to the Jardin du Luxembourg, where there might be a puppet show. It would be another long walk. Jean had already walked from the apartment down to the Seine, stopping to sit in the Tuileries for a rest, and then across the bridge, watching barges of coal being towed along the river, then past the École des Beaux Arts to meet Dmitrievna here at the café, and now they would walk up the hill to the Luxembourg, but she was sure that all this exercise must be good for the baby.

She drank a little more wine and watched two young lovers kissing on the street corner while a workman with stained hands and a dirty face rode by on a bicycle, a bag of tools on his back.

She was huge and immobile and could not believe that this was herself, this swollen ungainly creature, and the baby inside her rolled and hiccupped and kicked. Across the room sat Guillaume's cousin Gabrielle. She was a tall, broad woman with several moles on her face, and she had come to bring a long antique gown for this baby who was about to be born. It was some kind of family heirloom, heavy and ivory-white with fancy needle-work, and to Jean it looked like something in which a dead child might be buried.

She had gone through a spell of nerves when she was afraid that her child might be born dead, but now it was so active that she had no doubt of its strength. Its kicks, as just now, hurt her sometimes. Gabrielle had put a mournful look on her face and was reciting in a slow dramatic way the difficulties of her own experience of bearing a child. The endless pain, the doctor's despair. She pretended sympathy, but what she wanted, Jean could see, was to frighten her. Jean was a foreigner and an outsider and, if sufficiently terrorized, would accept a role in which she felt only humility and gratitude.

Across the room, in a dim corner, Guillaume observed all this. Now and then he tried to interrupt, but Gabrielle, not to be moved from her doleful narrative, bypassed his interruptions as if they had not happened. The chair he sat in had a high back, and it made him look smaller, a pale stiff figure in the shadows. The gown that Gabrielle had brought lay across her knees, a white shroud over which she delivered her endless homily. She moved from the terrors of childbirth to the dreadful state of the world, and then, by some insidious

rhetorical trick, back to the plans she had made for her own
funeral when the pain of bearing a child had seemed that it
must be mortal. As she endured all this, Jean's back was
aching, and she felt a little dizzy. The minute Gabrielle left, she
would ask Guillaume to take her out for a drive along the
Champs Élysées, then down Avenue Foch and through the
Bois de Boulogne. She must see happy people and the trees
and the sky. She would take out her largest, her most
outrageous hat, and when they got to the Bois, she would ask
Guillaume to stop the car and let her walk for a bit by one of
the lakes, big and awkward as she was.

Jean sat with the baby in her arms and listened to the loud
voices from upstairs. They had come to Les Sourcelles to
escape the anger and threats that were everywhere in Paris, but
the anger had followed them. Philippe was here, and he had
brought the deaf man, with his big nose and horrible staring
eyes, and the two of them were shouting at Guillaume that he
must do something, act or give money or sign something. She
didn't know what it was, but she knew that it was wrong.
Guillaume made her understand his faith that there was more
to living than what could be bought and sold, that each man
had a duty to the past. He could speak happily about it for
hours, and she liked what he said. When he went to the
chapelle expiatoire a few streets from their apartment, which
had been built in memory of the king, where the body had
first been buried, she would sit in the little park outside while
he went in past the white roses to make his devotions, but she
knew that he must do this. The others were consumed by their

hates. Robert, maimed, had reason, and she knew that even beyond his anger was his love for Guillaume. If he disliked and resented her she could live with it because of that love.

She could only sit here with the warm body of her child held to her breast and rock slowly back and forth and watch his soft face as he slept. He was called Guillaume like his father. She could hear a cold rain against the window. Otherwise she would have taken the baby out in the big English pram that Guillaume had bought. She knew that if she wanted to go out, she could leave the baby with Madame Roussel, but she hated to abandon him in a house that was so full of anger. She was fearful in a way she had never been before. She listened to the rain, and now and then she heard the voices from upstairs. She understood now the helplessness of women, and she wondered if there was another woman in the village like her, frightened for her child. She thought how her mother must have felt, with the three of them and a husband who got himself blown up, having to take favours.

A few months ago, an artist she met with Dmitrievna had wanted her to pose. She knew he wanted more than that, and she had told him that she had a husband and was going to have a baby. He was the first person she told, even before she'd told Guillaume. The words came out. He said that he'd never painted a pregnant woman and was very excited, but she had refused, and now she regretted it. He'd insisted that she and Dmitrievna come to his studio, and she'd seen his paintings, their unreal, exciting colours, and she wished now that she'd agreed to pose for him.

Dmitrievna had gone back to America to do a movie and earn American dollars. Jules was talking about another film, but she had agreed to stop when the baby was born, and besides, Jules was having trouble raising the money. Everyone was poor now, or afraid of being poor. Without telling Guillaume, Jean had taken her pile of francs to the American bank, and now they were all American dollars. She knew that Guillaume would disapprove, but she was not French, and she didn't need to be a patriot. She wasn't American either, but everyone talked about the value of American dollars, and she didn't even know if there was a Canadian bank. She thought of Canada as another place where people were poor, the way her mother was, having to depend on Ronald, who wasn't worth much. Jean had written to her mother to say that she was a grandmother now, and her mother wrote back a note to say she already was. Iris had quit school and got married the year before, and she had a little girl called Jean after her famous aunt. That made Jean think that she should write Iris a letter, and she tried, but it wouldn't come out right. She was still planning to do it one of these days. She didn't feel famous at all, and she was sure she wasn't. If she'd stayed in California, she might have been famous. The beautiful man who'd been her lover was famous even in France.

The voices were quieter now, and she held her child and listened to the sound of the rain and did not feel comforted. She went to the window and looked through the glass, past the drops of water, at the green garden.

Philippe sat across the room from her with his newspapers. Guillaume had gone off to a meeting of the directors of the bank, and the child was asleep in his room. The night before there had been riots in the city. Philippe and Guillaume had gone out in the dark, and she had stayed in the apartment with her little son, standing guard over him. When Guillaume came home, late, he said she should go away to Les Sourcelles. Robert was there, with Berthe and Berthe's brother to look after him. Paris was too dangerous, he said, but this morning she had decided that she would stay. They would go to Les Sourcelles for holidays in the spring and in the summer, but she wouldn't run away now. More than ever, the apartment was full of secrets. Notes arrived, Guillaume and Philippe were summoned to meetings and came back dangerously roused. Philippe had an apartment of his own, but he spent more and more time with them, as if he might need to be available at some crucial moment.

Philippe made no attempt to conceal his dislike of Jean and his distrust. He would sit in the same room with her, as he was right now, reading his newspapers and behaving as if she weren't there. She had thought of speaking to Guillaume about it but decided not to. It felt like begging, and she would not do it. She looked across the room. On the wood panelling of the wall were three landscapes by Corot, small vivid places in the countryside, grass and light. One with a river and a bridge. Beneath them sat a heavy wooden chair. Young Guillaume liked to try to pull himself up on it, but she was always afraid that he was going to fall and knock his head against the wooden legs.

The apartment was dark, too much old wood. At first she had found it comforting, like a long, complicated cave full of beautiful things, old silver and china, but she was unable to make it her own. She had hired a man to replace the wallpaper in the bedroom with a pretty pattern in light blue and bought a new bedspread to match, but it wasn't enough. The room was full of ghosts — Guillaume's first wife, and before that his parents, who had once lived here, and his grandparents as well.

Family was something different here, heavier. It was hard to remember that she lived in the modern world, that the galleries she went to with Dmitrievna were showing Matisse and Miró and Dufy and those distorted photographs Dmitrievna liked so much, that Jules Michaux and his wife lived in a villa that had been built for them, with furniture of bent wood and shining metal, walls with strange openings and oddly shaped windows, and a big bronze nude standing in the middle of the main room.

Philippe's mistress, Lucette, was an actress and singer, but she had never been able to convince him to see a movie. He regarded them as a plot by the Americans and Jews to destroy the classic French theatre. Jean looked over at the man who sat there in silence ignoring her, and thought how young he was, really, when you studied the face, and she was aware that his feelings were intense but shallow, that he had composed himself as he might have composed an essay on tradition in French politics. Lucette was older, and though she was frightened of him, his sudden rages, she also spoke of him with a certain condescension. Lucette was not her real name — it was a music hall name she'd picked up early on when she'd first come to Paris. She had an assurance that Jean disliked and yet almost admired. Lucette thought that she and Jean were alike and wanted to be friends, but Jean knew it would make things worse with Philippe and that Guillaume was uneasy about Lucette, preferred her slight vulgarity to be held at a distance. Respectable men kept their cheap women away from the rest of their lives. It was all very well for Guillaume to fall in love with a movie girl and marry her, but he expected her to move into his own circle, not to bring scandal into his world. Dmitrievna was a shock to him, but he accepted her as Jean's friend the way he might accept that an aging duchess wished to keep a bright, loud parrot at her side. Or perhaps Dmitrievna represented the modern world; he knew it was there and was astonished. He was a kind and worldly man, but he wished things to remain appropriately situated.

She looked at Philippe, at the perfect skin, a little pale, and the thick brown hair that still grew forward on the forehead, imagined touching the hair, the rather long neck. He was slender, and he moved well. You felt the body would be hard and muscular. Nature, she supposed, had intended her for a man like this, almost her own age, but as she looked away, she reminded herself that they disliked each other and that she preferred not to be in the same room with him. No, Lucette was welcome to him. What she longed for from time to time was not his rage and feverish intensity, the frowning of an angry boy, but some kind of lightness.

"The newspapers are full of lies," Philippe said suddenly, throwing the last of them down at his feet.

"Lies about what?"

"Blum. Blum. No matter where we turn, we find Blum — his bad influence, his love of intrigue, all that ambition and hatred."

Jean didn't speak. She had nothing to say.

"The government of France under the influence of a man without one French fibre in his being."

He got up from the chair and stood there as if he might come across the room and begin to beat her with his fists. In the distance, she heard the baby's cry. He had wakened from his nap. Though she knew that Andrée would go to him, she got up. She wanted to get away from Philippe, and once on her feet, she glanced toward him, and his eyes met hers, and now he looked not angry but puzzled, as if about to speak but unable to find the words. Or was it that? There was always something unspoken between them, and she was driven to interpret his looks, knowing that she might be altogether wrong. As she turned to leave the room, she thought he was still watching her, that he wanted her. Well, men did. All the angry talk had roused him. One strong feeling led to another, and since he could not have her, he would go and find Lucette or a prostitute and cleanse himself.

Andrée had reached the baby's room ahead of her and had him out of bed and was changing him, mumbling little endearments. In the night when he woke, it was lovely to know that Andrée would go to him, but in the daytime like this, Jean was a little jealous of the girl. Though she was only sixteen, she looked like a peasant mother, with her big breasts and fat behind, and she would cuddle Guillaume into her breasts and make soothing sounds, and Jean had to watch, frightened that her son would prefer this comfortable girl to his mother. Jean went and put her hand on his soft thick hair; he wiggled energetically as Andrée put clothes on him. As soon as he was dressed, Jean picked him up and held him against her to know he was hers, but he was impatient, and so she put him down on the floor and rolled his rubber ball toward him, and he took it in both hands and threw it, and she went for it and rolled it back, and then he rolled it again. Jean remembered playing the same simple game with Eg when he was a baby, though Eg soon learned to throw the ball farther away, where she had to chase it. So far, Guillaume was less aggressive, willing to throw the ball where she could reach it, although sometimes his arm would swing wildly, as if he thought he might send the rubber ball through walls and over rooftops.

Jean sent Andrée away and settled down to play with her son. He was such a pretty boy, with bright eyes and a lovely smile, the new teeth white, almost translucent.

"Such a pretty boy, such a pretty boy," she said to him in

English. Mostly she spoke French to him, but English was their game. He knew it was something different and special. So she babbled to him, singing little songs.

Before Guillaume left in the morning, he said she should go to one of the best couturiers and get a dress for a reception that they must attend next week. Two marshals of France and the president would be there. She was to charge the dress to his account, and to get something with a low neck because there was a fine necklace that had belonged to his grandmother that she would wear. It would look splendid against her beautiful skin.

She played with Guillaume, then decided that she must go and buy the dress. She went to find Andrée and have her take Guillaume to the Parc de Monceau in the big English pram. The kitchen was empty. It was the hour that Madame Roussel did her marketing. Jean went down the hall to the two small maids' rooms at the end behind the kitchen. The door to Andrée's room was partly open, and as she approached Jean heard the sounds that came from inside. She felt a cold excitement as she listened, and then — the door was unlatched and open a few inches — she reached out very delicately and gave it a little push. Andrée was bent over the small table, her skirt pulled up, her fat little legs spread, her toes barely touching the floor, and Philippe stood behind her, his trousers round his ankles, holding her hips with his two hands. The girl gave a great wheezing breath with each thrust. Jean felt herself responding, her legs pressing together, a nervous spasm making her bite back her own breath, then she turned away and went down the hall, walking with careful deliberation, and she picked up Guillaume, put warm clothes on both of them and went down the stairs to the little yard where the pram was kept, nodding to the concièrge as she went by her lodge.

As she pushed the pram along the cold grey street, she

wondered if Philippe had expected her to find the two of them. She thought probably he had.

Jean was in bed asleep when she heard Guillaume's voice talking to Madame Roussel. All month there had been fighting and riots, and he and Philippe were excited and enraged and at the edge of their nerves. Philippe talked to his friends at the newspapers, and they were all preparing for some great and terrible event, the end of the republic. Jean tried to understand and then gave up. There were too many names and too many rumours attached to each one. The fate of someone called Chiappe. Whether a man named Stavisky had committed suicide or been murdered. Everyone was attached to everyone else by a rumour or another rumour. The Radicals were to be driven out, and from chaos greatness would be restored.

The voices were quiet, and a door closed down the hall, Madame Roussel going to her room. Footsteps, the door opening. Guillaume was in the bedroom, taking off his clothes and putting on his sleeping suit.

"Guillaume," she said. "Are you all right?"

"I'm coming to bed," he said, and his voice was strange.

She could hear him hanging up his clothes, as he always did, and then he pulled back the covers and slid into bed beside her. She waited for him to come to her, but he lay still, and she could hear his breathing.

"Guillaume."

"There were dead men in the streets, Jeanne. It was like a war. Shooting and fires. They charged the bridge, again and again. Then the war veterans came and they joined. I thought it would be the end of everything."

Jean reached out and took him in her arms, and his body was rigid and trembling.

"Frenchmen killing each other," he said. "We've come to that. Philippe threw himself into the middle of it, and I was afraid I'd lost him. That he'd be killed. I ran into the crowd looking for him, and then the horses charged."

"Did you find him?"

"Later. I found him later. His leg was hurt in one of the charges, but he could walk. He wanted to go back again. He was sure that they could get across the bridge in one more charge. To the Chamber of Deputies."

Jean held herself against him to warm his trembling body, stroked him softly, but he didn't turn to her.

"What will happen now?" she said.

"I don't know. I was not meant for all that. Even Philippe frightened me, my own son. I thought about what would happen if they got across the bridge. But they were so brave when the horses charged. As I came back here, I was thinking about Robert. The war. I wanted to go to Les Sourcelles and talk to him."

Jean put her hands on his skin, stroked it gently, took his penis in her hand to try to rouse and distract him, but it lay soft and immoveable. His skin was cold, as if the death he had seen was inside him, breathing an unnatural coldness.

"We'll go to Les Sourcelles," she said.

"No," he said. "I can't run away. I didn't run away when the horses charged, I had to stand there. France was in agony, and I had to bear witness. I can't run away now."

"You said you wanted to talk to Robert."

"Yes, I will. I will."

Jean didn't know what to say or do to comfort him. He was someplace she couldn't reach. She was troubled and aroused. And so cold. She wanted to be warmed. She wanted a man on top of her, inside her, to shut out the world. She didn't know who that man was, except that she had never met him and never would. She thought of Philippe and Andrée. She said words to herself, the blunt brutal English words, repeated harshly inside her head, and she tried to put herself to sleep.

The big kitchen was warm, even though a cold rain beat against the window. The large coal stove, the fire fed and stirred to provide the heat for cooking, warmed the room as well. There was a faint smell of coal gas from the stove. Jean could feel sweat on her face as she worked. Young Guillaume was asleep upstairs, and his father had driven Robert to a *vignoble* where they would buy the new wines. Guillaume had brought from Paris a new wheelchair that could be folded and put in the car, and this was its first use. Robert was eager to try it, in spite of the rain.

Jean and Robert were not enemies now, though they were not yet friends. Robert adored young Guillaume, who adored him. The boy took it for granted that his uncle was crippled and scarred, and he would stand beside him and reach out to take Robert's hand. The first time he did it, his uncle took his hand but turned his head away, as if embarrassed, but now he was used to it and would reach out to the little boy. Because she was Guillaume's mother, Jean was almost forgiven for being an outsider. Also she had told him that her father had been killed in the war, though she hadn't told him how, and he accepted that as a connection between them.

When they arrived at Les Sourcelles this time, Jean had told Madame Roussel that she wanted to learn to cook, and now they were at work on a *terrine de caneton*. Jean was cutting the meat of the duck's legs into very fine pieces, which would be mixed with pork and veal and pounded and strained. On the other side of the table Madame Roussel was cutting up the giblets to put in the pot on the stove where she was stewing a knuckle and a calf's foot to make a jelly. At first she had been awkward and flustered with Jean in her kitchen and called her *Madame la comtesse* every time she had to tell her something, but gradually she had relaxed, though she still spoke in an impersonal way, as if Jean might be a group of touring journalists.

Her husband, too, had been killed in the war. He had been in the same company with Robert, though Robert had been an officer. Jean had told Madame Roussel about her father, but she had told her the whole story, about the accident.

"All the same, it was a death, and in the war," Madame Roussel said.

She was an oddly made woman, the top and bottom halves ill matched. Her upper body was thin, with long muscular arms and a flat chest, but she had short legs and heavy hips. Dressed in certain ways, she looked like a mistake, as if the top and bottom pieces of two different woman had somehow got attached. She wouldn't let Berthe in the kitchen when Jean was there, though it wasn't clear why, whether simply to avoid crowding or to prevent the girl seeing Jean doing such things. She was a quiet-spoken woman, but her word was law. It was comfortable to be with her because she was so certain about everything.

The flesh of the duck gave off a slight sharp smell as Jean

cut it and put it in the wooden mortar. She would begin the crushing, but she knew that Madame Roussel would take over. Jean's arms and hands weren't as strong, though sometimes she shocked Madame Roussel by lifting the heavy crock of brine.

Berthe had instructions to go to young Guillaume if he woke. Jean had been looking for an excuse to get rid of Andrée, and the summer in Les Sourcelles was the perfect one. She wasn't needed. They were all here to help with Robert, and Berthe had time free for the baby. Jean didn't like to leave him with servants, though Guillaume thought it strange that she wished to spend so much time with the boy, but she told him it was natural to her, the way she'd been brought up. She told him about all of them in that house by the water, Elmer Tisdale living in his boathouse and the men smuggling whisky (she didn't tell him about Bruce), and he found it extravagantly strange. He said he couldn't make out whether they were peasants or respectable people, and she said both probably. Jean knew that she was a puzzle to him, and sometimes she wondered why she had got married, whether it made any sense for either of them. For the ball where they met the president, she bought a dark blue gown with a silver panel let into the front, her arms and shoulders bare, and she wore very high heels to make her taller, and the necklace of gold that had belonged to his mother and grandmother, and she knew that he was very proud of how she looked, and one of the marshals of France asked her about being in the movies. That evening she was playing a part, *la belle comtesse de Seviède*, and she decided that when she had nothing to say, she would say nothing, and that worked very well. All night she could feel people looking at her. She knew that Guillaume was observing and being pleased, and when he came toward her out of the crowd, his eyes were brimming as if he might be in tears, she

knew that it was happiness and love, and at that instant, when
she should have been happiest, she remembered Delbert, who
was just a smart cameraman with a good line. Something was
happening in her chest, she knew what they meant about your
heart breaking, and she thought of Delbert hinting they might
get back together and of how she ran away because she didn't
want to, and she knew she couldn't under-stand anything, ever.
What she did was smile at Guillaume and whisper in his ear
that he was very handsome, and he was, his bright face and
fine moustache. When they left, a marshal of France bowed to
her, and she nodded graciously to him.

The wind had risen, and the rain beat even harder against
the glass. Guillaume and Robert would get soaked, but they
would enjoy it, and when they got back they would change
into dry clothes and sit by a warm fire. Jean scraped the last bits
of flesh off the bone with her sharp knife. She was worried,
when she let herself be, about the way things were. She knew
that Guillaume was spending too much on politics, and she
had the feeling that everything was going wrong. Everyone
talked all the time about politics and armies. Guillaume was
using things to prevent another pregnancy, and she knew it was
out of concern for his responsibilities. Once he asked her if a
trip back to Canada was important for her, and she didn't know
why he'd asked or what the answer was. She and her mother
wrote letters sometimes, and that was all.

In a blue hat and fine blue gloves, pale powder and dark red
lipstick, she was walking along unknown streets. A motorcycle
was parked at the edge of the road in front of a small café.

Beside the café the wall was covered with posters for medicines and cleaning fluids and aperitifs. The smooth muscular figure of a naked man raced into a bright distance exhorting her to drink a malt compound and be equally lively. Two boys in flat caps came out of the café with a bottle of wine, gave her a long look and went the other way.

She had no idea where she was. It was a way of being perfectly alone, to walk like this through the unknown streets of Paris. She supposed that she might have been frightened, but she was not. Each time, she found new places. She turned a corner and she was in a small cobbled square. Outside a window near her hung a bird cage, and she could hear the bird's long liquid song. At the corner of the square was a *pissotière*, and she could see the legs of a man at one of the urinals. Nearby stood a wagon, the horse waiting patiently for his driver to finish easing himself and once more take the reins. A woman with a baguette wrapped in paper ran from a bakery to her own doorway. Somewhere behind the tall houses, she could hear the sound of a train. She walked alone through the strange city while they all waited for a war to begin.

A car drove past her, and the wind from its passage brushed her skirt and legs. She crossed the square and walked into a long bare street. At the far end was a railway bridge, and as she went toward it, she could see that a small crowd was gathering, and she walked a little more quickly to find out what was going on. It seemed to take a very long time to walk the length of the street, and when she finally reached the crowd, she saw that they had gathered around an acrobat, who had spread his carpet at the edge of the road under the bridge and was performing for the group, mostly men and boys, that had come to watch him.

Two workmen in leather aprons moved aside to let her get

close enough to see. Standing close to them, she could smell the sweat of work on their clothes. The entertainer was a small man with short heavy legs. When he smiled at the crowd, you could see he had a tooth missing at one side of his mouth. His hair was thick and grew low in tight curls. He had clubs to juggle, and a number of chairs, and he began to pile these one on top of another, climbing upward as he did it, quick and adept, every movement beautifully neat until the chairs were piled six high and he was above the crowd. Then he balanced one final chair beside the one on top, and holding the back of one chair in each hand, he began to lift himself until he was in a handstand on the top of the chairs, his strong veined hands gripping the wood, his body almost motionless, back arched, perfectly balanced. Jean felt in her body the longing to do such a perfect thing. He began to come back down, and the crowd applauded, and she, too, a ladylike clapping of her blue-gloved hands before she turned away.

A fat handsome poet filled with rage, replete with it, like a stuffed goose. Ash from his cigarette fell on his necktie and vest. He brushed at it but left most of the ash behind. He was sitting across the table from Jean, with Jules Michaux and his wife Pascale between them.

"Better Hitler than Blum," he said. He took out another cigarette and put it between his lips, which curved up in a sort of smile as they took hold of it.

"Everyone is saying that," Jean said.

"I was the first. The others only imitate me."

"How do you know you were the first?"

"What does it matter? I was, so I was. We have given ourselves into the hands of communists, and France is no longer France. Half the country is on strike and the other half is trying to get money out of the country while they still can." His lighter flamed against the tip of the cigarette and he sucked smoke into his mouth.

"Will your rich friends not support you any more?" Jules said and emptied his glass of wine.

"My adorable rich friends will always look after me. But it's true that if Blum turns the country into another Russia, it will be a bad time for art."

"Eisenstein. Pudovkin."

"I was talking about art, not moving pictures." He turned to Jean. "You know that moving pictures have nothing to do with art."

"I thought we were talking about something important, like money," Jean said.

The man's eyes shone more brightly. He breathed smoke. Jean knew that the more offensive she was, the more excited he would be. It was a temptation.

"There must be an end to these strikes," Pascale said.

"They will give the workers what they want," Jules said. "It is hopeless."

"Everything of value comes from the top," the poet said. "Some are meant to give orders, some to take them. We are born to be what we are. I was born with words in my mouth."

Jean pictured a baby with letters falling out of its mouth, and it made her laugh.

"You laugh at me at your peril," the poet said. He was terribly worked up. If she got up to leave, he would follow her and try to drag her to where he lived and have her. She was a little excited by his intensity, although she hated him as well.

"I wish we had enough money to worry about where to hide it," Pascale said. She kept lighting cigarettes and letting them go out. She wore a wide black hat with a blue feather and a matching blue scarf at her neck. It didn't suit her. Her face was very thin and pale these days, as if she might not be getting enough to eat. Yet Jean had heard that her family was rich. Jules had asked Jean, when they first sat down, if Guillaume might invest in a film. She thought not. He was already worried about money, she knew, though he wouldn't send his money out of France. He was a patriot, and he thought it was wrong, but all their friends who came to dinner were talking about it. His cousin Gabrielle could talk about nothing else. She was offended that no country seemed entirely safe.

Jean had been hoping that Jules might offer her a part in a film. Time lay heavy on her hands these days. She spent hours with young Guillaume, and she loved to watch him grow and change, and she discussed household matters with Madame Roussel, and she read books, but it was not enough. The world was spinning off into a new madness, and she was silent. It was no wonder women took lovers. If she took this fat handsome poet, she would not be bored, for a while at least, though she would soon tire of him. To make a film would be better. The film Jules wanted to make was a murder story that took place among the canals, but to start, he would need enough money to alter the buildings so they looked right on film. What was real never looked real enough to the camera.

"I'd like to make a film about the strikes," Jules said. "To talk to the strikers about what they want."

"They have nothing to tell," the poet said. "They are the dupes of the communist agitators. France is no longer France. The country is in the filthy hands of the Jews."

All this talk about Jews. Until recently Jean never thought much about them. She'd never seen a Jew until she got to New York, and mostly they were in the stores, with their nice funny talk. Some of them worked in the movies, like Mr. Lasky and Mr. Zukor. At first she didn't know that Dmitrievna was a Jew. But now they were all brightly visible, as if by some change in the light. Hitler was sending more Jews into France, and Philippe was enraged. She wasn't sure what Guillaume thought. He said that some Jews were French and some weren't, and that was what mattered.

"But it can only go so far," the poet said, his bright eyes staring at Jean. "And then it will end."

Jean was looking down the boulevard from the café. The chestnuts were in blossom, and she watched the figures of the men and women walking beneath the branches alight with white blossoms and pale leaves.

"How will it end?" Jules said.

"France will rise against it."

"France is rising now," Jules said, "and it's not against the Jews and communists."

"I see the future," the poet said dramatically. "And don't you smile," he said to Jean.

"Was I smiling?"

"Smiling like a cat. You don't believe I can see the future."

"We all see the future," Jean said. "But it doesn't always oblige us by happening the way we see it."

"Show me your hand."

Jean looked at him, noticed the way a red vein ran jaggedly across the white of his eye toward the dark glittering pupil. She held out her hand. He took it with surprising gentleness, manoeuvred it a little, stared at the palm.

"The other one."

She held it out. Now he was holding the two of them. It was pleasant to feel the touch of his skin on hers.

"Yes," he said. "I might have guessed."

"What?" Jean said.

"I won't tell. If you read a palm without being paid, it is very unlucky."

"You are a very bad man," Pascale said.

"Of course," he said, laughing. "Of course I am."

Jean knew it was a game, and yet she couldn't help wondering what he had seen. Nothing. He only wanted to touch her hands, to make her interested, so she would go somewhere with him, and he would say that the hands showed she would be his lover. Still she regretted having given him her hands. What she knew about the future was that it was bad luck to imagine it.

She was in a nightclub during the war, and it would be the death of her, later, in front of a firing squad. The lights from the sides of the stage caught her body as she danced, and she was all flashes of dark and light, brightness and darkness shaping her, the costume revealing and concealing the way her breasts moved with the lifting of her arms, and her steps were carried by the waves of rhythm from the flute and little bells.

Marcel, the director, shouted, and the music stopped. Jean stood still on the stage and waited for him. She hoped that the dance didn't look ridiculous. They had brought in a choreographer from the opera to train her, and the two of them had worked very hard together. The choreographer said he had talked to people who had seen Mata Hari dance, and they reported that she was not a good dancer, coarse and simple, and that men came to see her because she was mostly naked, but Jean and the director had agreed that for the movie the dance must be interesting and artistic. He had hired a composer to write music.

Her dance was the prologue to the movie. It would be intercut with scenes from the nightclub, French officers talking and smoking while they watched her dance. The story was about a young French officer. He was betrayed by her. He couldn't resist her, even though he was engaged to a respectable girl.

They had already shot the scene in which Mata Hari was executed by the firing squad, and sometimes when they were shooting the other scenes Jean had the feeling that she was portraying a ghost, and she was, of course, for the woman herself was once real and now was dead. In the execution scene, the young French officer gives her a flower, and she holds it in her hand, and then she is tied to the stake, and they are about to cover her eyes, but she says no, no blindfold, but she will close her eyes so as not to disturb the riflemen, and there is a close-up of her with her eyes closed, and then there would be a cut to the next scene with the sound of the rifles firing. Marcel was very pleased with that.

"It will be very strong, Mademoiselle Cora, very artistic."

He had been talking to the cameraman and head electrician, and they were moving one of the lights, and now he came up to where Jean was standing.

"It is very beautiful, Mademoiselle Cora. Could we do it again?"

"And the close-ups?"

"Later."

Jean had tried to get him to shoot the dance with more than one camera, but he was obdurate, and she gave up the argument. He was an actor who was directing his first movie, and he had to be right about everything. She knew it was going to be hard for her to perform close-ups that would match and be convincing, but it was her first movie in a long time, and she'd decided not to be a bitch. She was surprised how easily Guillaume had agreed to let her do it, but he was distracted by all the politics, Hitler and Czechoslovakia and the posters threatening war.

The day the phone call had come to ask her if she would be interested in meeting this director, she had looked at herself in the mirror for a long time, finding the first traces of wrinkles at the side of the eyes, wondering if the eyelashes were a little thinner now. She stood naked in front of the mirror on an armoire and examined her breasts and belly. It was the body of a woman who had borne and nursed a child, and she examined it critically to be sure that she knew all its failings, and then she had dressed and gone to the first meeting. The director said she had an adorable accent which was ideal since Mata Hari was Dutch and never spoke perfect French.

They had met twice, and made an agreement. Jean had said they must hire Dmitrievna to design her costumes. They had trouble getting her since she was decorating a castle near Biarritz for a rich Englishman, but she finally agreed when Jean said she needed her help. If she was going to be a dancing girl, she wanted to be dressed by someone she could trust, and Dmitrievna had found some old pictures of Mata Hari and examined her costumes, then found photographs of temple dancers from the east. All the costumes she made were of fabrics that would photograph as a very deep black, but with silver jewellery or decorations. The costume for the dance was very sensual, flowing with her movements but not especially revealing.

"This is not the Folies Bergères," Dmitrievna said. "Mata Hari must be the perfect object of desire, not some trollop in spangles."

Marcel looked a little bemused when she made the announcement, but he looked at her sketches and agreed.

Jean tried to gather her concentration. There was a little tinkling of the bells and the flute blew a preparatory note. Though the chairs in the nightclub were empty, the actors waiting to be called for the reaction shots that would be done later, she tried to imagine eyes on her, herself the perfect object of desire. The assistant director called for quiet, the camera rolled, and the flute began its solemn winding tune.

She sat on the rocks at the edge of the spring and listened to the brisk cheerful sound of the water that bubbled out of the earth, water sacred to a lost god. Her son sat beside her. He was a strong active boy, but thoughtful, and whenever they walked here together, he would look into the water, finding it as hypnotic, it seemed, as she did. When they first arrived today, she told him about going to a spring when she was a little girl, and he asked questions about Canada, and they planned to go there someday.

Every day there were new rumours of war. Philippe had come to Les Sourcelles. He was being called up to serve in the army next month. Jean had come out partly to avoid him. She disliked everything about him but especially the way he was rough with her son. It was supposed to be a game, but it wasn't, and young Guillaume knew it. He would get a certain stubborn look on his face that said he knew Philippe wanted to make him cry and then mock him, and he would not cry. She could see that he was angry under his determination but frightened, too, by the rough games. Once when Philippe was being very cruel, Robert spoke in his rusty voice and told young Guillaume to come to him, and she could see that Philippe was about to say something mocking but did not. He was frightened of Robert, as they all were except the two Guillaumes, who simply loved him.

Jean tried to imagine Robert before he was maimed. He might have been beautiful and charming and full of gaiety. Or was he angry like Philippe even before the war ruined him? She might ask Guillaume. He would be pleased to tell her, and it would be good to have something to talk about. A silence had fallen on them. She couldn't explain it, and she thought perhaps it happened in all marriages. After a while you ran out of things to say. She tried to be interested in politics for his sake, but it made no sense. Guillaume was distant, and she thought he was far away even from himself. He studied the newspapers, and sometime he would take an atlas down from the bookshelf and look at one of the maps, his fingers moving from place to place, and she knew that he was planning battles. He would put the atlas back on the shelf and look toward her, ask some inconsequential question about their son, something to which he already knew the answer.

"Are you worried?" she would say.

"No, just a little concerned, as we all are."

When they were at Les Sourcelles, he was happier, and more likely to turn to her in bed, as he had last night, but it made her uncomfortable when she knew Philippe was nearby, as if he might be listening to them, and she was glad when it was over, though that made her sad.

She looked down into the bubbling water and thought how long it had come out of the earth here and how many generations had stopped to quench their thirst, back into the old dark history of which she knew so little.

"I want to drink, Maman," Guillaume said.

"If you wish."

He climbed carefully over the rocks and put his fingers in the water, then put them into his mouth.

"Does it make your fingers cold?"

"Yes, Maman, very cold."

Again he put them in the water and to his mouth, then he looked at her and smiled. He grew and became a person with his own stories. As they sat here on the rocks, or as he licked the cold water from his fingers, he was thinking, remembering. He looked at her and had thoughts.

Five

JEAN NODDED TO THE CONCIÈRGE and walked into the small courtyard. On her left was a door, and she opened it and started up the dark staircase. She had been to Dmitrievna's apartment only once before, and she remembered the dusty smell of the staircase. Today, walking in from the fresh spring air, the smell of old dust was even stronger, and she noticed a slight smell of oil, as if someone had spilled kerosene on the stairs years before, and it had soaked into the wood.

She had got a note from Dmitrievna asking her to come to her apartment this afternoon and had set out to walk there from the Boulevard Haussmann. It was a bright spring day, a blue sky with long pale clouds that she stood and watched for a moment as she crossed the Pont du Carrousel over the Seine, looking along the river toward the towers of Notre Dame.

She knocked at the door at the top of the stairs, and after a moment Dmitrievna opened it. She was dressed in an English-looking outfit, a double-breasted tweed suit with a long skirt, and on her head was a strange little hat that was also made of tweed and looked like a man's hat with a few extra feathers. Dmitrievna had spots of rouge on her cheeks, and the effect of the whole getup was theatrical and unconvincing. The apartment was in disorder. Beside the door were several suitcases.

"You're leaving," Jean said.

"Yes," Dmitrievna said. "It's not *un drôle de guerre* any more."

Two weeks before, the German army had moved into Belgium.

"What about the French army?"

"I have met the French army," Dmitrievna said. "They are splendid on horseback. That will not be good enough."

"Where are you going?"

"South, Spain perhaps, and I will try to get back to America."

"What about your friend?"

"She has matters of business to complete. We will meet in the south."

Jean looked at the woman, the tall figure in her odd plumage, the black hair and eyebrows, the eyes brightly fixed on hers. She felt frightened and wanted to beg Dmitrievna to take her along. She wanted to go back to being a girl in the movies, not to have a husband and son.

"You will be safe, little one," Dmitrievna said. "Yesterday I went to a fortune teller. The very best, and very expensive, and he laid out the cards for me, and what he saw was not what one wished to hear. But I will go now and do my best to defeat the cards. Perhaps it can be done. While I was with this man, I had him lay out the cards for you. It gave me some comfort."

The tall woman came to her and they held each other. Then Dmitrievna bent and kissed her on the lips. Jean could feel her teeth and could smell the rouge on her face, then the woman drew away. She went across the room and picked up a large package in brown paper, taped and bound with heavy string.

"You will keep this for me."

"What is it?"

"The paintings. My lawyer says that he will look after the

apartment, but I don't trust him with the pictures. Perhaps I don't trust him at all, but I have no choice. I will give you a key, and perhaps you can come here and think about me a little. If you care to do that."

Jean took the parcel from her. It was heavy and awkward.

"You will need a taxi," Dmitrievna said. "Do you have money for a taxi?"

"Yes."

Jean put the parcel down at her feet and looked around at the empty spaces on the walls where the paintings had been, at the open drawers, clothes and papers on the chairs. It was very frightening.

"If I do not come back," Dmitrievna said, "the paintings will be yours. They are works of genius, of course."

"No," Jean said. "You will come back."

"I will give you a piece of paper."

She looked around the room, found a pen and a sheet of paper.

"To say that the paintings will be yours."

"No," Jean said. She went and took the piece of paper and crumpled it, threw it on the floor. Dmitrievna looked at her, almost as if she might be angry. They were standing close together, and Jean could see that the woman's large bony hands were shaking.

"No pieces of paper," Jean said. "You will leave the paintings with me, and you will come back when you want them."

The silence went on and on, no traffic in the streets, no voices or footsteps, only the waiting. The radio produced nothing but static, and it seemed that the electric crackling was the sound in her head, the sound in the heads of all those who waited. Once, for a moment, a voice, speaking German, then it was gone into the blur of meaningless sound. Inside the closed shutters, the apartment was dim and lifeless. Young Guillaume was in his room playing with toy soldiers, a battle in which the French army always won against its enemies, but in the other game, played out across fields that were green with springtime, the French army was in retreat, and Paris waited in silence for the Germans to come.

Jean put her hands over her face and tried to think. She was here in Paris. She was married to Guillaume and had a son. There was a war in which men killed other men and sometimes killed the women and children as well. The Germans were at war and the French and the British, but the Americans were not. If you were American you were safe, or thought you were. The British had betrayed the French, or so it was said, and now the Germans were winning the war. Today they were coming to Paris, which was an open city.

You tried to go through it step by step saying yes, this is a fact, but then it made no sense again, and you were only confused and frightened and waiting and waiting for something to happen in the silent streets.

Until yesterday the streets were full of people in flight, cars and trucks and wagons, men and women on foot with parcels and bags, hoping to find a train. Families crying and bickering by the side of the road. Bicycles with people's possessions tied to the back and front, shouting everywhere, and the horns of cars as everyone ran to escape the advancing army. They had planned to go to Les Sourcelles, and they were putting things in the car, documents and the valuable jewellery, when Guillaume heard that the Germans were already there. Young

Guillaume looked at his father when he heard the words, his face puzzled and hurt, and asked if it was really true that the Germans were at Les Sourcelles and what would happen to his uncle Robert.

"It's hard to know, my son, what is true and what isn't. There are so many rumours. But they won't hurt your uncle Robert. Berthe and Antoine will look after him. He will be all right."

He had looked at Jean as if she might help him to believe his own words. She knew that he was frightened of what might have happened to Philippe. He was serving with an artillery regiment somewhere. There was no news of him.

They had continued to put things in the car, though neither of them knew where they might be planning to go. Those who crowded the roads were moving south, anywhere away from the fighting and the German armies. It was the headlong retreat of a whole city. All anyone wanted to do was run, and the panic was contagious. Jean could feel it in herself, an emptiness that invaded you and you wanted to run until you found another place where these things were not happening. They put a few more bags in the car and spoke, in a hopeless, pointless way, about where they might go. Jean thought of Jules Michaux's house in the south, but she had no right to think he would take them in.

It was then that Guillaume discovered that someone had stolen the battery from the car. He stood there in the small garage with a puzzled look, as if he'd been the victim of some clever magician's naughty trick. He stumbled over his words as he tried to say where they might get another battery.

"We can stay in Paris," Jean said. The words frightened her as she said them, and yet they felt right. If they were here and together, they could protect their son. She'd seen the frenzy of the men and women who were trying to flee, and she knew that some of them would kill to make their way and others would lie down and die. It was like a crowd fleeing a fire. Many would be trampled. Perhaps it was what the Germans wanted, to get them out on the open roads and kill them. There were stories about the German Air Force in Poland.

"Yes," Guillaume said, "we can stay."

As they unpacked the car, they could smell smoke from the big bonfires at the government buildings where they were burning papers. The last of the administration was about to go. They brought everything back to the apartment and closed the shutters, and Madame Roussel cooked dinner, and young Guillaume made up stories about how the French army would drive the Germans back, and he would hear the horses of the cavalry coming toward them along the Boulevard Haussmann. In the evening, the doorbell rang, and they all started and stared, but it was Guillaume's cousin Gabrielle, who hadn't been able to find a way out of the city. She babbled half hysterically, then dozed off in a chair. Guillaume took her to one of the maids' rooms, and they all went to bed. It was hard to sleep, and in the morning, the silence had begun. Jean wondered if she had been foolish to suggest that they stay. Every minute she expected to hear German soldiers battering down the door and coming up the stairs for them. She knew nothing about war, except that it set men free to do what they wished. Her father had never come back to tell her about war.

Gabrielle came into the room, looked at Jean as if this might all be her fault, heaved a vast sigh and walked away. Guillaume was in his study, writing. Jean wondered what he was writing, but it was a question she never felt she had permission to ask. When he sat there, he was alone with history. He could explain on paper how the politicians had led them into this war, how France had been betrayed by greedy men with no ideals.

The silence went on, more than an absence of noise, something like the pressure in your ears as you swam deep under water. The Germans were there, somewhere to the north, coming closer. She went to the window and looked down through the cracks in the shutter and could see a part of the pavement. Sunlight filled the street. She could go out and walk through the deserted city, nothing to accompany her but her own fears and desires. She put her ear against the shutters and listened. Nothing. Carefully she reached up and opened the shutters a few inches, looked out.

It was like the street in a dream, the trees in full leaf, bright green in the sunlight, a hint of wind, but not a human sound, nothing moving. Then a dog appeared, an awkwardly shaped dog, legs too long for the body, patchy brown and white fur. The dog was trotting along in a businesslike fashion, its head up, as if it was following the scent of someone who, deliberately or by accident, had left it behind. When it was past, she listened carefully, closed the shutters and waited.

She followed the man into his office and sat where he indicated. He went to his desk and shifted some papers to one side. At first he seemed to be trying to avoid looking at her, but then he looked up.

"What can I do for you, countess?" he said.

The American voice was a shock. She expected it, and still it was a shock. She took the magazine clippings from her purse and went and put them on the desk in front of him. He read them through, looked at her, looked back at one of the pictures.

"This is you," he said.

"Yes. It's me all right."

"I think I maybe saw one of your movies, a few years back."

"Quite a few people did."

"So you're Cora Heart."

She nodded. He looked at the paper on his desk.

"It says here the Countess de Seviède. That's the name you gave."

"I'm married to the count, yes."

"But you're an American."

"That's the problem."

"No problem being an American, you know that. Greatest country in the world."

He was smiling, but she didn't think it was because he'd made a joke.

"I'm not American. I'm Canadian."

"But you were in American movies."

"Yes."

"Mary Pickford, now, she's Canadian, too, I heard that."

"You see my problem."

"Your country's at war with the Germans. You're an enemy alien in France."

"They're interning British subjects."

He was studying her. He had a domed forehead and sunken eyes, a long jaw. It was hard to read his eyes.

"Why did you come to see me?"

"Can I become an American? Or get a paper to say I am?"

"Are you Jewish?"

"No."

"Well, that's one good thing. They do have a bee in their bonnet about Jews."

"Can you help me?"

"Do you want to get out of France?"

"I have a husband here, and a son."

He looked down at the desk. Looked up, then down again, then looked toward her, and for the first time he was a man looking at a woman.

"I don't see quite what I could do. If you were trying to get into the States, I might be able to get you some kind of a document that would get you in, since you've worked there before, a movie star and all that. But I suppose if you wanted to leave, you could just go back to Canada, easy enough. I might be able to give you a little advice about getting across the border into Spain. We know a few things. But I don't see that I can just make you an American."

"No, I suppose not."

"And there's always the chance that we could end up in this war. I wouldn't count on it, but you never know. That's not any kind of official position, you realize. But you can never be sure about anything. In a war. Though the war's over for France, I guess."

She couldn't think of anything to say.

"Your husband's a count?"

"That's right."

"Well, he must have some influence."

"Maybe."

He pushed the clippings back to her.

"Just use these," he said. "Tell everybody you're American. We'll never tell them any different."

She went and got the clippings and put them back in her purse. The man was standing, and he held out his hand to her.

"Are you going to go back into the movies?"

"I don't know," she said. "I don't think so. I made some movies in France. I might do that again. If they start to make movies again."

"Everything's starting again from what I can see. I think the French are just as happy they lost."

He was still holding her hand, but now he dropped it.

"Well, I've never met a movie star before," he said.

"And what do you think of them, now you've met one?"

"I think they're nice-looking girls," he said. The long jaw dropped in a wide silly smile. She turned to go.

"Good luck," he said.

Outside the building, a German soldier stood guard, and as she walked past, she avoided looking at him. She didn't want anyone to notice her lest they find out what she was doing there, that she was an enemy alien. There was a prison camp north of Paris where they were putting all the British. Guillaume knew someone whose English nanny had been taken away. He didn't want her to come to the American Embassy — he was sure she'd be safe because she was married to him — but she had to find out, and Guillaume was so lost and ill that she didn't feel she could trust him. She was terribly frightened that they would take her away from her son.

There were few cars in Paris any more, so the city was quiet and bare. People peddled bicycles across the grey city. The air was cold as she walked along the street, and she pulled her fur collar tighter around her neck. It was the coat she'd brought from New York with her, with the fox collar she was so proud of. It was old, but there was still the warmth of the fur against her cheeks. Winter was close now, and she was terribly frightened. Guillaume thought they would be better able to look after things if they went to Les Sourcelles, but it wasn't clear how they could get there. She walked past a building with more German soldiers in their ominous metal hats, and the black swastika hung over the cold street. It was all doubly foreign to her now. She went round a corner and saw a familiar figure coming toward her, a young woman in a black coat with a bright red hat.

"Jeanne!" she said. "Jeanne, have you heard?"

"What?"

"Philippe is coming back, and he's going to have a wonderful job."

Jean stood in line, her scarf and the fur collar of her coat pulled up around her face, her fingers curled up inside her gloves, her shoulders hunched against the cold, staring at the black fabric of the coat of the man in front of her, counting the threads in a small spot of wear on the shoulders. The store was supposed to have meat today, but so far none had arrived. She was standing in line at this store, and Madame Roussel had gone to another one. Jean had her ration book and young Guillaume's with her, Madame Roussel the other two. Each of them would bring back whatever was available, and then they would try to make it stretch out over the next week. There was still bread available and sometimes cheese. The coffee was adulterated and foul. Berthe's brother, Antoine, appeared from Les Sourcelles the week before with a bag of carrots and turnips, a chicken and a few eggs. A priest had told Robert about the shortages in Paris, and he had sent Antoine with the food. He had to carry it several miles on his bicycle to the nearest train station, leave his bicycle there and get a ticket to Paris with the money Robert had given him. He also brought a letter from Robert that said they should come to Les Sourcelles. When Antoine went back he took a letter from Guillaume to his brother, explaining that he wasn't well enough to travel but saying perhaps they would come in the spring. Jean tried to look forward to that, to think that her son would be better off, safer in the country, that the food would be better, and there would be fewer Germans.

The line moved forward a little. For a long time, the door of the butcher's had remained closed, and Jean began to wonder if there would be no meat, but if the line was moving, there must be something, though it might be gone before she reached the counter. Down the street, she could see a German soldier standing guard in front of a building with the swastika flying. She looked away. If she noticed them, they might notice her and demand her papers. She carried her clippings with her in her purse whenever she went out, and she went out as little as possible. Not that a German soldier was likely to be impressed by a few fragments from magazines, written in a language he didn't understand. She had hidden her Canadian passport. She wondered about destroying it but didn't. Anything might happen. Though now she could imagine nothing but this endless biting cold, the struggle to find decent food, Guillaume sitting in his chair, pale, coughing. Madame Roussel made soups for him out of bones and peelings, the last rice, a few dried herbs, and he would bring a cup to his mouth and sip it slowly and tell her that it made him feel better. Jean told herself that he was not old, not really, but the bones of his face showed through the flesh more each day. She could tell that young Guillaume was worried and frightened. Philippe, who was working for the commissariat on the Jews, came to visit and was smooth and loud and pleased with himself, shook his father's hand and said he knew a good restaurant to take him to when he felt better, and then went again.

Anything might happen. It wasn't just the Germans she had to fear. She could be denounced by anyone, a neighbour, someone she hardly knew who nursed a grudge. A bit of gossip might appear in the newspapers. There was a little note once about Jules Michaux, and the Germans came to question him. Jules could have given her away to help himself. He didn't. Or she didn't think he did. She saw him once in a café, and he waved to her to come and join him, and they spoke quietly so no one else could hear, and she heard about it all. The Germans promised that he could make films again. There were people he had to talk to.

In the morning she would wake and listen for some sound to tell her where she was, and then she would remember the war, but she'd get out of bed quickly, and she'd make a cup of hot milk for her son's breakfast and go to the room where he lay asleep and very carefully put her hand beside his face to wake him. She thought about the things he heard at school, about how France had been betrayed by the English and how the marshal had saved France by ending the war. He had a picture of Marshal Pétain on his wall. Guillaume said that a boy needed heroes and talked about the battle of Verdun and about the history of France.

Jean was pushing a loaded baby carriage along a country road in the snow, her son walking by her side. They were both shivering with the cold, but she thought that at the top of the next hill they would be able to see the village, and the road would be downhill after that. The baby carriage was piled full of bags and parcels. When she decided to leave Paris, she thought of it as the best way to carry things. She knew that the nearest train stopped miles from Les Sourcelles and that they would have to walk from there, and she couldn't imagine how the two of them would manage until she thought of the big English pram. It was in a shed behind the concièrge's lodge. The concièrge helped her find tools to take off the hood, then she packed their clothes and all Guillaume's notebooks and a few other things that seemed important. Hidden in the lining of a coat was her Canadian passport and the necklace that had belonged to Guillaume's mother. She thought that she had no real right to it, but she had taken it anyway, a souvenir of the ball when Guillaume had been proud of her.

Men and women she had met that night had come to the funeral. There had been many people there, but it was no help. The priest stood and knelt and spoke in rapid Latin that she didn't understand, the people knelt and stood and bells rang and they went to the altar rail. Guillaume's coffin lay among them. She watched Philippe moving forward, then a strange woman in a wide hat and the fat handsome poet she had met at a café. She tried to think why he was here. On the way out of the church, she had seen an old woman in a black hat and veil, kneeling and sobbing, her hands clasped in front of her. She asked Gabrielle who it was, and Gabrielle told her it was Madame de Coulanges, Guillaume's mistress. She wondered how often she had seen him since their marriage. She wanted to talk to the woman, but she had nothing to say. None of it had made any sense, and she had kept herself silent and held the hand of her son, who was brave all through it, though she knew he cried when he went to his room at night.

She had decided to go to Les Sourcelles because she was

frightened of Philippe. He came to the apartment the day after the funeral with a German, and Jean watched the German's stupid sly face, and the way he looked at her breasts, and she had never been more frightened in her life. She thought that Philippe was offering her to the German, the day after his father's funeral. By the end of the next day, she had packed everything and told Madame Roussel that she was leaving. Madame Roussel would stay in Paris and look after the apartment.

Jean was tired from pushing the carriage, and her feet were wet.

"Let's stop for a minute, Guillaume," she said. "I want to rest."

"I'm not tired, Maman."

"You must be very strong then, because I am."

"But you're pushing my baby carriage."

Jean stood for a minute, looking across the field covered with snow. There was a patch of woodland at the end of the field, and under the grey sky, the trees were sharp outlines of black. There were German soldiers at the station where they got off the train, and one of them had smiled at her when he saw her with the baby carriage piled with bags, Dmitrievna's parcel of paintings tied on top, and a very old coat of Guillaume's laid over it all. She gave the soldier a quick smile and then turned away. She had no travel documents, wasn't sure if they were needed. She knew that Philippe could tell her, but she was too afraid of him to ask. She wanted to be settled at Les Sourcelles before he learned she was gone. Once they were with Robert, they would be safe. He was a war hero, and they would leave him alone, and the village was small and unimportant. Or so she thought, and hoped her thought was true.

Once last summer, when the Germans first came, she and Guillaume were invited to dinner with some of them and some colleagues of Guillaume's from the bank. It was a good meal, and everyone was very gracious. She had asked Guillaume to introduce her as an American, and she felt almost safe. The Germans all called Guillaume *M. le comte* and asked about his book on the Dreyfusards, and Guillaume, his face flushed and feverish, talked about it too long, until she could tell that the Germans were getting bored. One of them, a handsome blond, kept staring at her. After that, the Germans had ignored them.

She took the handle of the carriage and began to push. The road was uneven, and the carriage bounced in holes and twisted away from her, and she would catch it before it tipped and turn it straight again. Her wet feet began to ache from the cold. It had been a long bad winter. She hoped that the house at Les Sourcelles would be warm. She thought of standing in the kitchen there with Madame Roussel, the two of them red-faced and sweating as they made a daube of beef and braised leeks. Ahead she heard a noise, and at the top of the hill a motorcycle appeared with a German soldier driving and someone in the sidecar. She pushed the carriage to the side of the road.

"Guillaume," she said. "Stay close."

"We're not afraid of the Germans," the boy said.

"I am."

The motorcycle came toward them, and she could make out that it was a young girl in the sidecar, bare-headed, her hair blowing loose, her coat gathered and her shoulders hunched for warmth. The face of the soldier was hard to make out under his helmet, and Jean kept her eyes a little averted. He appeared not to look at them as the motorcycle went past, but the girl gave a little wave of her hand, and then they were gone. The soldier's mind was no doubt concentrated on getting the girl to a convenient bed. Jean felt envious of the two of them, and lonely. She pushed herself to walk faster. It was growing late, and she wanted to get to the house before dark.

She stood in the warm summer night and listened to the aircraft passing overhead, moving toward the east, toward Germany, where they would drop their bombs on the German cities, then return to England. The return was less predictable, though sometimes later in the night the noise would come, and she might hear it as she lay in bed. That was mostly what they knew of the war, that and the shortages. Sometimes they listened to the BBC and tried to believe what they heard. In Paris, it grew worse all the time, the rationing and failure of supplies. Here in the country, there was enough, though the diet was repetitive and mostly plain. Jean and Berthe took turns cooking, and as the harvest of fruit came in, they preserved what they could of it. There was not enough sugar to make jams, though once Antoine found a farmer with some honey, and they made a strange confection of strawberries and honey that might last the winter. Antoine foraged in the countryside on his bicycle and occasionally took what he found to the railway station, where there was a man who sold food in Paris on the black market. The man bought produce from Antoine and others and then took it to Paris, where he had regular clients with the money to pay. Sometimes Antoine would trade the food for black market coal.

Berthe and Antoine had become Jean's regular companions.

The brother and sister looked alike, tall and thin, with big hands and long noses. They were very close, and Jean sometimes thought they communicated by some sort of silent language, from one brain to the other. What one knew, the other knew immediately. One of them would explain things to Jean when they felt it necessary, but there were long spells when nothing was said, and Jean was growing almost used to that. There were days when she feared she was losing the power of speech. Robert had accepted her now, but with his ruined voice, talking was an effort, and he contented himself with few words. He spent all his time with his brother's notebooks, trying to make them into a book that would explain everything. To break the silence, Jean and Guillaume would babble to each other. He would come home and tell Jean all the rumours he had heard in the schoolyard, what the Germans would do next, whether the planes they heard at night were British or American, and once about the bombing of Paris.

She listened to the planes in the blackness of the night, heard the rumbling in the air and felt it against her skin. Her whole body was electric with it, and with the pain of being untouched. Now and then, at certain terrible hours, she thought that she could die from it. Earlier this evening, she had gone looking for Berthe, who had taken Robert off to bed a while before, and she had come on them in Robert's room, the man's twisted body lying white and naked on the bed while with one hand Berthe gently touched his face, the other stroking his penis, which was large and erect. Berthe's eyes were closed, and Jean noticed that Robert's hand was somewhere under her skirt. Jean turned away and made her way down the stairs and out into the garden.

They pleased each other, and of course why not, it was fine and right, but it made Jean want to cry out for her own loneliness. Why was there no one to touch her? Even Guillaume had reached the age when he didn't want his mother to hug him. Jean felt that she understood all the stories about men and women turning to stone. First you were on fire, and then the fire burnt out and you were a cinder. Now she was on fire, every inch of skin burning.

A little light shone from the kitchen window, and she crossed the lawn to the small stone barn. She could hear a soft clucking from the henhouse behind. The barn was left open now. Antoine had spoken to Robert, who had given him permission, and Robert had explained to Jean that sometimes a British or American flier might spend a night there. They needed to do nothing but leave the door unlocked.

Jean didn't know if anyone had ever stayed there. It was understood that they didn't need to know. Once in the spring she thought the pile of straw in a corner looked as if someone might have slept on it, but she couldn't be sure. She opened the door of the barn and went inside.

"Hello," she said, in a soft voice. She spoke in English, and she almost believed that a man would answer, some young American pilot, and that she would go to him in the dark, never see his face or know his name, and they would comfort one another.

"Hello," she said again. "Hello, mister."

There was no answer, and she could tell from the feeling of the air that the barn was empty. She went back outside. It was a windless night, and the sound of the airplanes was softer now, and soon it would be so soft you couldn't tell whether you were hearing it or imagining it. Small things moved in the night. Soon she might go in and turn on the radio and see what she could find. Right now her ears felt so alert and attuned that she might pick the signals out of the air.

Jean cut the paper carefully with a sharp knife she had brought from the kitchen. Since she had arrived at Les Sourcelles, Dmitrievna's parcel of paintings had been under her bed, but the night before, as she lay awake, listening for the sound of aircraft, listening so hard she began to imagine things — the sound of a motor, German voices as they came to search the house — she decided that she would open the parcel and hide the pictures where they might not be found, in secret places in the attic and the barn.

When she had cut the outside wrappings all around, she lifted off the top layer. Inside were three canvases still on wooden stretchers, and between them others, loose sheets of canvas, separated by layers of soft cloth and more paper. Jean lifted the top canvas. She remembered seeing it on the wall of Dmitrievna's apartment soon after she had bought it.

"I have abandoned the American dollar," Dmitrievna had said. "I have considered it, and I have lost my childlike faith. We will have paintings instead."

Jean studied the canvas, and the speed and vivacity delighted her. At first she was slow to learn about Dmitrievna's things, but then her eye understood, and now, in hiding from war, her eye was hungry and quick. One by one she took out the pictures and spread them about the room, the ones on wooden stretchers leaning against chairs, the canvases lying on the bed. There were some paintings she had never seen, and a small group of drawings in a folder that were new to her as well. For a few minutes she admired them, then she tried to think where everything might be safely hidden.

She went out to the barn and dragged in a ladder. Berthe, who was in the kitchen, stared at her, and Jean explained that she must get to the attic. Without asking any questions, Berthe helped her carry the ladder up the stairs and set it where she could open the small trap door that led to the attic of the house. Jean could tell that she was curious.

"Better not to tell you," she said.

She went back down to the kitchen and got a candle. Once in the attic, she lit it. Whatever she had expected to find, she was surprised at the emptiness of the long low space. It had a stale, dusty smell, and there was a single wooden chest. Anyone searching the house would open it immediately. She would have to find other places, the barn, the chicken house.

She closed the trap door, fetched Berthe again, and the two of them returned the ladder to the barn. Just as they returned to the house, they saw the wheelchair coming in the front door, Antoine bringing Robert back from church. She was familiar with Robert now, and the scarring and the blank eye and folds of flesh were ordinary, and she could read the expression on his face and knew he was upset. Usually going to mass calmed and uplifted him. Antoine's face was harder to make out, unsurprised.

"What is it?" she said to Robert, and he looked at her with his one eye, the eye murderous. She looked at Antoine.

"Criminals," Robert said. "Degenerates."

"The Germans?"

"Yes."

"What have they done?"

"They took the church bell," Antoine said. "Germany is short of metals, and France must contribute its church bells to the war effort."

"Degenerates," Robert said again in that harsh struggling

voice. "The bell was cast in the sixteenth century." He turned to Jean. "You've heard it, that lovely bell ringing out over the fields."

"Yes."

"Never again. Four hundred years. It rang the angelus every day for four hundred years. And now silence."

Robert had friends, not close friends but rich and titled friends, who lived a few miles away. They invited him to come for dinner, and, having heard that Jean was at Les Sourcelles, they invited her too. It was understood that, in spite of the shortage of petrol, they would send a car for them. There was nothing for Jean to wear on such an occasion until Berthe found in a trunk an old dress that had belonged to Robert's mother, an elegant black dress, and when Jean tried it on, it was almost her size, except it was too long, and too big in the hips, and she and Berthe shortened it and did a little remodelling so that it looked more modern. Berthe was a good seamstress, and Jean had seen enough costumes fitted that she knew how to make the adjustments.

They managed the dress, and everyone, Guillaume and Berthe and even Robert said that it looked beautiful, and Berthe got Robert dressed in his best suit, and when the car came, it was driven by a German officer in uniform. Jean was sick with fear, but she behaved well, concealing everything, and she knew that the officer was admiring her and making excuses to stand close to her as, with Berthe's help, they got Robert and his chair into the car.

The German spoke French, though his speech was a little

hesitant. You could tell that he was thinking about his words before he said them. He knew that Jean had been in the movies, the rich and titled hosts had told him that, and she wondered if he knew that she wasn't French. Now the Americans were in the war, it was no help to be thought American.

At dinner, there was good food and wine. The nicest of the three German officers, the one that came to pick them up, sat beside her, and she could feel the warmth of his body as he leaned over to fill her glass again, even when she said no, and she wanted him to touch her, but she couldn't trust him or trust herself, and she was glad when one of the other officers began to boast in an unpleasant way and she could concentrate on that. After dinner their hosts suggested that she and Robert could stay the night, and she wasn't clear whether the German officers were staying here or not. She looked to Robert to decide. She had noticed his face as the German officer talked, and she believed that he was offended and angry, though he had remained calm. It was the Germans who had ruined him in that other war. Robert spoke politely in his damaged voice, thanked his hosts for the dinner and asked if they might be driven home. There was some dispute among the Germans about who would drive, and for some reason a different officer won out, and Jean was just as glad. He was a man more easily ignored, and even when he took her hand and kissed it before driving away, she was cool to him.

In the night she thought about the nicer officer, and her dreams were hot and disturbed.

The war was nearly over now. Everyone said that. The Americans were coming closer all the time, but the Germans were more dangerous now they were losing. They weren't polite any more. Jean stayed in the house as much as she could, and when she went out, she didn't go much farther than the garden. Antoine had dug up part of the lawn, and he'd planted every bit of seed that he could get, split every seed potato carefully to make sure that each section planted had only one eye. Jean helped by weeding and picking off bugs.

There were things going on that Jean wasn't told about. Berthe and Antoine communicated in their silent way, and Berthe explained to her that it was safer for Jean if she didn't know. And Jean had never told anyone where Dmitrievna's paintings were concealed. Sometimes Antoine looked at her as if he wanted to tell her what he knew, and one day, as she saw him look at her like that, she realized that he was younger than she'd always thought. There was something a little boyish in his unspoken but vivid excitement. She wondered if they confided in Robert. It would provide a pleasure for him, trapped in his chair. He was still working over Guillaume's notebooks, extracting and copying, preparing the book that must be published.

Jean stood up from the garden where she was pulling weeds and stretched. It was a fine cool day, and she was aware of a sense of physical well-being. She felt the way her skin touched her clothes, the strength of the body beneath. She stretched out her arms and turned until one hand caught a patch of shade from one of the old chestnuts, and she studied the way the light and shade dappled her skin. No one was watching her. She stretched her arms another way and turned to look up at the sky.

There was a distant sound, growing louder as it came across

the sky, and she saw two airplanes appear over a hilltop. They were different shapes and had different markings, one German, one British or American, and at first they were coming straight at her, and she wanted to run and hide behind the stone walls of the house. Then both of them swooped upward, and she was aware of a popping sound that must be gunfire. The two young men who were flying the planes were trying to kill each other. War, she said to herself, this is war. It's close now. The engines snarled and coughed and the guns fired, and then one of the planes was smoking and falling like a crazed thing, then disappeared behind the hilltop, and in the air was the soft thump of an explosion, and one of the young men was dead, and that was war.

Six

The voice went on and on.

"He never took one franc, not one centime except his salary. He could have had so many bribes. He could have taken anything from the apartments of the rich Jews. The others did. He could have been rich, but he just wanted to do his duty."

Jean looked at the woman who sat across the room from her, her eyes swollen with tears. She was pouting, embittered.

"They killed him because he did his job."

Jean and Guillaume had reached Paris the day before. She could have stayed at Les Sourcelles, but when they heard that Paris was liberated, that the Americans were there, she had to return. The last weeks everyone had been on edge, waiting. A group of German soldiers withdrawing through the town after a losing battle had found an empty house, broken in and stolen anything that looked valuable. There was more traffic on the road and the sound of guns not far off. They knew that they might find themselves in the middle of the fighting at any time, and for three days she kept Guillaume in the house all day, afraid to let him out, but then the guns moved off, and there were no more Germans to be seen. It was unnaturally quiet, and then in the morning, Berthe and Robert came back from church and reported that they had seen an American jeep, the soldiers waving to them, and that was their liberation. They had survived, and with the news of the liberation of Paris, the compulsion to return to the city was too great to resist. From the train they saw smashed buildings, the wreckage of tanks, piles of rubble, windows that looked on emptiness. In the suburbs there was bomb damage, but towards the centre of Paris, there was less sign of war, only a strange quiet.

Across the room Lucette was sniffling and blowing her nose. A week before, someone had broken into Philippe's apartment and shot him while Lucette was asleep in the bedroom only a few feet away.

"It was the communists," Lucette said. "Once the Jews were taken care of, Philippe was helping to deal with the communists. He had sources of information. People told him things. They trusted him."

After Philippe's death, Lucette had come to the apartment on the Boulevard Haussmann, and Madame Roussel had taken her in. For days she hardly got out of bed, but now that Jean was here, she was determined to tell her story, and there seemed to be no way to stop her talking. She had been over it all last night, and now this morning, half dressed, she had come to find Jean to tell it to her again.

Jean wanted to go out into the city, see the American soldiers who had replaced the Germans, to remind herself that they were safe. She had taken her old Canadian passport from its hiding place. Paris was bare and impoverished, but as they came from the Gare St. Lazare, pushing the old baby carriage loaded with their possessions — one last time, she told herself, soon there would be taxis on the streets — the sun was shining, and a few leaves lay on the pavement. The city smelled different than she remembered it.

She wanted to go out and find some American soldiers and

speak English with them and ask about the movies. She wanted to go to Dmitrievna's apartment and see if it was safe. It was heartless of her, she knew, to be unmoved by Lucette's grief, and she did her best to pretend, but Philippe was a man who hated and frightened her, and she felt, more than anything, relieved by his death. Life had been postponed since that day when she had looked out into the silent dreaming streets and waited for the German army to come. Now she wanted to move on.

"If only I'd wakened up," Lucette said. "I might have been able to stop them somehow."

"They might have shot you, too."

"I don't care. I would have died to try and save him. What good is it for me to be alive? What good am I to anyone?"

She began a soft wailing. Jean knew that she should go to her but couldn't bring herself to do it. The woman sat there, her skirt on, but bare-legged, no blouse, and her pink slip showing through the dressing gown she had pulled around her. Her face, without makeup, was puffy and pale.

"You'll stay here," Jean said, "until things get worked out."

The wailing went on. Jean stood up.

"I'll get you some coffee," she said.

She knew there was no coffee, and quite possibly none of the ersatz, but she had to get out of the room. As she walked down the hall toward the kitchen, she realized that her son Guillaume must now be *le comte de Seviède*. It was a startling thought, and she wondered if Guillaume himself had worked it out. Probably. He was a quick minded boy, and he was interested in the family's history. He and his uncle Robert would sit for hours at Les Sourcelles and discuss these things. She was afraid that Guillaume's sense of the family honour would be a dangerous thing for him. She must go to someone,

perhaps someone at Guillaume's bank or Maître Léon and
find out about these things, about money and property. After
her husband's death she had run away, but now it was time to
start again.

Jean searched the kitchen, and in a tin she found something
that was probably the last of some imitation coffee. There
wasn't much, but if she boiled it and strained it, there might be
a little flavour and colour. As she waited for the water to boil,
she thought for the first time of Philippe's death, the sudden
noise, the shattering of bone and flesh, the blood, Lucette
staggering from bed, her thin body in a nightgown, seeing her
lover.

The bubbling of the water shook the small pan on the gas
burner. Jean dumped the brown grains in and set it back. That
soft bubbling was like the sound of death. Empty, impersonal,
uncaring. When she had done her best to make some kind of
beverage out of the brown stuff she had found, she took it to
Lucette. As she arrived in the sitting room, she saw her son
kneeling beside the woman, trying to hold her in his arms as
she cried.

"It's all right, Guillaume. I've made Lucette some coffee."

He looked toward her with a look that was unreadable,
and the look frightened her. She didn't know what he was
thinking. He was all she had, and, for a moment, he was a
stranger.

Everything was changed yet nothing was changed. Jean
walked along a street that was full of other people, and she felt
the chill of autumn in the air, and the Germans were gone,

but the winter was as much a threat as the winters before. Gradually there was a little more food, the promise of coal, but fighting was still going on to the north, and although there was hope, the future was being postponed. Maître Léon could tell her nothing very clear about Guillaume's estate, but the way he shook his head and sat in silence made her suspect that he was only waiting to tell her the bad news, that perhaps he wouldn't let himself think it through. She had already accepted that there would be nothing. She had gone to the American bank where she had put the little money of her own and was almost surprised to find that it was still there and that it had grown. It almost seemed as if those dollars must have been lost in all the chaos of war, and the discovery that they hadn't was illuminating in a way that couldn't be explained. She wasn't foolish enough to think she had been clever, but she had a new understanding of how simple cleverness might be, how easily it might be learned.

There was no sign of Dmitrievna. Before coming back to Paris, Jean had once more packed up the paintings and drawings and put them on top of the load on the English pram, and she had looked forward to delivering them to her tall astonishing friend. When she went round to the apartment, she found that someone else was living there, and the concièrge explained that when all Jewish property had been seized and redistributed, first a truck had come from the Germans to take all the furniture and dishes and silver, and then these people had come to her and insisted that it was now their apartment. There was nothing to be done. Jean kept the key that Dmitrievna had given her.

Jean was restless, ready for some event that wouldn't occur. So today she took herself off to the Salon d'automne that was being held at one of the hotels. She wanted to see the Picassos that had caused riots and were being kept under guard. She found them and discovered that she had seen others like them in Dmitrievna's collection and at galleries before the war. At first she had felt she had no right to judge what she saw, but now she realized that she had taken it all in and perhaps understood. As she stood in front of a Picasso portrait of a man, a cubic body, the face distorted, jaw twisted sideways, everything painted in flat planes of colour, she was unastonished and read the man's face as she might read any face. In a still life, the flatness of the fruit in a bowl, the odd perspective was a kind of gaiety. Perhaps it was the fact that Picasso had joined the Communist Party that had caused the uproar. The paintings themselves made her cheerful. If they were brightly modern, well, everything was now, and she liked it that way. She had grown to respect, even love, Robert's loyalty to the past, his determination to maintain its words and its ways, but herself, she didn't belong there.

As she studied the Picassos, she found she expected to hear the voice of Dmitrievna behind her. They had gone to so many galleries together. "I have experienced boredom," she remembered Dmitrievna saying once when they were at a second rate exhibition. "There is no need to go on repeating the experience until it loses its charm."

The remembered voice was so clear that Jean turned and looked behind her, but there was no one there. She snorted with something like laughter and left the exhibition. Now she wandered through the streets, looking at the patterns of dead leaves, startled at everything she saw.

Ahead of her a group of well fed men in American uniforms crossed the street and went into a corner bar-tabac. As she got closer she saw them at a table by the window, studied the faces. Then she walked in, felt the warmth on her skin, smelled the thick tobacco smoke and the spilled wine. She walked up to the table where the three men sat and looked directly down at one of them. She concentrated, trying to remember, get the voice right.

"I do believe that must be Mr. Delbert Hunnicut," she said. The face stared at her.

"Sweet Jesus Christ," he said.

"No, Uncle Del," she said. "That's not who it is at all."

Jean pulled open the door of the hotel and walked the length of the short hall to the stairs. There was a smell of cooking from the small apartment where the owner lived with his wife and his two children and his wife's mother. There was a bell on the door that rang when she came in, but nobody looked out through the lace curtains. She came every day at this hour. On the first floor, there was a long set of windows overlooking the small courtyard. It was a grey winter afternoon, and not much light came down in the well between the buildings. The walls were uneven and hadn't been painted for a long time. In this light especially, they were dim and rough.

Another landing, another set of stairs, a smaller window. Darkness closing in. She was climbing almost to the top, to a small room under the eaves. She took a deep breath and climbed on. When she reached the room, she knocked lightly on the door, and it opened inward. Delbert stood and looked at her. There was a bottle of wine open on the table beside the bed, and by it a candle was burning, looking a little sad in the grey afternoon light. Del noticed her looking at it.

"That's to warm the place up," he said, and she laughed.

They were always cold here except when they were in the narrow bed together. Delbert came and put his arms around her, and she held herself tight against him, and he stroked her back and kissed her face. He took off her hat and threw it across the room as she kissed his mouth.

"You taste like wine," she said.

"Want some?"

"Not wine. The other."

They kissed some more and then withdrew from each other to undress. Delbert had put on some weight, and his body was thicker in the middle than when she'd first known him. A little fat over the kidneys and a hint of a paunch. She reached out and stroked his belly.

"You're a fat old man, Uncle Del," she said as her hand moved over the soft skin and curling hair. "You've had too much high living."

"Just get your damn clothes off," he said, "and get into that bed."

"Yes sir, Uncle Del."

But she couldn't stop looking at him, his thinning hair at the back of his head, the deep lines beside his mouth. She had to memorize him, the way he was right now, because he wouldn't be here much longer, and when he went he wouldn't come back. The way the hair grew on his chest, the way he held his mouth, the pale colour of his skin in this light. He was climbing into bed as she took off the last of her clothes and got in with him. She was shivering, but the two of them clung tightly together, the wonderful feel of skin against your skin.

They went on for a while, mumbling a little into each other's faces and hair and ears, and later there was the final moment with all its grand opera and greed and repletion. She found herself softly kissing the side of his neck, both of them a little breathless and not wanting to move. Finally they slid apart, and she lay against his chest and licked and bit him a little. Over his shoulder she could see the pattern of the lace curtains that she looked at every day, and she thought of how the curtains would be here, but the two of them would be gone.

"When is it?" she said.

"When's what?" he said, pretending he didn't know.

She said nothing, waiting for him.

"Tomorrow morning," he said.

"That's too soon."

"Not a damn thing I can do about it."

"Just stay here."

"Can't do that."

He was an official army photographer. He'd come ashore with the American troops in Normandy, got blown up in a car but walked away from it, came with them all the way to Paris, and he had a few days to make pictures of Paris being happy about the liberation, and then he got a couple of weeks leave. She was stroking his back, looking for the sore spots from when he got blown up. She liked to touch them and feel him flinch. She found one and he gave a little shout.

"You get a medal for that?" she said.

"For what?"

"For being all banged up."

"Yeah, I got the famous Banged Up Medal for Old Photographers."

"You deserve it. They could make a movie about you."

"Who'd play the part of you?"

"Some pretty young thing."

"Hard to find one with such a sweet ass."

"I bet there's lots around. You could audition them all."

"You bet."

"Just tell your wife it's part of the job and it has to be done."

Del had told her the first day that he was married. It turned out he had a son just about the age of Guillaume. She almost wanted to take him home and show him her son, but Guillaume was too smart for that. He'd know right away, and he was so loyal to the memory of his father that he wouldn't like it one bit.

"You tell your wife about me?"

"No."

"You didn't confess about how you found this little girl out in the country, innocent as parsley, and taught her your dirty ways? You didn't tell her that, Uncle Del?"

"Not a word."

She bit him on the shoulder, bit him hard so it would leave a mark, and he lay there trying not to respond until finally he shouted and pushed her away, but she grabbed hold of him and held him against her breasts and kissed him.

"You got to make me happy again," she said. "Maybe twice."

"How about dinner?"

"Not till I'm ready. Not till I've had enough of the other, and I might never have enough. I'll keep you at it till you lose some of that fat."

She kissed him as if she'd die without, pulled him over on top of her, and for a moment, as he was getting himself back in place, she looked at the room, stained where water had leaked in, at the way the dim last light from the window made a shape on the old plaster, at the pattern of the dirty lace curtains, at the pale yellow flame of the candle, and at the bottle of wine that they'd drink later on.

" Old Baxter Dunphy never mentioned in his sermons that heaven would be like this," she said.

"Who?" he said.

"Mind your business there, and don't be trying to talk and do it at the same time. You know you're not smart enough for that."

He gave a little snort of laughter, and his mouth came down on top of hers.

Jean sat in the Jardin du Luxembourg on a summer day, and the leaves of the large trees were bright green, and the grass was green. The gardens were being repaired after the disorders of the war and the occupation. Between the trees on the long paths of gravel, a few figures moved. A sound of hammering from far off. Men and women sat, as she did, in the straight chairs, some with a book or a newspaper. It was a warm beautiful day, and she could not stop shivering. There had been rumours, worse than rumours, and she had tried not to listen, but today she had picked up a magazine, and she had seen the pictures. Dmitrievna had never got in touch with her. Jean had asked Jules Michaux about her, and a couple of gallery owners who had been friendly with her, but none of them knew anything except that she had set out for the south, planning to go over the Spanish border. Jean had written to America, to people she hadn't seen for years, and to her surprise the one to answer was the beautiful actor she'd known all those years ago. It was a friendly, ungrammatical letter that said he wasn't getting much work any more, he'd invested his money in a restaurant and it was doing pretty good, and nobody he asked had heard anything of Olga Dmitrievna for years. They thought she was still somewhere in Europe.

A woman in a purple hat walked by, leading a small dog with bulging eyes. Jean felt a sudden passionate hatred for the dog and the woman. She watched them until they went out of sight behind a tree.

Her husband had died, his death was part of the disorder of the war. She thought of him now with a sorrow that she hadn't felt before. All her concern had been for survival, for how to save her son. Now she thought of her husband Guillaume, his deliberation, his careful kindness, his royalist convictions that were like some insistent oddity of dress. It was possible that she had never understood the man at all. There were times when she looked at her son, who was growing up now, who looked a little like his father but more like a photograph she had seen of Robert as a young officer, and she thought she didn't know him, even though he had been created inside her body. Guillaume and his uncle wrote letters to each other, and the boy was planning to become a professional soldier. It was incomprehensible to her. She understood nothing. She had married a man, taken him inside her and borne his son, watched him die, and she didn't know him. Loved him maybe but didn't know him. She knew Delbert, knew him too well altogether. She imagined him back in the States with his son on a hot summer afternoon, fishing in a stream where there hadn't been a fish for twenty years, shooting the bull.

You looked around you one day, and you were well on the way to being forty years old, and it was hard to credit how you'd got here and that you couldn't just go back and start over again with a different ticket to a different destination. You got on a train, and it took you a long time to realize that there was no return ticket. You got to the next station and went on from there.

Trains full of Jews with no next station. Everybody said

they'd never known what was happening at the other end. There were no Jews around Les Sourcelles; it was easy not to know. Philippe must have known. He had finally found a due object for his hatred. Philippe putting that brilliant ungainly woman on a train to be stripped and starved and murdered. The tall, bony, black-haired naked figure that had met her at the door in California now lying among the dead in those pictures.

She didn't know. There were still refugees moving all over Europe, struggling to cross borders, lost in the ruins. She might still come back and announce her disapproval of all that had happened. In the meantime, Jean had her own way to make. Maître Léon explained to her that Les Sourcelles, although it was mortgaged, could be saved and would belong to her son when he was grown up. Robert was safe, and if she wanted to go and live there in genteel poverty, that could be arranged. Apart from that there was nothing.

Marcel Toussaint, who had directed the movie about Mata Hari, which, as far as she could tell, had never been shown anywhere, was raising money for a new film and had spoken to her about acting in it. She wasn't sure she could do it any more, stand in front of a camera and let herself be seen. It was laughable. It was what she had done when she was a pretty child. She knew it would embarrass her son if his friends were to see her in a film, and she hated to think what sort of part she might be given. Still, if she was offered money, she might do it.

What was worst was that she knew that Dmitrievna would forgive her. If even now the woman were to appear with a terrible story about what she'd been through, she'd forgive Jean instantly, and that was what was worst. Though Jean knew, in the cold part of her mind, that Dmitrievna would never come back to forgive her or not, that she had vanished with all the others. Olga Dmitrievna no longer existed, and Jean did exist, and she had used Dmitrievna's paintings to start herself in business in this little art gallery on a small street near the École des Beaux Arts. Guillaume gone, left with nothing, she'd been a little desperate to know what to do for money, not wanting to go back into the movies or even knowing if she could.

She had told Maître Léon the truth about the paintings when she first had the idea of opening a gallery, and he'd given her advice about how to proceed. She thought perhaps he felt some responsibility for the fact that Guillaume's money had been lost, and he gave her good advice. It would be a dangerous business — too many things were turning up that had been filched from Jews who had fled — though he said that she had a right to the pieces. He thought it was foolish of her not to have let Dmitrievna write the piece of paper. When she opened the gallery, Dmitrievna's paintings were to be put on sale only in ones or twos. It took time and the last of her American dollars to acquire other works of art, but once open, she knew that she could bring out another of Dmitrievna's things every few months. If Dmitrievna had family, they were far off and unknown; she was stealing from strangers. The greatest danger was that the French government might find some way to claim the pictures.

A few months before, there was a little party for the opening, and Guillaume, who was almost a man now, very grave and proper, had helped her greet the guests, looking handsome in his suit and tie. Berthe had brought Robert by train from Les Sourcelles, and although Robert had no interest in the pictures, his presence gave the gathering an air of consequence. He had lent her his dignity for the evening, and she was grateful.

It was an unsettling business. One day she saw a small man looking in the window of the gallery. He stared intently through the glass at a small cubist oil, then opened the door and walked across the room to stand in front of it. A short bald man with dark skin and deep lines on his face, and when he turned from the painting to look at her, as she sat by her elegant small table on her elegant small chair, she met his black animal eyes and pretended to herself that she didn't know. Dmitrievna had bought the painting from his studio, and he might remember and ask questions. If he did, she would simply tell him that she had been given it and was now forced to sell. As he looked at her Jean was aware that she wanted to go toward the man and touch him, that she was convinced his skin would have a slight smell of spice. You wanted to touch him as you might a certain kind of small animal.

Then he turned and was gone, and she was relieved, though for the next week she was frightened that he might send a dealer or the police, but nothing had happened.

The hardest thing, she knew now, was not selling paintings, though that could be a long slow dance, but finding good material to sell. The dealers loved to gossip, but they kept their secrets. Jean went to auctions, not only in the slender hope of finding something good at a reasonable price, but also to hear the gossip, to be part of it. When the gallery opened, she invited those she had dined with as Guillaume's wife. She was *la comtesse de Seviède*, and if the name could help her, she would use it.

She went to shows of students and young artists. She had been amused and flattered when one young artist showed signs of wanting to seduce her. No doubt he wanted to be able to tell stories about how he'd had a countess on the floor of his atelier. And he had. He was rough and not especially gifted as a lover, but she'd been in a mood to accept his youthful presumption. When they were done, she dressed herself again in her pretty underwear and brushed off her dark skirt and repaired her *maquillage*. She'd offered him a show in a few months time, though she suspected that he would be a nuisance when it came to business matters, and she'd had quite enough of lying on cold floors. There would be girls enough to join him there.

The big apartment on Boulevard Haussmann was lost, and Madame Roussel had gone to live with a sister somewhere in Brittany. Jean and Guillaume had a small apartment halfway between the gallery and the Lycée Henri IV, where he went to school. He was still determined to join the army and defend France. He had friends at school, and yet he kept himself apart, as if he felt a need to be alone with his destiny. Like Robert, he was determined that a book be published to represent his father's ideas, and Jean had promised to help with money if she could. There was something almost monastic about Guillaume. As if he had been born out of his time. She could see nothing of herself in him except a look about the eyes. He was boyishly chivalrous toward her, affectionate but determined as he tried to perfect her French.

She heard a noise in the courtyard behind the gallery. It was a small yard, and there was some dispute about who had the right to use it for storage. Those in the apartments on the lower floors were convinced that they had more rights to the ground, being closer to it, but this was eagerly disputed by those higher up, most especially a widower named Racicot who worked in a government office and behaved as if this gave his utterances the same authority as those of the president of France. He had a bicycle, which he never used but which he insisted on storing in a sheltered corner of the yard. This made it difficult for anyone to reach the doorway leading to the stairs. Once one of the tenants of a lower apartment had dared to move it. The culprit was never found, but M. Racicot delivered a letter to the door of each of the suspects, a letter written in French so highly formal as to be almost impenetrable which made a number of large but undefined threats. Since the back door of her galley abutted on the small courtyard, Jean had received one of these letters. She had taken her copy home to show Guillaume, and it made him smile, which was a rare enough thing. She wondered if she should go out and try to see what the noise was about, but she didn't want to find herself in the middle of a feud, so she ignored it.

A woman stood on the street outside, a small dog on a leash. She looked in the window, and Jean smiled at her. She had come in twice before and looked around at the paintings as if that was not the point of her visit at all. Likely she had something to sell but was delaying that announcement. It might be something suspect, or perhaps she was only embarrassed at selling a work of art because she was short of money. If she came in today, Jean would offer her a cup of American coffee that had been sent to her, and the coffee would allow the beginning of a conversation, and she could be led to the point. The dog would have to be watched. He looked like the spoiled, stupid sort who, given the chance, would piss on the furniture.

Under the wind, Lake Ontario was running east in white-capped waves. It was a chill metallic green but dark blue under the shadow of the clouds that moved across the sky. In the distance, against a horizon of black clouds, she could see a pale rainbow. Beside her, where the reeds and grasses rose from the water, there were little tongues of light. A sudden darkening of the shallows, wrinkled and crossed by patterns of ripples.

Across the dying leaves and grasses fell the long slanted autumn sunlight, silver at the edge of the clouds. The rapidly changing sky was blue, grey, white, and there was a constant sound of wind in her ears. A small flock of ducks leapt into flight from the surface of the water, gained height and curved away downwind.

She had come out without a hat, and the wind blew her hair across her face. It was astonishing to be where she had grown up, to stand where she had stood thirty years before. At the edge of the big lake, everything was large and sudden. You felt the wind blowing all the way from the arctic.

Jean turned and walked back toward the house. Three weeks ago a letter from her sister Iris had reached her in Paris. Ronald had died a couple of years before, and now it had become clear that their mother was ailing. She was in hospital and not expected to get back out. Jean had found enough money to buy a ticket to Montreal. On the boat, she decided that she would be the Mystery Lady who spoke to no one but moved slowly and silently once a day around the deck. At dinner, if she was with the English, she let on that she spoke only French. If she was with the French, she said she spoke English. She found books in the ship's library, read one novel after another, sipped whisky, and treated it all as if it were another movie. It was something she'd learned to do.

She left the ship in Montreal and found a taxi on the dock to take her to Windsor Station. From the train, she looked at the distances of the landscape, the rawness of it all, the bright paint of the houses, and it was hard to accommodate its strangeness. When the train stopped at Belleville, Iris and her husband were waiting for her on the long platform. The husband's name was Gord, and he was a tall, silent, smiling man with straight thinning hair. She and Iris looked at each other and tried to remember that they were sisters.

She got into their big comfortable car, and they drove along the country roads, and there was a kind of familiarity now. The landscape was something she might have dreamed and half forgotten, the fields of dead grass all bent one way, the dark grey of an abandoned log barn. They took her to their warm, crowded house, where she met nieces and nephews, the girl named after her, and everybody treated her as if she were a celebrity, and she couldn't quite find a way to make them easier. Gord called her countess, and she said none of that, but they still weren't easy. The only time she felt natural was when they took her to the hospital to see her mother. She was shocked at how old and sick the woman was, but the uneasiness and worry on her face were familiar, the quick, careful glance that saw you and then turned away, the small hands. Jean bent and kissed her on the cheek, and her mother looked fussed and pleased, and Jean sat down in the chair beside the bed, and her mother told her how Ronald had got his finger cut when he was out fishing and did nothing about it, and the next thing they knew he was full of blood poisoning, and the next thing he was gone. Never was good for much, Jean thought to herself. Her mother said had she been out to the house yet, and Jean said no, but she'd go out and see Eg one of these days. Her mother asked was she going to stay in Canada, and she said no, she didn't think so. After all, her son was in France. Her mother puzzled a little over this French grandson she'd never seen, and Jean told lies about how when he was older they'd both come and visit her. They both knew that her mother wasn't going to live much longer, and soon she was too tired to talk any more, and Jean left, but she went back to the hospital every day, she told her mother stories about her life. She told her about Guillaume and the war. It sounded different when she told it, and it was hard to recognize the things that had happened. Jean had never thought of herself as one for crying, but every day when she walked out of the hospital, there were tears in her eyes.

She'd put off going out to the old house. Eg didn't have a car, so she had to wait till Gord had the time to drive her out. They called yesterday to let him know they were coming, and Jean had said maybe she'd stay for a day or so, if that was okay.

Jean turned from the lake to walk back to Eg's house. After Ronald died, her mother had moved to an apartment in town, and Eg had been left to himself in the old place. There were three pairs of boots by the front door, piles of newspapers and *True Detective* magazines on the couch, and a shotgun propped up in the corner behind a chair covered with dirty dishes. On the big round table were three packs of cards and a cribbage board, and Eg said she'd have to leave by Friday or be ready to put up with the men who came round to play cards.

What bothered her was how badly her brother was crippled. Her mother had written her once about how sick he'd been and how he'd never walk right, but she hadn't heard about the accident when he'd been working on a roof, shingling, and had fallen. The way he walked was laborious and awkward, and he'd never find regular work, but he did odd jobs when he could get them, was caretaker for a couple of summer cottages that people had built further along the shore. He was still young, but you only noticed that when you looked in his wide grey eyes. The clothes he wore and the way he walked made him seem like an old man.

A skein of ducks crossed the darkening sky. Tomorrow morning, one of the neighbours was to drive her into town. Tonight, one last time, she'd sleep in that old bedroom with the low ceiling. Eg had a bed off the big room downstairs. They'd had electricity put in the house since she'd left, and there was a little lamp with a pink shade on a table in the corner of her room, something Iris must have chosen, probably saved up her money for it. Or maybe her mother bought it. It was years since Iris had gone off to marry Gord.

The wind tossed the trees and leaves blew fluttering to the ground. Tonight Jean would hear the wind against the tin roof, and beside her would be the empty room where her mother had slept with Ronald, and before that with her father.

Jean opened the door. Her brother was sitting in a stuffed chair, a *True Detective* magazine in one hand, a cup of tea in the other. He was turned almost on his side, either to catch the light from the window or because it was the only way he was comfortable.

"Well," he said, "the lake still there?"

"Yes, Edgar, it's still there."

The brown teapot sat on the corner of the stove.

"Can I have a cup of that tea?"

"I expect you could."

Jean went to the cupboard to get a cup. She knew exactly where they'd be. This had once been her home.

She looked at the figures across the table from her, Jules and Pascale and the fat handsome poet, and she remembered another afternoon. The same four people in the same café on the same street under the same trees. Jules and Pascale were settled in Lyon now. He had given up the movies and was the manager of a factory owned by Pascale's father. He would not explain what the factory manufactured and dismissed the question with a certain disdain. The two of them were well dressed and looked rich and unhappy. They had sold their bright modern house in the hills near Aix-en-Provence, and they had a house at Lyon above the Rhône. They were in Paris to look for a small apartment. Jean looked at them and tried to understand their unhappiness and then thought that perhaps it was not unhappiness, it was only the way time made people more defined, more limited. Twenty years ago, there was more to the future, the air was shiny with choices to be made, but now the choices had been made. Perhaps it was only that.

The poet was fatter and had spilled ash on himself for so long that he was all greyed by it. His anger was deeper and narrower now, and he was no longer handsome. He glared at Jean with something that might be desire or only the memory of desire. Once there was something about him that was bright and evil and tempting, but not now.

Jean, too, must have become more what she was, something defined where there had been possibility. She looked at the poet, who screwed up his eyes against the smoke of his cigarette, and she remembered things he had said on that other afternoon. She looked upward at the sunlight coming through the leaves and at the cars parked across the street, and at two men who stood talking by the doorway of an antique store. One of them was a doctor who had come to her gallery once or twice. He had bought nothing, and she'd been unable to make out if he was serious. She thought perhaps he was assessing her, not the pictures. The first time he had come in with his wife, the second time alone.

"You have all abandoned your talent," the poet was saying to Jules. "I will be the first to admit that film is a bastardized and inconsequential kind of art, but still it was your calling, and you have abandoned it."

"And you have not abandoned yours, you wish us to know," Pascale said.

"No, I have not. Nor have I given myself to the false poetry of surrealism or any of the other fads."

Jean noticed that the doctor was looking across the road toward her. When he saw her notice him, he nodded his head gravely and went back to his conversation for a moment, then turned and came toward the table. Now she had no doubt about his interest, and as he was crossing the street, she liked the way he walked and the look on his face and thought that perhaps he would become her lover.

She was too much alone. People came to the gallery, and there was Guillaume, but he was growing away from her, and at the gallery she had to be on the watch all the time, to sense who wanted to buy, who wanted to sell, always a little concerned that someone would recognize one of Dmitrievna's pictures and make a fuss, though when it came time to explain the provenance of those pictures, she always mentioned Dmitrievna's ownership — she didn't want to be selling pictures of questionable authenticity, that was the worst thing of all — but she let the impression get around that she had bought the collection before Dmitrievna left Paris. There had been enough unseemly doings in the war that most people were prepared not to ask too many questions.

The doctor was standing beside the table, and she introduced everyone. He asked if he might sit down with them, and he ordered a whisky. Of course. He was just that kind of man, and she didn't mind that there was something predictable about him. He would be orderly and sensible, would perhaps already have a small apartment somewhere, and it was there they would meet. He would remain devoted to his wife and children, but he would always treat her with dignity. Like her husband with Madame de Coulanges. There would be no surprises, and they might stay together for years. Yes, she thought, that might be very agreeable, and she turned and looked at the man, the shining, clean-shaven cheeks, the quiet brown eyes, and again she thought, yes, he would do nicely, and hoped that she wasn't wrong about his intentions.

The street was narrow and steep and the cobbles uneven. On each side, houses with thick wooden doors pressed close. The September sunlight was bright and warm, but the street where she walked was cool in the shade of the stone houses. The windows had heavy wooden shutters. Now and then as she climbed the hill, she would get a glimpse over a stone wall into a garden with flowers and a fig tree. Or she would look down on the rooftops of red tiles, at odd angles to each other so that it looked like a cubist painting, the geometry, the unity of colour. They had been here only a couple of days, and the streets of the village were still a maze to her. She turned a corner now and found herself in a little square. There was a tree growing in the square, its leaves very green against the walls of pale yellow stone, and under it a stone fountain, but the fountain was dry and looked as if it had been so for some time. The bottom was filled with a rubble of dried leaves and twigs. Beside the fountain was a bench, and Jean sat herself down there. She hadn't met a single person as she came along the narrow streets, and the empty square increased her sense that the town might be deserted. She was the only one who hadn't heard the news of the plague.

That must have happened in the days of the Black Death, villages discovered empty, though there would have been the stench of rotting flesh, well-fed rats running in the streets. Here the air was fresh and on the breeze, she thought she could smell the tang of the herbs that grew wild on the hills, thyme, rosemary, fennel.

As if to reassure her, the figure of a dark thick-set woman appeared out of an alley and crossed the square, went up three stairs and through a door. For the first time, she saw the small sign and realized that the doorway led to the post office. She would write to someone. She opened the purse she carried by a strap on her shoulder to see if she had a pen. Perhaps she would go in and buy an air letter and write to Guillaume and tell him about this square, and it would remind him of France, his beloved France. He had come south once with some young officer friends when they were on leave before going to Indochina, and she imagined him sitting on this bench in this square.

There was no pen in her purse. Well, she could buy an air letter and write it later. Alain had a pen. It was a black fountain pen that he carried in the inside pocket of his suit jacket. She knew such things about him now. As time passed, she learned more details. He had a history and a geography. The dark mole in the centre of his back, the line of little hairs down his belly. A certain change in his breathing when he grew angry.

She hadn't asked him how he had made an excuse so that they could have this week together in the Vaucluse. One afternoon as they walked from her gallery to the apartment they used, he had asked her if she could take a week's holiday in September to spend with him, and she had agreed. It wasn't something she'd expected. So they had been together for three days now, driving down and then staying in the little house he had rented. She had never spent a night with him before. When she woke in the dark, frightened of everything, frightened for her son, she didn't know if she was allowed to wake him. He did work hard, put in long hours at the hospital and in a clinic in a working class area, and perhaps he needed to sleep soundly on this holiday, not be troubled by his mistress's fretting. She didn't know. What she did was move toward him, turn so that her back touched the warmth of his body, and that was some comfort.

There was so much to learn about a human being. Only this morning she discovered that he was a communist, or at least voted for the Communist Party in every election. Her years with Guillaume had left the residual feeling that the communists were creatures out of some spiritual underworld, though she knew that they had been the heart of the resistance, and she saw references in the newspapers to the amount of support they had among the professions. Picasso was a communist, and Sartre.

She had been tempted to tell him about her husband's politics, but he would have scoffed. They had bickered for a moment about the war in Indochina. Jean would have said she had no politics, but it was her son's war, and she must be loyal to her son. She didn't think it would ever be necessary for Alain and Guillaume to meet, and that was just as well, for it would not be a happy meeting. You began with a lover who had the right air, whose manners and tone pleased you, and before you knew it, he had become a human being, with all the difficulty of that.

The woman who had entered the post office came back out and hurried away to her house and her duties. The square was silent except for the soft perfect sound of the wind in the leaves over her head. It was the time of year when the mistral might begin to blow, sweeping down out of the Alps to tear the ripe figs from the trees. Beside her on the stone rim of the dry fountain, there was a tiny lizard, perfectly still, clinging to the rock as the dapple of sun and shade fell over it. For a long time it was still, and then, obeying a signal from some mysterious source, it moved quickly away and disappeared into a crack between two rocks.

At the edge of the square stood a two-storey house, and past the angle of its corner, she could see a distant hillside, the pale silver leaves of an olive orchard. The country of oil and wine and above it the fierce blue sky. Sun dazzled her eyes, and she closed them for a moment, and when she opened them again, there was a dark figure at the edge of the empty square, watching her. It was Alain, distant and foreign in his dark suit, looking at her as if she were some incomprehensible being that had appeared out of the light.

As she lay in bed, aching and chilled, Jean realized how seldom in her life she had been sick, but now *la grippe* had laid her low, and there appeared to be nothing to do but lie here and endure. Late yesterday afternoon, Alain had come to see her. It was the hour at which she would have gone to the apartment and met him and made love, and she thought that he was a little irritable at seeing her helpless and unwell, but it might only be that he disliked illness. When he first told her this, she said she thought it was a very strange and unlikely thing for a doctor, but he believed it made him a better physician. Since he disliked disease, he worked harder to cure it. This struck her as a slightly comic claim, but Alain had little sense of humour and none about himself, so she accepted his words at face value.

It was odd to see him in her bedroom, in his dark suit, sitting in a chair, his large hands clasped in his lap. She had never invited Alain here, had instead gone to the apartment that he rented not very far from his office, a place that such a man kept to meet his mistress in decent circumstances. Sitting across from him, here, made her aware that she had never made the place her own. There was furniture from the home she had shared with Guillaume, although most of that had gone to his cousin Gabrielle. There were a few things she had bought. Yet even though she had a little money now and contact with fine furniture and pictures, the apartment looked as if she had only recently moved in. Or as if it might be rented furnished. There had been great difficulty finding it, and long negotiation with the daughter of the previous owner, and that had perhaps helped to create in Jean a sense that her presence was temporary, had prevented her from finding any style that was appropriate and personal.

Today, lying in bed, weak and uncomfortable, trying to lose

herself in sleep but finding her sleep oppressed with heavy discomfited dreams, she thought that it was a weakness in her that she could not take possession of the place, that each piece of furniture was too small or too large, that too many of the walls were bare, that the wallpaper was dim and unwelcoming. It wasn't ugly, it was only nondescript. She lacked the largeness of soul to own what was hers.

Alain had sent some ill-tasting mixture from the pharmacy, but if it was going to do any good, the effect was still to come. The malady was more in charge of her feverish body today than yesterday. She wished that Guillaume were with her. He was such a dutiful boy. He would have brought her *tisane* and read to her, as she had done for him when he was little and had a terrible bout of measles. Alain might come by later, but he would be impatient. He was a straightforward man, a little proud, not without kindness, but he could not unbend to comfort a mistress whose face was flushed and whose nose was running. Perhaps she should invite him into her bed. It would be good to touch someone, but no doubt she would infect him with *la grippe*, and he would pass it on to his wife and family. Chills came up her back, and she pulled the covers more tightly around her, and thought that she didn't care a *sou* whether his lovely family got sick. All the better if they did.

Sick, you were aware of how much of what kept you going was the mere accident of good health. It gave you the illusion that you existed as some particular and exceptional entity. Take away health, the appetites weakened, and nothing made sense. You were forced to lie still and think, even if thinking wasn't something for which you had a talent. Because you were sick, you learned that you must grow old. You were no longer the beautiful child who gave herself to the camera. She had a horror of pictures now, not because of the way she looked —

she was a well-tended woman — but because she had lost the innocence that had allowed her to let herself be seen. Even with Alain she was a little shy, though she liked to look at him, to study the particular human features of this particular man.

The chills had stopped for a little now, but there was an aching all through her head and neck. It went on. It went on. Everything went on. She needed a change. Recently she had hired a young woman, Gilberte, to look after the gallery when she was away. She was a plain little thing, though she had enormous breasts that made men stare. Her presence meant Jean could go away for a few days if she wanted. Perhaps it was time for a trip to Les Sourcelles, walks in the country. Robert was looking much older now, and he and Berthe were, in their way, like an old married couple. They made Jean welcome, and Robert would talk with her about young Guillaume's future and about the dead Guillaume's book. That still. He continued to believe that one day the book would appear, that it would strike France with the force of a revelation, but none of the publishers would have it, and neither she nor Robert had the money to pay for its publication. Jean suspected that it would, in fact, appear so out-of-date as to be merely quaint.

When she was better, she would plan a little vacation at Les Sourcelles. She began to sweat now, her face hot with fever, and it was hard to believe that the careless days of good health would ever return.

She could not imagine Indochina. She knew so little of the world. She had lived in a few places, but there were so many thousand others that she had never seen and never would, places where people with different skin and startling ways of life went on about their business, knowing nothing of her as she knew nothing of them. You saw pictures in the magazines, but those pictures could not make it real. Indochina: she imagined a place with jungles and mountains and strange temples, but she could not be sure if it was like that. Dainty women and thin muscular men. That was what you saw in the pictures, but they couldn't tell you all the particular colours of green. She tried to imagine a slow river running through an intricate jungle, but she didn't know how to shape the leaves, what the shadows were like further back among the trees, whether there was a sound of birds. There must be, but were they bright coloured or small things that hid in the shrubbery? Perhaps both. There were boats on the river, slender boats poled over the brown flatness by slender men. Yes, she must have seen such a picture.

Imagine her son there. That too was difficult. He wrote from time to time, but his letters didn't offer the kind of details that she could understand. His account of it all was very abstract. He wrote about France, the history of empire, how he was learning the difficulties of command. She imagined a letter that contained all the things he didn't tell her. There is a bird singing outside the barracks, and its song is *tu-toi, tu-toi, tu-toi*. I have a Vietnamese sweetheart, and the scent of her body is like green tea. At night when I lie awake I remember the sounds of the old house at Les Sourcelles. She was sure there must be things like that, but Guillaume did not tell them to her. Still, he wrote faithfully, and when she answered she tried to imagine what might be of interest to him. She read the newspapers so she would understand the politics, and she asked Alain what things a dutiful young officer would wish to know. Alain had two daughters but no sons, and he was sometimes interested to hear about Guillaume and his old-fashioned ways.

She kept a map of Indochina by her bed, and at night she would lie in bed, before she was ready to sleep, and try to imagine Guillaume there. She studied the rivers, how they ran through the countryside to the sea, and she tried to memorize the names of the mountains. A map gave you the idea that you knew something you didn't know at all. You studied it, and there were shapes and names, but if you had never been there, you couldn't understand what it might be like. She studied her map, and she thought the strange thoughts that come late at night, when you know that the past is a dream like any other, and it's hard to believe that you have ever existed at all, when you think that there are millions of people thinking thoughts at that moment, and you know none of their thoughts, as if you were already dead and were only an occasional passing memory, as she might remember her husband or her mother or Dmitrievna, who were no more real to her now than the characters in a book she had been reading earlier in the evening.

The day had gone by as days did. She had negotiated for a Seurat drawing that might or might not be for sale, and while sitting in the gallery in the afternoon, she had done some of the bookkeeping necessary for the payment of her taxes. When she closed the gallery, she had met Alain at a bar and they each had a whisky, then walked to the apartment where they made love and talked for a while about his younger daughter, who worried him, and about a mad patient who worried him even more, and then she had caught a taxi and come back to her apartment and cooked andouillettes and sauerkraut and drunk some wine and read her book.

This was what you did. The late afternoon sunlight coming through the narrow street to fall on the pavement and the tables and chairs outside the bar could only be called beautiful, and Alain's body was familiar and satisfying, and the food and wine were a slow pleasure in the mouth and a warmth burning inside, and yet there was something that could not be said, could not, perhaps, even be thought, the thing beyond all this, the reason that men and women read books, as if to find in the shape of those stories the shape of their own.

She put down the map, turned out the light and settled herself for sleep. This was always, for her, the strangest moment of the day. Sleep was a mystery, blankness or the arbitrary narrative of dreams. Why should it be necessary, this retreat into unconsciousness? Perhaps she was frightened by it since she slept alone. Though she was not altogether sure that she would have preferred to have Alain there beside her.

You lay alone in the darkness, and in a while your eyes would close, and you would vanish into the solitude of the body's automatic responses. The lungs breathed, the heart beat, and if suddenly the heart stopped beating, nothing would be any different, only one kind of unconsciousness exchanged for another. She remembered when she was very young her grandmother teaching her to say her prayers before she went to sleep, and she understood that necessity. They called sexual climax the little death, and she had never known why. Sleep was the little death, experienced every day, a retreat into silence, to a place where you were not. Before that long journey, it was a time to set things in order.

She wondered what prayers her faithful son said each night. Whether he lay in a bivouac listening to a rustling in the jungle or on a chill plain in the mountains, listening to the night sounds that might be enemies and waiting for morning and the familiar bird that sang *tu-toi, tu-toi, tu-toi*. She tried to find words that might be a prayer on his behalf.

She moved only when she was told to move, spoke only when she was told to speak. If Robert had not sent Berthe to her, she might have starved, have lain in bed emptied of tears and unable to open her eyes or feed herself. The tears came slowly, then you were nothing but tears, and the body tried to break itself apart with sobbing, and yet it couldn't, and you fell into a dry sleep, and in dreams it was all different, you were deluded into some kind of happiness, and then you woke and after a second remembered and longed for the worst dreams that did not contain *this* worst. You thought if you could scream loud enough and long enough, the thing would not be, that by main force you could turn the globe backward, time would reverse itself, this would not be. That was what your screams were, the huge effort to reverse time, to stop the earth in its course, but the weight of it pressed at you, pressed until the screams weakened and became hoarse sobs.

Grief was a sickness, incurable and fed by memory. To remember was unbearable. Not to remember was unbearable. Something must change. This could not be, and the sobbing would begin all over again. She had known him so little, really, her child and yet such a strange being, though she was always touched by his uprightness, his stiff sense of honour. He was so clear, so determined, she would think, and she would see him alive and for a moment believe. So easy to believe that, natural and right as it was. He was young, and the young lived. The leaves did not fall in May. No, not ever. This is a thing which will not be. I will not let it be. One day, some mother, in the giant power of her grief, will stop the earth.

I will not breathe.

I will not live.

I will stop the earth.

As she was lying in her bed, pale and exhausted and unable to find sleep, she saw the shadow of a figure beside her in the darkened room. She could not see at first who it was and had no idea how it had come to her, and for a moment she thought that this was Madame Death, the great mother, come to give her peace, and then the figure lay down on the bed beside her. She heard a voice, recognized Berthe, and would have drawn away from her if she could, but there was no escape. The woman took her in strong arms and held her with a terrible force, their breasts crushed together, and she felt shocked and captured, aware that she had never in her life so much as touched Berthe's hand or arm, and now she was imprisoned in her body. While she wanted to pull away, felt she couldn't breathe right and would bite and scratch to escape, she knew that she must let it be, that she must allow herself to be touched.

She didn't understand how Robert, who had loved the boy so much, could bear to send Berthe away from him to Paris. Antoine was there, Berthe said, and would look after him, as if it were that simple. She held her and would not let go, would not let her die.

Now Jean took orders, and her body lived a sort of life. Once Alain came, and she mimed a conversation of some sort. Gilberte arrived for instruction about the gallery, and she said something or other, she couldn't now remember what it was. Day after day, Berthe told her every single thing to do, and if she wasn't told, she did nothing, and the observing part of her waited for Berthe to show some irritation at this passivity, but there had been none yet. A colonel came to speak for the French Army, and she told him he was a very stupid man.

What she wanted to know, the one thing she wanted to know, was whether any other woman might have loved Guillaume, whether somewhere in Indochina another woman shared her tears. There was none in France, she was sure. Guillaume might have been too shy to tell her about a mistress, but Robert would surely have known. If there was any kind of love.

What she wondered — the first living thought that had come to her — was whether, by some grace of natural being, a girl, a small, dainty Annamite girl, might carry his child. One day she would ask Berthe to get in touch with Robert and have him make unofficial enquiries. He still had contacts in the army, and now he was *le comte de Seviède*. Perhaps someone would tell him the truth, some last kind truth.

She looked down at the river that flowed on and on. The city was pulsing with the rhythmic beat of the slogan. *Algérie Française, Algérie Française, Algérie Française.* All week there had been tanks in the streets, and marching men, and the city resounded like a beaten drum, once more fallen into one of those states of enchantment that seized it in almost every generation, as if the quiet alleys and orderly streets heard a message from history, the whisper of contagion, the word that it was time to rise once again. She had read how the delirium of Paris had made the revolution. She had herself sat waiting with her baby in the apartment on the Boulevard Haussmann while Guillaume and Philippe had gone out into the night to join the crowds besieging the National Assembly. Now it was the army that had risen. They had come back from Indochina in defeat and were determined to avenge that defeat in Algeria. Her son's ghost marched with them, but only to remind her that he was gone, that his body had been left behind in that far country, lost in the endless green and a long intolerable silence. That she continued to live, that she satisfied her appetites was a mere vulgarity, a cheapness, but it went on. She had grown thin, but now she was herself again, or someone who resembled that woman.

When she saw the tanks, she hated them. The army killed her son. He wished to be the perfect knight who defended the soul and purity of France, and he was young and good. When she saw the tanks, she saw them running their heavy treads over the shining ghost of that young knight. The beat of the slogan struck him down. She could not blame the thin brown men.

She tried to explain this to Gilberte, at the gallery, after they had seen soldiers massing on the boulevard this afternoon, and Gilberte had lifted her head to the length of her neck, puffed her big chest and begun to lecture her about the higher cultures and the duty of France to civilization. Jean had been seized with a terrible rage. Everything in front of her went out of focus and at the same time closed in, as if she would have to shatter glass to break free. Her arm rose as if to smash it all. She felt the skin on her face go cold, and Gilberte stepped back from her, frightened, her mouth unable to finish the word that she was forming. Jean found the door as if it might be her last act before suffocating, and she ran along the street, gasping for breath and with a terrible sound coming from her throat. Beside her there was some public building with an armed soldier standing guard in front, and as she passed by she began to shout at him, the worst filth that she could speak, and even as the words came out, she knew that this was insanity, the army was already maddened, in full spate of rebellion, and the man might knock her down or shoot her. She turned and ran. She ran and walked and walked until her breathing began to slow a little, then she walked further, staring at the faces that came toward her, as if one of them would be familiar and comforting. She wished that Berthe had not gone back to Les Sourcelles. What she wanted was to go back to the apartment and find her there, silent and certain.

She had made her way down to the Seine, and she stared at the river and tried to let the flowing of the water calm her. A barge passed by, with laundry hanging on a line over the deck at the back. Last week there had been a report of a murder on one of the Seine barges. A jealous wife had drowned her husband. Small facts, other people's lives. She looked along the quai. Most of the *bouquinistes* had stayed at home or were part of one of the demonstrations that would break out in the streets, but one man sat there on a chair beside his open stall of books, bent over, staring at the pavement, waiting, offering the past for sale, no one buying.

She had an appointment this afternoon with a man who might sell his collection of drawings. He was an old doctor that Alain had met somehow, and he lived alone in an apartment in Vincennes with an old dog and the drawings that he had picked up over the years when he had practised on the edge of Montparnasse, some of his patients from among the artists who lived nearby, some from the *grande bourgeoisie* of the Faubourg Saint-Germain. The artists had come to call him Dr. Drawings because he would always take drawings in payment for his treatment, and there were stories that he had picked up this and that from his rich patients as well. He and his dog were both much decayed, but they could still be found each morning walking slowly at the edge of the Bois de Vincennes. Alain had met him, in some way she had never understood, and learned that he hated museums and tax collectors and might be prepared to sell drawings, or be paid on the understanding that the drawings would be taken and sold after his death. That was a dangerous way to do business, but if the collection was good enough, she might be willing to do it. She could have Maître Léon draw up an agreement.

She must prepare herself to go back to the gallery and see Gilberte. She was afraid that the insane rage might come back. Or she might find that Gilberte had quit. Locked up the place and left her a note. No, the girl was too ambitious for that. Nothing but a good marriage, a marriage into a family with money and preferably a title, would take her away. Talking to clients, Gilberte always referred to Jean, silkily, as *Madame la comtesse*, though Jean herself rarely used the title. In business, she was Jeanne de Sevièede.

It was possible that she disliked Gilberte. Perhaps that was the source of the outburst. It was possible that she disliked everyone in the world. The idea of going back to the gallery and seeing that face with its slightly protuberant eyes and thick lips was repulsive, but it had taken a long time to persuade Dr. Drawings to come to see her, and she mustn't miss him; he was worth money to her, and for now money was all there was. She had twice gone to his apartment in Vincennes and stood in the dark hall while he held the door and refused to invite her in. She had left a card, and a week later she had received a short note. She had written a reply to that and received another note. At last they had made this appointment.

A jeep full of soldiers drove by. A flock of pigeons passed through the grey sky over the grey-green powerful river, and she wondered why she didn't go down the steps and drown herself.

What would she do with Alain's apartment now that she had it? Rent it. Make money. There was a moment when she was ready to turn it down, but that would have been foolish, and after a certain time of life you gave up such foolishness. It might, she supposed, be thought one of the great watersheds in life — the moment when you accepted the necessity of prudence, even its moral worth in the scheme of things. One turned from *cigale* to *fourmi*. One learned to love money.

She looked out the window across the small courtyard at the pattern of roofs and gables and chimney pots. And beyond them the pale spring sky. And beyond that the space where the Russian satellites whirled round the earth observing, learning this and that, spying perhaps on the American enemy. The promise that men would go up there and sail around the earth.

The light gleamed on the metal roof opposite, and a curtain blew in front of an open window. Someone had come home from work and opened the window to let the spring air blow in, perhaps to blow across a bed where two lovers lay naked and entwined. If she opened the window in front of her, she could listen for their little sounds over the noises of the city traffic.

It was the hour when she came here with Alain, but now she was alone. His wife had inherited a large property in Toulon, and he had agreed to move there with her and open a new practise. There was enough sickness everywhere. Alain explained the reasons that it made sense for him to move. He had always liked the south, was ready for the ease of life there. He did not say, though it was clear enough, that he had no reason to stay in Paris, apart from Jean herself, and that one didn't alter one's life for a mistress. However, he had spoken to his lawyer, and the apartment where they had spent the hours together would be hers.

The coolness and calculation of it all had given offence. They were sitting by the window of a café when he told her, and she had stared along the street and seen an old man, a *clochard*, lying at the edge of the pavement, a wine bottle clutched to his chest. A young girl walked by him in a very short skirt, her legs bare, her young body moving with an easy assurance, offering itself with all its beauties fresh and intact. It was a little parable of youth and age. She was in the world between, the world between expectation and despair, the world of calculated choices, a mistress being pensioned off, but kindly. She wondered whether Alain would find himself a new woman in Toulon. Probably.

She had taken a drink from the glass of whisky in front of her and arranged her thoughts. What was most dignified was to remain as cool and detached as the man. So she asked him if he was sure he could afford such a gift. Her gallery was doing well enough. She was in no danger. With equal coolness, he assured her that particularly after this new inheritance had come to his wife, he was well able to give her the apartment, and he would be pleased to think of her in comfortable circumstances. He reached out and put his hand on hers in a rare gesture of public affection. An image passed through her mind of a horse falling and dying in the street. She could hear a distant voice singing.

They had risen from their chairs in the café that afternoon and walked, as they always walked, to the apartment where they undressed and joined themselves together as men and women did, knowing all the ways to please, but she was aware of an emptiness in the rooms around them, an emptiness that had always been there, though not always acknowledged. They moved carefully in the landscape of their pleasure, with a certain formality and poise. This was not new, but her observation of it was.

There would be no farewell at the Gare de Lyon, no letters, only an empty space in the day.

As there was on this later afternoon as she stood staring out the apartment window across the roofs to the pretty sky, as she planned to take away a few things that she didn't wish to abandon, the table by the bed, a small chair where she had often sat to pull on her stockings after they had made love, and then to rent the apartment and invest the money.

She lay on her back and stared at the hospital ceiling, where there were patterns of small cracks and something that must be old dirt or perhaps a discoloration of the plaster. She imagined various ways of framing it and putting it up for sale. Increasingly art was whatever was called art by an artist. Her response to this was double: a delight in the liveliness of it all and a slightly cynical sense that it was only a series of tricks. All this new and brave work was the reason that she had come to New York, where she had almost died.

The tall black nurse who was in charge of the ward this morning looked in the door, and Jean said good morning. The woman smiled and disappeared. Yesterday she had promised that Jean could be up today and start to walk. The first step in getting out of the hospital and back to Paris. She had been enjoying New York, but she couldn't afford to stay now. Fortunately, Gilberte had bullied her into buying insurance for the trip, but the doctors had assured her that there would be a slow convalescence, and she must get herself back to her apartment for that.

The bleeding had started in her room at the hotel, and at first she had thought that the blood and cramps were only her menstrual period. Her periods had become a little irregular, but they went on, though she had reached an age where they might come to an end. There were occasional moments of unease, but she had congratulated herself on finding her way into the menopause with comparatively little difficulty.

Less than an hour after the bleeding started, she knew that this flood was something different and dangerous. There was no one to call. She sat in a chair, towels under her to soak up the unceasing flow of blood, and she began to shake with chills, holding herself as still as she could while she tried to think, but she was dizzy and sick, and there was nothing to be thought, and at last she simply picked up the phone and told the abrupt and unfriendly girl at the desk that she needed a doctor.

A few minutes later there was a knock on the door, and then a key turned, and the manager appeared, a short bald man with a large nose and double chins and a brisk, almost military manner that was like an ill-fitting suit of clothes.

When he asked what the trouble was, she tried to explain, and he astonished her by blushing. Made uneasy by this female problem, he became even more brisk and military, and before she knew it, Jean was in a cab on her way to a hospital, afraid that she might bleed on the seat and at the same time too frightened to care. At the hospital, she was surrounded by strange faces, an old Italian man with a huge moustache who was holding his chest and praying loudly, a Puerto Rican mother with a tiny baby that cried endlessly, a black woman who stared insanely at everyone around her, a black boy with a broken arm that he held in place with his other hand, wincing with pain whenever he moved. The order of the world gone wrong. She felt even more frightened as she waited for someone to see to her, but finally a young Jewish doctor took her into an examination room and asked questions, gently palpated her abdomen, ordered X-rays and called in a specialist.

Hysterectomy: did that mean she was old? She looked at the pattern on the ceiling. She hadn't succeeded in working out anything with the two New York galleries where she had been negotiating, and now she hadn't the strength. In a year or two, perhaps, she would come back to New York. Or perhaps it was unnecessary. More and more Americans came to Paris, and they would always buy the high modern if she could get the work into her hands. Matisse was dead, though Picasso appeared to be ready to live forever, and anything by either one of them would always sell. In the gallery at the moment there was an attractive little cubist piece by Juan Gris. It was valuable, and she was certain she could find a buyer, but now she thought that instead she might keep it.

She closed her eyes and tried to remember the little painting, and when she opened her eyes, there was a tall man standing by her bed. He was slender and elegant, wearing a good but slightly old-fashioned three piece suit and a dark tie. For a moment she wondered if he was an undertaker come to assess his chances, but there was something familiar in the blue eyes.

"Do I know you?" she said.

"You once did."

It was the voice she finally recognized.

"Paul."

He nodded.

"How did you get here?"

"I heard you were looking for me."

She'd forgotten. When she first got to New York, she had mentioned him to one of the gallery owners as an old friend, and the man had recognized the name. Paul had a reputation. Jean had spoken of getting in touch and then forgotten.

The two of them sat on a bench in Central Park. Paul had brought her here in a cab for her last afternoon in New York. She was still weak but strong enough to return to Paris. Gilberte would meet her at the airport and drive her into the city, and she would settle in her apartment and wait for her strength to return. Sometimes, in the shakiest moments, she thought it never would, that from now on she would be deteriorated and incapable, but the surgeon had assured her that, within months, she would be as strong as ever.

It was an early summer day, and she could hear birds singing, and the leaves were freshly green. Sun shone, and two old men stood on the path, arguing vehemently, and a young black man rode by on a bicycle. Little pieces of the world. The mood of strangeness that could catch you in a new place or after sickness. What had always been obvious became entirely unlikely.

One of the old men began to walk away, the other watching him and muttering, then following along. That was how she thought of them, old men, but how much older were they than the man beside her, how much older than she herself? She had abruptly entered the age of bloodless infertility. It was as well that we didn't see ourselves clearly.

She closed her eyes for a moment and listened to the

birdsong, the noise of traffic from the edge of the park. New York. Far off the scream of an ambulance. Here people lived high in the air, looking out and seeing the sky. A city of fantasy and rage: that was what she thought the day she arrived from Paris, which was terrestrial, secretive, pragmatic.

"Are you famous?" she said to Paul. She spoke without opening her eyes.

"Well known in certain circles."

"Are you in love?"

"What questions you ask, Jean, sitting there with your eyes shut."

"If I opened my eyes, I might not ask them."

"I always found you a delightful girl."

"And now you find me a delightful *femme d'un certain age*."

"Yes, I suppose I do."

"You didn't tell me whether you were in love."

"No. I have a friend, but I couldn't claim to be in love. Are you in love?"

"What an odd question," she said, and opened her eyes and looked toward him. His long slender face was pale, and his short hair was almost white. It made his blue eyes brighter.

"You have a beautiful face," she said.

He smiled.

"Thank you for bringing me here, Paul."

"Did you come to Central Park when you lived in New York with Del?"

"Not often."

"Do you have someplace in Paris where you go and sit in the sun?"

"The Luxembourg Gardens. Not like this. Smaller and quite formal, with gravel paths and sculptures."

"I've never been to Paris. But I've seen the pictures."

"Come and visit me. I'll show you everything."

"I've hardly ever been outside the United States. New York has always been home."

"Are you still taking pictures?"

"Not so much. I've been making drawings."

"Do you sell them?"

"I've never tried."

"I could give you a show."

"You haven't even seen them."

"Paul, I know you. Anything you did would be fine."

The two old men had walked a certain distance in silence and then turned and come back, and now they were talking together like the best of friends. Paul had turned to look at her, and his eyes, so surprisingly bright, held hers. He started to laugh.

"Just a little girl from the country," he said. "You once told me that's what you were."

"True enough. Let's go and see your drawings. There's time before I have to catch the plane."

"No. They're a secret."

"Why?"

"I don't know. I'll think about it some, and one day I might send a bunch to you. Or maybe not."

"Why aren't you famous, Paul? You're a wonderful photographer."

"Only movie stars are famous. And politicians. And maybe singers. But like I told you, I'm a little bit well-known. That's good enough. Everyone in the Village recognizes me."

Jean closed her eyes again. She tried to remember coming to Central Park. She knew she had, but no memory would come. In the distance, beyond all the bird sounds and over the soft rumble of traffic on Fifth Avenue, she could hear a trumpet playing a long high line, a tune she knew but couldn't name.

Crazy to be heard. She felt a sharp pain in her abdomen along with the constant ache there since the operation. A piece of her was missing. She was a new kind of woman now.

What happened in life was death. It was astonishing that Robert had lived so long after that first terrible wounding. Men and guns had tried to destroy him and had come very close, and yet he had survived, with his ruined body and harsh voice and one eye, and then somehow had lived on and on. She felt sure that it was, in some part, the way he had been cared for by Berthe and Antoine. Their devotion had made him live. That and his own devotion and simplicity, the nobility of his faith. Jean remembered how frightened of him she had been at first. The last time she had visited, he had been pale, with white hair, and age had taken the harshest edge off that crow's voice. He had taken her hand as he used to take her son's.

Now the old house and the title would go to some distant cousin. Jean had first met him at the funeral. He was a thin man with old-fashioned eyeglasses and a rigid manner. He had stood among them as the priest chanted the more or less forbidden Latin words over Robert's body. *Requiem aeternam dona eis, Domine.* Robert had loved his church and been loyal to it, and it saw him out of the world with dignity, breaking the rules of Vatican II for his sake.

After the requiem mass, Jean had walked through the town where one or two of the older people spoke to her. Then she had gone for a few miles down country roads, a wind rustling the leaves over her head. She had passed the little stone house where Antoine lived, and where Berthe would presumably join him. She remembered Berthe coming to her after her son was killed, and as she did, an idea came to her. She returned to the big house and found her way to the kitchen where Berthe was preparing food.

"I would like you to come to Paris and live with me," she said. Berthe looked at her over the long nose with the same unmoved stare she turned on everything. "For as long as you want. You came to me before, when I needed you."

"I'll talk to Antoine," Berthe said. Jean wondered if Berthe looked forward to a life with her brother in the stone cottage. They were more like two versions of a single person than two separate people.

Jean walked to the front of the house, to the room where Robert's wheelchair sat empty by the window. The cousin who was to be the new count came in and tried to make conversation. He avoided asking when she was leaving, though Jean had the sense that he was hoping she would mention it, and she did so, saying that she would trespass on his hospitality until the next morning if that was acceptable. He was a little effusive and went away.

Jean found her coat and went out of the house again, this time going up the road to the spring and sitting on the rocks by the edge and listening to the eternal, cheerful sound of the water. Her son's spirit, if it were anywhere in the created world, would be here. The water chattered like a happy child. She sat for a long time and thought nothing.

When she got back to the house, Berthe came to her and announced that she would move to Paris. For a certain time, at least.

Seven

BEYOND THE ROW OF WHITE refrigerators was the plate glass window of the store, and beyond that rue Papineau, a busy street in the east end of Montreal, the half-known city she had chosen when she decided it was time to change her life. The snow was falling more thickly now and blowing along the street. It had snowed almost every day since she arrived. The store on the opposite side was a blur of yellow light. Behind her she could hear the voice of the proprietor talking jovially about the big storm that was forecast and telling her she better get home. She stepped out into the blizzard and turned toward the corner to find the bus stop, wondered about trying to find a cab, but thought that in this weather it would be impossible. She had come across the mountain on the bus, and it was probably easiest to get back that way.

A few steps along the street, she stopped to pull her coat more tightly around her neck. No scarf; she was unprepared for the assault of the Canadian winter and must buy one soon. She remembered a clothing store of some sort by the corner where she had got off the bus a few minutes before, the first flakes starting to come down as she stepped to the pavement. Dark figures moved past her, hunched against the wind and snow, bundled up, shapeless. The wind stung her face. A door opened, and she felt warmth from the room within, heard noise. It was a tavern, and two men were coming out, one short, almost withered, the other taller, burly. The big one, drunk, tripped and fell, and the smaller one let out a string of mumbled blasphemies and began to try to haul him to his feet. Jean moved to the edge of the sidewalk to pass by. Cars drove past, headlights on, the wheels quiet on the snow. She saw a cab, but by the time she had raised her hand to wave, it was gone.

Bent against the wind, like all the others who were out in the storm, she studied the pattern of footsteps in the fresh layer of snow, as if it might be a code she could interpret. She caught a glimpse of a man inside a furniture store standing close to the window and watching those moving through the blizzard like blinded animals. It would be so easy to get lost in this, and the awareness of danger sharpened her sense of adventure. When she reached the corner, she saw a bus coming and risked running across the street on a red light to make sure she caught it, running all the way to the stop. Just as she was about to climb the steps of the warm, lighted bus, she caught a glimpse of a *felquiste* slogan on the brick wall beside her, and as her eyes traced the letters, a tall thin young man passed, walked away into the snow, and for a second she was convinced it was her son Guillaume. It was her son about to vanish in the snow. She stood still, watching him as he disappeared, wanting to call out. The bus driver was speaking to her, *Madame*, he was saying, *entrez, là*, and she obeyed, lost sight of Guillaume in the blowing snow.

She made her way up the hill to Place d'Armes, the square that was the beginning of the old city. In front of her, the massive entry and two square towers of Notre Dame Basilica, grey stone in the cold daylight. Since the first day she had arrived in Montreal, the weather had been cold, and there was always snow on the ground, and she would sit in her apartment and think that maybe she was a fool to have come here, though it was the dead season in Paris as well, chill streets, rain. She might have stayed in Paris if she had not suddenly felt deserted, Berthe deciding that she must go back to the country to look after Antoine, who was in poor health, Gilberte entering a belated and ill-omened marriage and going off to Grenoble, that and the opportunity to sell the gallery all coming close together made her think it was time to move on. No longer young but still stricken with restlessness, she had packed up, bought a ticket and flown across the ocean to a country that was once her home. She had decided on Montreal because she had the habit of living in French. Something in her wanted to go back, but not all the way, just as far as this borderland, a new nowhere. She arrived in Montreal in a snowstorm and took a room in a hotel where the broken TV set showed its pictures only in wild shades of green and purple, and she set out to rent an apartment and settle.

She looked back across the square to an elegant domed and columned temple of finance, the old Bank of Montreal building, and she reflected that this would be her last city. In the meantime, she was to meet someone who advertised himself as a theatrical agent. It was all very strange. One day recently she had picked up the newspaper and found a little story about this man. She called him, with the strange feeling that she had become a crank, a crazed eccentric, but he listened and agreed to meet her at a restaurant in Old Montreal. When she hung up the phone she read the newspaper story again. It was one of those little anecdotes that columnists came up with about local characters, and she wondered then if this purported agent was a fraud, conducting his business out of a restaurant. She was old enough to be foolish if she chose.

She had brought the few clippings that she had saved, including the ones she had carried around Paris in the early days of the war in the hope of being taken for an American. She had bothered little about these things, but the scraps of paper were evidence of something.

Beside her was the restaurant where she was to meet this man, Alfred Payne. It was a bare place, yellow walls with nothing hung on them but a couple of calendars, its name, *Polonaise*, in plain letters on the window. The light behind the wide plate glass windows was bright and fell from long fluorescent fixtures. The tables were scattered around the room, as if at random, and at the table closest to the kitchen sat three men, smoking, a full ashtray in front of them. She sat down at one of the tables close to the front and picked up the menu, though she had no intention of eating. The food was eastern European, and when the waiter — or maybe he was the cook, or both — came to her from the table in the corner, she surprised herself by ordering a bowl of goulash soup. She was hungry after all, it seemed, and the warmth and spice would insulate her against the cold day.

The two men at the table in the corner were looking toward her, and she found herself annoyed and was about to say something sharp when one of them approached and sat down across from her. He held out his hand.

"I'm Alfred Payne," he said, and when she reached out her hand, he bent and kissed it, smiling as if he was pleased with himself for having thought of the gesture. He had long hair, golden brown with a reddish tinge, and a large moustache of the same colour. His bright eyes were the same colour as his hair, and the slight pallor of his skin emphasized the sienna glow all around it. From the kitchen, the man in the apron appeared with her goulash soup and set it on the table in front of her. She regretted having ordered it. She would have to sit and eat with the man across from her. She spread a paper napkin in her lap.

"Hey, Woitech, bring me one, too," the man said. He was nodding his head. "And coffee, Woitech," he shouted to the kitchen.

She enjoyed the bite of the spices in her mouth. After every spoonful, Alfred Payne looked toward her and nodded and smiled as if encouraging a recalcitrant child. Woitech arrived from the kitchen with another bowl of the soup and a pot of coffee and filled a cup for each of them, and the man across from her tucked a napkin into the neck of his shirt and bent over and began to shovel the food into his mouth, spilling some on the napkin with each bite.

The other man from the back came by the table, doing up a leather jacket.

"I'm going," he said. "I'll see you over there."

"Right on."

"Don't spend too long talking with the nice lady. We have to get the rest of that set up."

He went out.

"Theatre?"

"Stagehand. A regular paycheque."

"And your agency. Do you have many clients?"

"William Morris wasn't built in a day. I started out with a couple of topless go-go dancers. I think what they really wanted was more like a bodyguard. A girl shows her tits and everyone thinks she's a pushover. Negotiating through me gave them a little dignity. So I ended up with half a dozen girls. I treat every one of them like she was the queen. Then I heard about this little cheap movie. Guy I know was the gaffer. They were doing some night club stuff, and they needed a couple of girls. I was on the set checking that out, and I talked to the producer, ended up handling all the extras. It grows."

She finished her soup. This was absurd, a man who protected topless dancers. Still, when he asked, she took the clippings out of her purse and pushed them across the table. The man looked at them, his bright eyes intensely focused on the page, his short thick fingers holding the paper flat on the table. His fingernails were bitten down short.

"You were a movie star. A real hundred-dollar bill."

"I went to France and spoiled it."

"You make movies in France?"

"A few. Mostly I got married and did other things."

He was staring at her, grinning.

"Far out. I ought to go and out and find prints of some of your old movies, eh?"

"I don't know if you could."

"Can I keep these a couple of days, maybe get some copies made?"

"Why not?"

"The movie business isn't all that big in Montreal. We got the Film Board, Norman McLaren cartoons, documentaries, and they do what they can, a feature now and then. The French do some. You willing to work as an extra?"

"I just don't want to be bored."

"This could be an opportunity," he said. "This could be a genuine opportunity. I'm going to call my sister."

"Why?"

"She's in Toronto. CBC. She knows some people. Tell them I got a silent movie star who's smart, still looks great."

Ridiculous that the flattery pleased her, but it did. He pulled a card out of the inside pocket of his coat and handed it to her. The print on the card was a little smudged. Then he took out a small black notebook and a fountain pen. He took down her name and address and phone number, writing them in a tiny neat hand in a corner of a page. Then he looked up at her, his head on one side. With all the hair and the bright eyes, he looked like an amiable puppy. He stood up and shook her hand and nodded and smiled his way to the door, then stopped and looked back toward the kitchen.

"Woitech," he shouted. "Put the two soup on my tab."

Jean was waiting for Marie Duguay to come and meet her for dinner in the hotel dining room. They had driven here together from Montreal, where Marie lived in the apartment upstairs, though she was full of complaints about it and was always making plans to move. She was younger than Jean, recently widowed and not showing much sign of grief, though her endless worries about her health might be grief displaced. They had met now and then in the front hall, and one day Marie had invited her up for coffee, and an hour later, they had planned this weekend trip to *le bas Saint Laurent*. Marie drove, with a good deal of nervous lurching, but they had arrived safely enough and gone to their rooms to settle in, and in a few moments Marie would knock at the door. The dining room offered fresh sturgeon taken in the river nearby.

Jean was always enlivened by a new place. As she waited for the knock on the door, she was looking across the wide stretch of the river, and the light that came down through the clouds made the line of mountains on the north shore black and solid. There was a narrow terrace at the foot of the closest hills but not enough land to farm. As the dusk came on, she thought she could see a light over there against the darkness of the escarpment. Then it was gone. The river, still shining with the reflected light of the sky, flowed northeast past the little group of rocky islands called the Pilgrims. Between her window and the river was a hundred feet of land and then a dike that contained the water of high tide, and below the dike a long stretch of marsh. Some of the marshes on the tidal flats had been harvested, the water controlled by *aboiteaux*, the one-way wooden drains built into the dikes to let water out of the salt meadows.

The black shape of the mountain range was the end of vision, and you looked across the gleaming metal of the river which had flowed there for a few thousand years; in the seventeenth century the little sailing boats from France came off the ocean and down the gulf to make their way to Quebec and beyond. Champlain, the settlers and traders: on the road here from Montreal, they had seen the traces, the high gables of old houses, the roadside Calvaries. She too had crossed her oceans. She had reached the Pacific, had taken ship across the Atlantic. Years ago when she was coming to Canada to see her mother, her ship had passed along this river. She had waved to the tiny villages, the white church spires. Now she stood in one of the villages, watching. Her father's ship had sailed off to war from Quebec, and he had never returned. That was so long ago, and he was a young man who never got to be old. Nor did her son. There ought to be a sunlit land of heroes where the two could meet and find some language in common to lament their violent passage from the world. Where their hands might clasp in a bright room safe from history.

When they went to the dining room, Jean would pose the questions about Marie's unlamented husband that until now had remained unasked. She liked hearing people's stories.

It was one of those evenings that made you feel as if eternity was possible. The summer night was holding itself in readiness, but it did not come, only atom by atom mixed more darkness with the rays of the setting sun. The air was full of light, and the trees in the square reached out for it as if they might invent a new dimension. There would be night, but not yet, not yet. In the distance, she could see the high glass buildings of the downtown. On the other side of the square, a girl and a boy were passing a joint back and forth, and when it was finally done, they wrapped themselves around each other so tightly that they might have been a single creature. A tall man with a cane was passing by, and he looked at her and smiled.

A basket of vegetables, peas and new potatoes, lay at her feet. Earlier she had gone to the market at Jean Talon, and on the way back on the bus she had passed a cinema and impulsively got off to watch the film that was playing. Then she had come here to the square to sit and watch the rest of the world.

The summer streets were full of people walking, and for some reason she imagined that they were all making their way toward the river, as if the long evening made them know that Montreal was an island and sent them to the water to watch it find its mazy way toward the ocean. The paths of the park were a small pattern, and each time a figure moved under the trees, it was startling and new. The leaves were thick and a copious jumble of shades of green, thousands assembled to decorate this one tree. She felt that she might be waiting to rise and enter a beautifully framed image from a film, and as she pictured that, she saw the other life as a schoolteacher in Picton or Belleville, marrying a local man, having two or three children and sometimes wondering if everything might have been different, if she might have been in the movies, gone to Europe. The two women looked each other in the face, and of course neither was quite real.

She was about ready to go to bed when the loud knock on the door came. As she walked down the hallway, a second knock. She looked through the glass, and there was Alfred Payne with a woman. He'd been to the apartment before to deliver contracts. She'd been a little astonished that he'd found her any work at all, but she had done a few appearances as an extra and a couple of speaking parts. She opened the door.

"Great," he said. "I was afraid you'd be tucked up. This is Bobby," he said, indicating the woman. "We need to talk to you."

There seemed to be nothing to do but step aside and let the two of them into the house. Alfred pulled an open bottle of cheap wine out of his jacket pocket and held it out to her.

"You got some glasses?"

Jean was inclined to resent the intrusion, but Alfred was smiling his wide doggy smile and looking trustingly at her with his bright eyes, so she directed them to the front room and went out to the kitchen and brought back three glasses. Alfred got up from his chair, filled the three and passed them round.

"Santé," he said.

Jean sipped the wine, which didn't taste like wine at all. Bobby, who was wearing a black leather miniskirt and black high heels with long bare white legs, was sitting on a straight chair in the corner of the room, very upright, her feet pressed tightly together. She had a wide mouth and large shapely lips, which were covered with white lipstick, and her eyelids were coated with silver eye shadow, a lot of mascara on the lashes. The eyes were a pale brown, and her dark hair looked as if she cut it herself with a razor.

"We're here," Alfred said, "because I take you for a sophisticated woman, a woman who has seen something of the world."

She wasn't sure whether to answer. Let him go on.

"Bobby here is one of my clients. You can probably tell that she's a dancer."

Bobby was having trouble sitting still in her chair.

"Tell her," she said. "For fuck sake tell her."

"Okay. I am." He turned back to Jean. "There's a guy coming to the bar where she's been working. He's developed what you might call an obsession with Bobby here, and Bobby is not interested."

"He smells, for fuck sake," Bobby said, "and his idea of conversation is to tell you he's got such a big gizmo."

"You're not charmed," Jean said.

"But the guy is persistent. Somehow he found out where Bobby lives. First he sent her flowers, and this afternoon, he's at the door."

"I was just going out," Bobby said, "so I told him to wait downstairs for me, and I went out by the fire escape and called Al."

Jean took a drink. It still didn't taste like wine. She felt as if she ought to be annoyed by all this, but she wasn't. It gave her a certain silly pleasure.

"I went to the club tonight, and we made an arrangement with the manager. I said he better do something about Mr. Gizmo or he's never going to get any more dancers. Bobby did her show and we took her out the back way where I had a cab waiting, and the manager of the club is going to speak to the asshole in question. Or have somebody else speak to him."

"He scares the fuck out of me," Bobby said.

"In the cab, I tried to think where we could take Bobby for a couple of days. It would be easy enough for Mr. Gizmo to find my place."

"So you came here."

"I thought you could handle it."

"How long?"

"Two days. By then the guy is *mis à tabac* and told to hit the road. If that doesn't work, I have a friend who's a cop who might do me a favour."

"All right, as long as neither of you tells anybody that Bobby is here. I don't want any wild men arriving at the door."

Bobby was staring at her.

"Really? I can stay here?" she said.

"For a couple of days."

"I never thought you'd do it."

"I told you," Alfred said. "She's a great lady."

"There's a room by the kitchen," she said. "I don't know if the couch is very comfortable, but it will have to do."

"Far out," Alfred said and tossed off the rest of his wine. He was at the door, ready to leave, his bright eyes at their brightest, his smile vast. Almost before they knew it he was gone.

"I'd better find you some sheets and towels," Jean said.

The girl followed her as she went down the hall to the closet and pulled out a couple of sheets and a pillow. She remembered buying them when she got to Montreal and wondering who would ever use them.

"I never even thought you'd do it," Bobby said.

"Why not?"

"Well, why would you?"

"Call it an adventure."

She turned out the lights in the front hall and went into the back room, and again the girl followed her. She folded a sheet around the cushions on the couch, put another one over it and spread a blanket on top.

"Who's that?"

She was pointing to a picture of Guillaume, a rather formal portrait in his uniform.

"That's my son."

"Where's he?"

"He's dead."

"You have any other kids?"

"No."

"I want to have three."

Jean looked at her, the bare legs, the face with too much makeup, the black T-shirt tight over her breasts.

"How old are you?" she said.

"Twenty," the girl said. Jean didn't believe her.

"You like dancing in bars?"

"I like the money. Yeah, I like it okay mostly, how they look at me. Except I don't like this jerk."

"I hope they can get rid of him."

"Al said maybe he could get me a gig in Toronto or Ottawa for a while so I could get out of town."

"I'll show you where the bathroom is."

She did that and picked out a towel and washcloth.

"I'm about ready for bed," she said.

"Yeah, me too, I guess."

The girl looked into the bedroom as they passed the door. When they reached the little room, Jean put the towel and washcloth on a chair.

"You masturbate a lot?" the girl said.

"No."

"I do. All the time. My sister says there's something wrong with me."

"You think so?"

"No. Not really. I was living with a guy for a while. I didn't do it so much then."

"What happened to him?"

"He found someone with bigger tits. That's what he said."

"I'm going to bed, Bobby. I'll see you in the morning."

She left the girl standing in the middle of the hallway looking puzzled. She went to her bedroom, closed the door behind her, and prepared herself for bed, taking off her own makeup with cleansing cream and a Kleenex. Usually she washed her face with soap and hot water; they said it aged your skin, but she no longer cared. If she was old, she would be old. But having left the girl on her own, she didn't want to go back out to get to the bathroom. Leave her to find her own way.

She lay in bed, wondering what Bobby was doing, whether she had got into bed and fallen asleep or whether she was wandering around the apartment to get her bearings. That's what I would do, Jean thought, wander a little until I felt at home. She imagined the younger woman taking off the high heels, inspecting the kitchen, standing in the front room, picking up a book to see what Jean was reading, looking out the window, seeing a car go by and being frightened that the man had found his way here. Then quickly making her way back to the little room, closing the door and getting into bed.

When Jean woke in the morning, the apartment was quiet, and she got herself up and ready for the day without hearing any sound from the girl. To get to the kitchen, she had to pass by the door of the small back room. Bobby had left the door wide open, and she saw her sleeping face on the pillow, young and bare.

In the kitchen she made herself a bowl of fresh fruit, bananas, apples and pears, with a little cream, while the kettle boiled to make coffee. She cut up enough fruit for two bowls and put one in the refrigerator. She had two crusty rolls, one for each of them. She enjoyed breakfast, had always been someone who wakened easily, and she liked the simple plain tastes at this time of the day. She was impatient for the girl to wake, curious to hear more about her. It was a while until she heard her get up and walk down the hall to the bathroom. The shower ran for a long time, and then there was silence, and finally footsteps coming back.

"Bobby," she said.

"Yeah."

"There's coffee, if you want it."

The girl appeared in the kitchen doorway, a towel wrapped around her. Her bare legs and shoulders were pale and damp.

"Do you want to borrow a dressing gown?"

"Is that okay?"

"I have an extra one."

She went to the bedroom and pulled a white terrycloth dressing gown out of the back of the closet. She handed it to the girl, who dropped the towel and put it on as if the nakedness of her pale perfect body meant nothing. She took the towel back to the bathroom and joined Jean in the kitchen.

"Would you like a bowl of fruit?"

"Just coffee."

"If you change your mind, there's a bowl of fruit in the fridge."

The girl nodded. She looked around the room and out the back window to the row of poplars.

"It's quiet here," she said.

"Your place isn't quiet?"

"No. It's right on the Main. There's always something, trucks or somebody shouting."

"You hear more traffic in the front room. Did you sleep well?"

"Yeah. I had this crazy dream about meeting myself when I was a baby and telling myself what an ugly baby I was."

"Do you try to explain your dreams?"

"No. My mother was always talking about her dreams and whether they meant she was going to get money or meet some handsome man. I thought it was stupid. I mean, they're just dreams, you know."

For a while they sat in silence drinking their coffee.

"You lived here long?"

"No. I came here from Paris last year."

"Paris. Was that really great?"

"It was a life."

The girl looked at her. The pale brown eyes were wide and might have hidden almost anything. Without makeup, there was something stark and primitive about her face.

"Where do you come from?"

"Halifax," Bobby said.

"Do you go back?"

"Why would I?"

Jean refilled the two cups.

"Let's go into the front room," she said. She picked up her cup and the girl followed her. Jean sat on the couch, and the girl took the chair opposite her. Jean had brought little from France, and sometimes the room felt bare, three pictures on the white walls, a small cubist painting, a drawing, and a photograph taken inside a large bare warehouse with a view out the window, a girl naked in the corner of the room. Bobby was looking at the painting on the wall beside her, an earnest, puzzled look on her face.

"What's that?" she said.

"It's a little cubist painting by a man named Juan Gris."

"That's modern art."

"Yes. He was a colleague of Picasso and Braque. In Paris."

"You know those guys?"

"I once saw Picasso. I didn't talk to him. He came into my art gallery."

"You had an art gallery?"

"I couldn't afford to keep paintings, but that little one I kept. I gave myself a present."

"You like it?"

"Yes, don't you?"

"I don't know."

She stood up and walked toward the couch and looked at the two pictures that were there, the drawing and the photograph.

"That's me," Jean said. "I was an artist's model for a while."

The girl studied the pictures, then looked at Jean as if struggling to make the connection. She went back to her chair.

"I don't know what I'm going to do today," she said.

"What would you do if you were at home?"

"Make a couple of phone calls. Go out and look around the stores. Buy a magazine."

"You can do that here."

"I don't like to go out. Not till I hear from Al. I don't want that guy to find me."

"It's a big city."

"Not big enough."

"I'm going out to get some groceries, and while I'm gone, you can sit and think of stories to tell me when I get back."

"What kind of stories?" The girl's face had that bare primitive look again, the eyes wide and fierce.

"Any kind you like."

Jean put on a light fall coat and went out the front door. There was a sharpness in the air, and the front walk was covered with dark red leaves. She breathed greedily as she walked to the supermarket. On the way back, the warm sun shone in her face.

When she opened the door, she heard voices, and for a second she was worried that the man from the bar might have found them, but then she recognized Alfred's voice.

"All set," Alfred said. He must have just washed his long thick hair. It looked as if it could give off sparks. "I've got Bobby a gig in Ottawa, starting tonight. By the time she comes back, the jerk will be taken care of. And I just got a call from Toronto. Some guy who swears he's seen one of your old movies is making a little feature, and he'll pay your way down. He says he's got something perfect for you."

Bobby looked at the man, who was so pleased with himself he looked as if he might burst with it. The girl was smiling too.

"I just told him, 'Al, you're a fucking angel,'" she said.

They all smiled.

It was a snowy winter morning, and she was listening to Radio-Canada, a discussion of the films of Claude Jutra and whether he would somehow be ruined now that he was working in English Canada, in the English language. She found she preferred listening to the French network, and she had seen some of Jutra's films. As she listened to the discussion, which was growing eloquent and rancorous, she wandered from room to room of her apartment. Beyond the bedroom window snow was falling, the pattern hypnotic. She stared. She touched things, to know they were there. Opened the small box where she kept her jewellery. It was a long time since she'd looked in it, and as soon as she opened the lid she knew something was wrong.

The antique gold necklace was gone. The one that she had worn, shining against her perfect skin, to the ball where her Guillaume had been so very proud of her and a marshal of France had stared hungrily at her bare shoulders. She never wore it, but she had carried it with her, not only because it was valuable — she had sometimes imagined another war, selling it for food — but because it was her last connection with those years, with the man she'd married. Something had been taken from her, something golden.

Now what to do? There was no question of who had taken it. That girl, Bobby. Quick little fingers. She could call the police, or she could call Alfred and ask him to try to get it back. He might still be in touch with the girl. Or did she remember he said once that Bobby had disappeared? Yes, that was it, she'd been keeping bad company in the months after she had stayed with Jean, and then one day she had vanished with no explanation, and he was afraid that she might be buried under a highway somewhere. Dropped in a hole the night before the highway was paved, that was how those people got rid of dead bodies, and pretty young girls were expendable. There was always another to be found. Jean remembered the girl standing slender and naked in front of her as she put on her dressing gown. That pale beautiful body had been abandoned somewhere by hard careless men. Someone had taken possession of the necklace. It moved on from hand to hand.

She could call the police and report the theft. They might check the antique shops, pawnbrokers.

No, she thought, no. Let it be gone.

It was unseemly, of course. What might easily be her final appearance before a camera in a commercial advertising a treatment for hemorrhoids. She had never watched it, but cheques arrived from time to time as they renewed the contract to show the piece for a few more months. A cheque had arrived in this morning's mail. It was a parable, she had said to herself the day she set off to the studio for the filming. Once I was a creature of possibilities, now I am the embodiment of small disasters. The commercial had been made in Toronto, and she believed that it was not shown in French. She was as glad that Amélie, the woman who came to clean for her twice a week, would not see it. Amélie called her *Madame la comtesse* since the day she had seen an envelope from France addressed that way. It did not displease her to be given that title. *Madame la comtesse* would not suffer from piles, though stiffness in the joints was evident from time to time.

Would the hemorrhoid commercial be her last appearance? It might. Alfred Payne had suddenly married one of his topless dancers, and the two of them had gone off to California to become famous. So here she was, once again in retirement. A director at the NFB talked about an important film that he wished to make using her, but she expected it would go to the limbo of lost stories to join all the dreams forgotten by morning, all the anecdotes untold, the novels planned, the other world that god intended before he grew distracted by this one.

She went to the kitchen to open a bottle of wine, and as she stood with the corkscrew in her hand, she remembered buying it in a neighbourhood shop in Paris after her old one broke. She could remember the light of the store, and the smell, that vivid inconsequential moment.

She walked into the church where she came to remember her dead. The old church was here and the door was open, and she came. A church was an empty room, a silence, a history. Even when she was young, she had preferred the church when she was alone there. Now when she came here she didn't pray, but she went slowly through the list of those who were lost, named their names to herself and considered her own astonishing longevity. Marie Duguay had gone the year before while on a visit to a daughter in Florida. And before her all the others. Then there were those who might or might not be alive, who had simply vanished from her awareness. She did not go to visit her brother.

The city was full of huge Roman Catholic churches, most of them relics of the late nineteenth century, when the power of the church and the parish priest was at its height, when the Pope was declared infallible and the priest gave orders and made demands. You heard stories about the greed and heartlessness of

the priests then, the sum they would demand and receive to
bury a poor old woman, but now the great stone churches
were empty. The one where she sat went even further back
and evoked the days when the priests held the city as a
seigneury, part of a colony that brought the crusading faith of
the counter-reformation to the Huron and Iroquois nations and
sent shiploads of fur to France. Stories that she had been told in
school. Now religion had been replaced by political enthusiasm,
Monseigneur de Laval replaced by Monsieur Lévesque, one
bishop by another. She remembered from his first election, the
failed referendum, the kind of reverence in which the man was
held. She knew better than to think that history repeated itself,
but she remembered her son's passion for France, a passion that
he had learned from his father and uncle. Perhaps Catholic
countries could never abandon the sacred, could only displace it.

A priest in a cassock crossed the chancel and disappeared
through a small door. She had been brought up among protes-
tants of a narrow and committed vision, and in those days,
priests were strange animals, with their Latin masses, their
celibacy, the dread secrecy of the confessional, but now she had
no fear of them. Her husband and her son had been Roman
Catholic, and she had got to know Robert's friend, the curé of
Les Sourcelles. Whenever she heard church bells pealing over
the streets of Montreal, she was taken back to Les Sourcelles.
An empty church offered enough silence, and as she left, she
always dropped a few dollars into the collection box. Once the
churches died out altogether, she wondered where men and
women would find the silence. Perhaps they would no longer
need it. That was the thought of a crotchety old woman, of
course, with her aching hips and increasing irritability.

Name them, her dead, starting with her father so long ago,
and in naming them see how possibility had become inevita-

bility and then vanished. *Some there be who have no memorial, who are perished as though they had never been.* Like an author's characters who are invented and then excised from the final draft, and only he knows that they might once have existed. When she was gone, who would remember those she remembered?

Mickey Shapiro was talking on the telephone when she walked into the shop; he waved to her and indicated a chair. She sat down, leaned back and closed her eyes, but when she did, everything began to spin, so she opened them again. She had met Mickey when he had a store a block from her apartment. Once or twice she gave him advice about paintings and they became friends. He'd moved recently to a smaller store which was crowded with dainty china and showy glass. A white and green epergne sat on the edge of a table beside her, begging someone to knock it over and smash it. She was in that dangerous state, from tiredness probably, when she wanted to imagine things broken. "I don't like what the market's doing these days," Mickey was saying. "It's jittery. I'm thinking of just taking the loss on that stuff and staying liquid."

His stockbroker again. He claimed he had only a few dollars in the market, but then Mickey cried poor over everything, the lousy rental market in Montreal brought on by separatism, the crippling taxes levied by the Quebec government. People who were good with money worried about it; they were like protective parents to their investments.

"I've made up my mind," Mickey said. "Sell it and buy me a T-bill. Talk to you later."

Send the troublesome child to boarding school. He hung up the phone.

"Good afternoon," he said. "You look tired. You want some tea?"

"Please. I could go to the tea shop up the street, but the company's better here. And you're better looking than the woman who runs it."

"I wasn't a bad-looking guy once, but I put on weight."

"Lovely eyes, Mickey. Lovely warm eyes. I've always told you that. How are your children?"

"They keep going to school because they can't find jobs, but they're okay. You haven't been in for a while. You been sick?"

"No, but I don't go out as much. I get tired more easily."

Mickey was plugging in the kettle in the back room.

"You know what somebody tried to sell me yesterday?"

"What?"

"A box full of Nazi stuff. Swastikas and iron crosses. Memorabilia, he calls it. I couldn't believe it. I just looked at the guy. Finally I said to him, My name is Michael Shapiro. And he looks at me. I'm a Jew, I say. He still didn't get it. The guy is maybe thirty, a young hustler. He doesn't get it. Hitler and the Jews means nothing to him. Finally I said to him, Get the stuff out of my store, then go read a book. I think these young guys live on Mars."

"I saw them wearing those things, Mickey."

He brought the teapot on a tray and tried to find a place to put it.

"I was just a kid," he said, "but I remember all the quiet talk, the letters, the phone calls, trying to get out an uncle, a cousin, then it was too late."

She closed her eyes again. She was remembering her little

son bending over a spring of water and catching it in his cupped hands and trying to hold it to bring to her to drink because they'd walked a long way, and she was hot. By the time he reached her, there was no more than a little dampness left in the soft bowl of pale skin and small bones, but she bent over it and wet her lips and kissed the fingers, and he ran back to fetch more.

She opened her eyes and looked at Mickey, who was pouring tea into a cup. Behind him, beyond the glass, was Montreal, was the world.

Eight

THE EDGES OF LANGUAGE were blurred until the trains came to a stop, and then you realized that the people near you were speaking something that might be Spanish or Russian or Bengali or Urdu or Polish. She would study the faces and try to make out where they had come from. Recently there were more of those half-Indian faces from somewhere in south America. Lovely girls from southeast Asia. All these figures moving about in tunnels under the city. She went among them as a little safe adventure, out of a need to keep moving, to see the moving world. She would walk at her slow careful pace from her apartment down to the metro station. If she went at the right time of the day, she could get a seat, and she would watch the people as they got on and off, the families, the young lovers, the students reading their texts.

She was old now, and if she happened to find herself in a crowded car, someone would offer her a place. She had learned which stations were emptiest, which most crowded. Sometimes she would get off and change to a different line, ride it to the end, see it empty and refill for the return journey. Some parts of Montreal were known to her only by the underground geography of the subway stations, though in pleasant weather she would disembark at some promising stop, walk a block or two and then come back to the station. You emerged into a strange place, searched among the new streets, caught a glimpse of lives lived.

She was growing tired now, tired of being shaken by the train's starts and stops, of being out in the world. This driver was one of those who did everything abruptly. It was when she was tired like this that they would come to her, the watchers, the ones she knew, who sought her out in the long tunnels. Now, just as the train began to leave the station, she saw one of them, such a beautiful man, with his composed, empty face, standing perfectly still as she passed by. *Farewell, my dear.*

The train leapt ahead into the darkness of the tunnel. She waited for her own stop and made her way out. A heavy woman pushed past her and jostled her a little. It would be a long way home. If necessary, she could get a cab from the station.

On the way to the escalator, an old man was playing the violin, not very well, a hat in front of him for coins. She dropped in a quarter and mounted the long escalator that rose higher and higher through a concrete tube, with an iron wheel of lights in spherical white glass balls hanging above, heavy and ominous, like some huge spider.

There were secret places to go on certain kinds of days, as long as her legs would carry her. On a cold day, she would make her slow way on foot, then by metro, then on foot again, to the Jewish Public Library. It was a warm place to sit and watch things happen around her, to hear the voices. She would take down a book from the shelves and perhaps read a few pages, but also she would watch and wait. It was a place where people knew each other. She had become a familiar face over the years, and one or two of the librarians would smile, though she never spoke.

A few tables away a man bent over a book. He was thin, and his back was hunched from years of bending over books or ledgers. His head projected forward from the bent spine at the end of a long stretched neck, like the head of a turtle. On his head was a yarmulke, and he wore a dark jacket over a grey sweater. His glasses hung a little away from his face as he bent forward to read. He had good features, with a shapely, dark mouth. He looked alert and intelligent, and yet there was a quality of impersonality, as if he were one of those ancient tortoises with bare unblinking eyes.

Outside the wide windows at the side of the room, she saw a few flakes of snow. Time to leave soon and get herself safely home.

She looked back at the man, who was turning a page, and there was something she wanted to ask him, and then she understood why she came here, why she had been coming here for so long. Of course. Comfort and warmth, a bright room, but more than that, she was searching, waiting for her to arrive. Of course. *Are you coming now? Where are you? Where are you? Oh I know, but still, where are you?*

"Ça va bien, madame la comtesse?"

"Comme toujours, Amélie, comme toujours."

No one but Amélie called her that any more, though she had a perfect right to the title. One of her names. A lifetime of events behind her, and before her a dim November day, watching Amélie clean the apartment.

From the time she had wakened, she had felt the ghost of an arrival. She told herself that it was only the awareness that this was one of Amélie's days, that she would hear the door open and the familiar voice, no more than that, but it was more than that after all. A brainstorm, no doubt, some electrical accident in the aging circuits, the faculty of intuition feeding on itself. This morning as she lay in the bath, she looked at the skin that hung loose on her frame, the way it sagged and wrinkled, and she imagined a camera trained on her, making an observation on her progress. She had once been young.

She heard a car stop outside, and she pulled herself up from the chair to make her way to the window to see who was coming. A camera in the corner of the room watched her, the camerman cranking evenly, and she wondered why he was using such an old-fashioned machine. To match the earlier footage, it must be that. Final scenes which would be cut into one of the old prints.

A man walked from the car along the sidewalk. His walk was familiar, but he was differently dressed now, in a grey suit and without the beret. Still she would have known him. He moved out of the frame.

She turned from the window and looked to her right, at the drawing. She had carried it with her for years, a memory of something. The young woman's body with its smooth skin and rounded flesh lay soft and open, and the man saw this, and his quick hand recorded the contours of her legs and belly and breasts and the contours of his own desire, his delicacy and hunger and awareness. Something happened, and lines on paper kept it. Softness and ease and charm. Sometimes she pretended that she had forgotten the past, but it was there, though now some of it was very far off. The time before she was *madame la comtesse*, and the time before that.

Soon, she thought, the drawing and everything that she had loved would have to endure existence without her.

You should have been used to it a long time ago, but you never got used to anything. Sometimes she felt herself watched, the presence of the camera, though she was herself, she supposed, the eye watching. You saw yourself in the vision of that eye, fabulous, immortal as thought, dying. It was said there were those who could tell dream from the rest, and memory from dream or faith, and the tree was there because you ran against it, but the more sleep, the more dream, and sleep was always at the edge of her eye. Good child, sweet animal I was, come back, you cried. We are lonely for you, and they have put you somewhere, and you are lost as the pattern of wind on water in the instant of its passing.

Among other things, she was turning to stone. You tried to move a leg and nothing moved, and again you willed the action, and slowly a foot crept forward, and you thought how once this was beautiful and strong, all hair and power and sweetness, and now it was rusted and inept. You see, my dear, how it has come upon us that once were slender and quick. You with your little camera that saw me as so beautiful until I could not believe that you would not want me, but you were in some parallel universe, beautiful as a wolf, and only moved for your own kind, and yet how you knew me, so I had rather be naked for you than anyone. Good day, Sir Wolf, and your fur so long and thick, and good day, you say to me, and your eye so bright.

The creature observed her from across the room, and she studied the long snout that must be testing her smell and understanding her that way. He waited as a wolf will wait, and she was surprised at the knowledge that he would speak. She spoke his name, and thought she heard him answer, but the voice was quiet, and in a while she realized that the animal was speaking another language, one that she didn't know, something from a far country, German perhaps, and when he paused, she spoke his name again to encourage him. Tell me how I was beautiful as you saw me, that girl I was, white as all the girls who go into the forest and meet the other world. As she lifted her foot to move toward the smiling beast, her hip grew stiff and betrayed her, and she swayed, off balance, about to fall, and put out her hand and caught the wall and straightened herself, and as she did, she found that she was thinking in French, as if in answer to someone who had spoken to her, a rusty voice and a bright eye, *qu'as tu, mon cher?* as he stood on one leg by the window, one wide wing spread, the other broken, the sharp beak open, the one good eye luminous with what might be pain or rage, hopping forward, trying to use the spread wings for balance, the conversation between their thoughts swift and dangerous, an epic of *noblesse* and falling, falling out of the air.

She sank toward a chair, farting, exhausted. Solitary and unreal, a whim, a fancy, nothing but words, she could be that. The tree that was there because you struck against it would not remember you. You said love, but it was enough to be seen or dreamed. The powerful legs and shoulders, a man as solid as a plough horse, not one word to be said, the shape of muscle under the skin, haunches and the long smooth back, the horse that bears all, warrior and wagon, plough and harrow. Slaughtered to fall in blood. He stood in his slow animal patience, struck the earth with one hoof, the skin flicked over a muscle as if at the touch of a fly.

She opened her eyes from a sleep busy with other dreams and knew he was gone. She turned her head toward the voice that skittered over the air like a flight of swallows and saw the black figure on its long legs, stepping forward and back, all quick unease, but she entered into conversation, since she knew now that she would be answered, and the dainty bird called out its strange old name with quick insistence, eyes moving quickly from side to side for danger, what would break her again. Then the long legs began to dance, and the eyes to blink, and there were other creatures around her, Bergkönigs they were, on their heavy feathered feet as they came closer and closer to the smiling spindly creature, and one by one they leapt on her as she danced her silly dance and tried to bear their weight, and Jean rose from the chair to go to her and help, but they vanished, and she was never heard of again.

Her stomach hurt, and she gave a little belch and tried to remember if she had eaten. Was Amélie coming today? It was damned annoying to have no brain any more. What was it, muck in the arteries, no blood getting up there, something like that? You remembered what thinking was like, but you couldn't do it. Time was a mess, with everything getting out of order. Yet some things were clear. She thought of that horse standing there, powerful and patient, not saying a word, and she knew who that was, and she remembered his name. Turning into animals like that. An unlikely sort of affair. When Guillaume was a little boy, he liked fables, and his father would read him La Fontaine, who wrote such elegant French.

She would go to the kitchen. Amélie made sure that there was food, and she'd have some bread and cheese and make a cup of coffee. If she could do that without setting herself or the house on fire, that would be an achievement. She wondered if it was important which ones turned themselves into animals to come to her. No sign of Delbert. No doubt what he'd be, one of those slow old dogs who liked to lie in the sun and just now and then walk to the nearest tree to lift his leg. She saw him curled up on the couch, one eye open, pretending to be wise as a foxy old grandpa, which he probably was by now, opening his mouth to yawn, still had all his teeth, big red tongue to remind you of all kinds of things, and mumbling to himself a few old sayings which about summed it all up. So long, Delbert, time for lunch. But he followed her along the hall, wagging his tail.

What would she herself become? Her transformation. No knowing that. Suppose the wheel was to turn, and she was to be reborn in another skin, what would that be? She'd never been any good at party games. Fish, lizard, nanny-goat, stone. She farted. Her hip gave an ugly twist. Outside the kitchen window, the poplars were coming into leaf, the astonishing unfolding of that golden green. Sunlight was a wall of brightness in these vivid atoms. As had been. As will be. Imagine that she was not there, and the leaves opened all the same. She would not be there to know she was forgotten. The actors walked out of frame and went who knows where. The little dolls tossed aside. Someone turned a page and the book was over.

Nine

ESTELLE DUNPHY IS a hundred years old, and she remembers just about everything. She doesn't talk much anymore. It takes too much energy and there's no one worth talking to. The nurses and the other women at the home treat her like some kind of puppet, dressing her up and showing her off to visitors, pointing out the letter she got from the Prime Minister on her hundredth birthday. They act as if she had no brain left, and she doesn't much care. But she remembers everything. For example, she remembers Baxter's sermons, though she couldn't say why. They weren't interesting. She herself didn't altogether see the point of the things he said. It was a little bit as if he was talking in some kind of code that he understood and nobody else did. Well, maybe some of them did, but Estelle didn't. Baxter wasn't any kind of a preacher when she first met him. He had the little store where his father always had it, and it seemed like something they could make a go of. He had that red look about him as if he'd just been boiled, but she figured she could get used to that and she did. But the preaching was a shock. Maybe it was just because the church was handy, kitty-corner to the store. That's what she thought at first. Someone once told her that preachers, by and large, had the itch on them more than most men, and preaching was some kind of substitute. Estelle didn't know most men, in fact she'd only ever known

Baxter, and she didn't make a habit of asking other women how it was with them, but Baxter's itch was out of all reason, or so it seemed to her, and if the preaching was enough to keep him off her for a few days, well then it was a good thing. She went across to the church with him and she listened, and now she could remember the sermons. Well, not surprising, he only had about four of them. He'd written them out in pencil in a school notebook, and then he learned them by heart, and if he got lost, he'd stand there and get more and more red and sometimes start over again at the beginning. It was probably a good thing he didn't preach for too long before they found a real city minister to come by after he'd finished at his own church. Those sermons were just one of the things that Estelle remembered that did her no good at all, and remembering that, Baxter's preaching time, she remembered the only time she ever caught him with another woman, which was then, with that girl who came to play on the piano. It was the day after the funeral for Bruce Docherty, or what was left of him after months in the lake. Estelle walked into the church, and there were the two of them, sitting there in straight chairs facing each other, and Baxter was taking candies out of his pocket and putting them in the girl's mouth. She saw his fingers up against her lips and tongue, and the girl was crying, not moving at all, not making a sound, just tears running down her face while Baxter put candies into her mouth. Estelle got him out of there and back to the store, and she picked up one of the meat knives and held the point so he could feel it on his skin and told him if he ever got too close to another woman again she'd cut him like a young calf and feed them to him. Baxter was full of claims about how innocent it all was, but she'd seen the girl's tongue, and she knew better. Not long after that, and it was no accident, the first of the boys was conceived, and Baxter had given up preaching by then. Once they had the two boys, the store wasn't enough, so they moved into town, and Baxter got on at the basket factory, and she clerked in a bakery on the main street. They said that girl had gone into the movies.

Plums. Why had that word come into his head? Edgar wondered. Plums. He'd never much liked to eat them. They always looked so good, but there was that sourness when you got to the pit, a sourness that spoiled the sweetness that had gone before.

Greengage were the best, and there used to be a tree a few miles away, on the road toward town, but he expected that it was cut down by now. Edgar hawked up a lump of phlegm that was rattling in his throat and spit it into the coffee cup that sat on the arm of his chair. Across the room a young woman with big muscles was throwing herself around on television. He left the TV on, but he seldom turned on the sound. He was about ready for more coffee.

When his neighbour drove him to the store, the way she did once a week, he might ask her to drive by where that plum tree had been. He could remember the taste of them and the rubbery texture, the way they were almost the same colour as the leaves, as if they were hidden, something you might not notice. He remembered that from when he was a boy. There was just that one tree at the corner of Stenner's apple orchard, the corner where the drive turned to go to their house. It would be almost the season now, and he could imagine one of those little sweet plums in his hand, that soft green colour, and how small they were.

Edgar pushed himself up from his chair. His right leg, the one that had been bad since he was a kid, ached as soon as he was on his feet, and he knew the other one would start when he tried to walk, damn legs, damn them. He leaned on the counter to take a bit of the strain off his aching legs, and he stared out the window. A quiet rain was falling, a rain with no wind to impel it, and drops made a pattern on the surface of the water, which was almost white except for the splashes of the drops, and those were black and silver.

Whenever it rained, he wondered if the roof was leaking. He hadn't been upstairs for years. In the few seconds he'd been standing there, the direction of the rain had changed, and something in the clouds, and now there was a different kind of shine on the surface of the lake, and the splashes where the rain hit were darker. He'd been looking out that window for seventy and more years, since he was big enough to climb on a chair, and the water had never been the same twice.

The kettle boiled, and he poured it into a clean cup with some instant and stirred. He kept a bucket by the back door to piss in, and he wondered whether to go now while he was on his feet or try to hold off until he'd drunk his coffee. They kept telling him he wasn't supposed to use the outhouse any more, that it was too close to the lake, but he didn't see how they were going to stop him. During the day he used the bucket to void his water and at night he took it out and dumped it on the grass near the door. If they put him in jail for it, he'd get better food. Edgar had never been much of a cook. Never been much of anything, except a watcher and thinker. Times he'd thought he was pretty good at that, knew things before he was told, good nose for the weather. Back when they were still fishing the lake, before it was all poisoned and dead, sometimes one of the boys would come and check with him, especially if they were going a distance out in the fall, when the weather was unreliable. He had a feeling for it, though that was partly the leg, which had its regular aches and pains. Bad enough from the sickness, but then he'd fallen off a roof where he was shingling and broken both legs, and he was never too much on his feet afterwards. That kept him out of the army and mostly kept him home. It wasn't easy to get work, but he had the house, and when the boys came to play cards, he'd get a percentage of the winnings of anybody who was up at the end. A lot of years in this old house watching the way the weather came toward him across the water. He thought sometimes about who'd get the house — he was the last one left, both his sisters gone — and his neighbour told him he should make a will and make sure it wasn't the government.